*Alaska's Alei*

Book 3

# REDEEMED

## TRUDY

## SAMSILL

# Acknowledgments

- *To Almighty God, who has given me life and the passion to write. May my passion bring You fame.*

- *To my husband, Steve. For all of the unwashed clothes, unswept floors, and quick dinners, I do hope you know how very much I love you. Even though my cooking and cleaning has suffered since I started writing, you have loved me anyway and continued to believe in me and my fledgling writing skills. Without you, I wouldn't be who I am today. Still holding out for that moose hunt!*

- *To my darlings. My four children, I love each and every one of you! Your differences and unique life-stages make me smile every time I think about you. You have no idea how your encouragement and support have kept me typing away, believing I could do this. Thank you for being the best children on the planet!*

- *To my editors/family/friends. My mom, Jane; sister, Amy; friends, Sharon, Jana, Angelia, and Risa , you each have a special place in the writing and editing of these books. Thank you for your tireless reading, questioning, proofing, cheering, and encouraging!! I need you all for this to happen.*

This book is dedicated to my Grandmothers,

Vera and Melba,

Who both have
Greatly encouraged me
To finish this series
before

"the Good Lord takes them home!"

*He has redeemed my soul from going to the pit,*
*And my life shall see the light.*


*Job 33:28 (NASB)*

# CHAPTER 1

*End of July, 1968*

This was the night. After spending the last three, long, miserably cold, late evenings of hiding in the wooded shadows, he knew this had to be it; he couldn't mess things up now. Thankfully, his patience had paid off tremendously. Hour upon hour, crouched low and blanketed in the cold, dark, Alaskan night, he knew this was the time. And he was confident that he knew exactly which room she was in.

From his hiding place, the man watched the last of the windows wink out at *Rita's Place*. Just a little longer and he would make his move.

Sitting in the ever-darkening shadows, the man reflected on his extreme appreciation of Rita and her girls. Little did they know, the young, pretty things were money-makers for him as well, not only working to provide money to line their own skirt pockets and those of their caretaker, Rita. He had secretly used the girls in the lipstick-red painted house for his own gain.

Not wanting their sick need to be discovered by the townspeople, much less their own wives and children, the local men in Seal Harbor paid the now hidden man to arrange the girls for them. Their lust and their seedy longing for pretty women were his gain. He was sort of a "delivery man" with the goods consisting of young girls. He couldn't feel too guilty about it. The girls had chosen this way of life; no one had forced them into it.

Coming back to the present, the man slowly and silently stood to stretch his tired limbs. With the lights out for over an hour now, he decided to get the deed done. Creeping as stealthily as a black panther, the man, who appeared equally as black from his hood to his shoes, stole silently to the edge of the back fence. Lifting the gate latch slowly to ensure it didn't creak, he eased the gate's door open and propped it ajar with a rock. Better to make his exit as easy as possible.

The house was now within thirty feet of him. Stepping in the shadows, he made his way to the window, knowing the girl slept within that very room. Ducking below the window's ledge, the man stayed in place for a while listening, hoping he hadn't disturbed the inhabitants. Easing a hand up to the window sill, he checked to make sure his eyes hadn't deceived him.

They hadn't. As with the previous two nights, luck would have it that the window was opened just enough to get his fingers through to silently push it further up. Reaching a black-gloved hand for the edge of the windowsill, the man slowly shoved it up, flecks of white paint falling off the window frame. Through the now opened window, he could see two figures sleeping on twin beds, one girl smaller than the other. Knowing the girl he wanted was larger than her overly slim sister, he studied the sleeping girls a bit longer. Yes, he knew which one was Berta.

An owl hooted in the distance causing him to almost jump out of his skin. Stepping back into the outside shadows, the man stilled his breathing and waited for his heartbeat to return to normal. Slow and steady.....no rushing.....he could do this. Never before had he committed such a feat, but he knew the time had come.

Time to cause a distraction in Seal Harbor. Time to let Andrew know the threat was real and make certain he kept his mouth shut in the future.

Easing the window up an inch or two further to accommodate for his bulky frame, the black-clothed man slowly and stealthily swung his leg into the room of the first floor bedroom. He knew he had to be absolutely silent in his movements. Hunting most of his life had paid off in this moment as well. The old floorboards remained quiet under his feet. Standing completely still and taking shallow, quiet breaths, he rehearsed the plan once more in his mind. Creeping to the bigger girl's bedside, the man silently withdrew a cloth from his pocket.

Shoving it into her mouth and pressing his body on top of hers, he found her ear and whispered, "If you scream or move, I will kill your sister."

Something sharp touched the side of her neck, and instantly the girl stilled under him. Fear consumed her. He could feel her fear as every muscle in her body tensed and then froze in unison.

Slowly he rose from her and crammed the cloth further into her mouth. Listening for the other girl in the room, he only heard her continued light snoring. Grabbing both of his captive's arms, he quickly twisted them behind her back, slowly pulled her to a standing position, and forced her onto her tiptoes.

"To the window," he hissed in her ear. Feeling her stiffen in pain, the man eased up on her arms and guided her toward the window's ledge. A nudge was all it took for her to be convinced to move forward. He had rightfully played upon the girl's fear of injury to her sister if she did anything wrong.

Hanging tightly onto her arms still twisted behind her back, he carefully and quietly guided Berta to step one leg through the open window. Knowing time was of the essence, he had to get them both away from *Rita's Place* as quickly and as quietly as possible. Pressing a knee into her back and nudging her firmly from behind, she climbed the rest of the way through with the man right behind her, the cold night air greeting them both.

Terror and dread like never before paralyzed the girl's foggy mind. Not unaccustomed to being afraid for herself, Berta could hardly move for fear of what would happen to her sister. Her body responded in kind, completely stilling beneath the strong man's grasp. She *couldn't* leave Ana. But she had no choice, and to resist would bring her sister harm. Another sharper nudge let Berta know he meant business. Allowing herself to be pushed forward to the woods, her mind took over and began flashing snatches of dark images from days of horror she and Ana had survived as young girls.

Pain and fear rolled in her gut and wanted to push its way from her mouth, but the cloth kept her cry muffled. A clear thought rushed to the outer edges of her confused mind. *Thank goodness, Ana is still safe and sleeping.*

Her feet hurt as he pushed her along the uneven ground. Thankful she had slept in her socks, Berta wished she had left her robe on as well. The nightgown offered little protection in the night air. Her body began shaking, both from alarm and cold. Her legs quivered so violently she nearly collapsed.

Roughly the man tightened his grip on her arms nearly bringing her up off her feet. She had no idea where he was taking her.

4

Berta chided herself for not paying attention to where he was leading her from the beginning. The only thoughts she had at the beginning of this living nightmare were for Ana's safety. Occasional stabs of pain as a stone or branch tore at her feet, arms, legs, and face tore Berta's mind away from her sister who would be so very terrified when she woke to Berta being gone.

Now other thoughts quickly tumbled through her confused mind as she wondered which customer she had made angry enough to kidnap her. What had she done wrong? Was this the drunken man who she inwardly hated that had requested her services earlier in the week? She didn't smell alcohol on the man, only the stench of body odor. Who had kidnapped her and why?

Berta found herself tripping over limbs and brush in the woods. She thought of struggling against the man now that she was farther away from the house, but before she could formulate a plan, a flashlight's beam blinded her vision. Someone else was now in the woods with her and her captor. The light's beam winked off as quickly as it had been turned on.

An evil chuckle escaped the other man's lips. "Good job! This will keep the fool quiet," Berta heard the man with the light say. Not able to catch a glimpse of either man's face, she made a mental note to take in every detail she could. Then the next thing she was aware of was intense lightning flashes of pain as something hard connected with the side of her head. Feeling her body being lifted like a ragdoll, Berta passed out in the arms of her abductor.

Freezing cold and completely disoriented, Berta could not determine what had happened. Her splitting headache and the constant throbbing in her right shoulder was a haunting reminder that something wasn't right. Reaching a hand to her temple, Berta knew from the dried blood and knot that had formed above her hairline that she had been hurt. But who had done this to her? Trying to ease herself into a sitting position only made her world spin furiously. Nausea consumed her body, and she wretched violently from the pain and dizziness.

Rolling to her other side to shift her weight off of the bump on her head, Berta thought she would pass out as tiny pin-pricks of light danced before her closed eyelids. Behind these tiny lights, Berta saw an image from long ago that caused her to shrink even smaller on the cold, wooden floor underneath her quivering body.

*Huddled in the dark recesses of a tiny, smelly shed, Berta had one arm draped around Ana's skinny shoulders and her other arm covering her head. Bracing herself for one more blow, her body tensed as she heard the padlock slam into place from the outside of the shed. He had left. Thankfully, she had only received four smacks this time instead of the usual eight or ten. As long as Ana remained unhurt she could endure the blows for them both.*

*Hatred so strong she could taste its metallic bitterness in her mouth, Berta did her best to shush her crying sister. At thirteen and twelve years old, the two girls had endured these bouts of rage from their drunken father many times before. But since their mother had disappeared weeks before, Berta's anger with their mother's unexpected and unexplained departure had slowly turned into admiration.*

*Her mother had somehow escaped their raging father; maybe they could too. Trying to keep from losing their young minds, the two*

6

*girls spent hours alone in the pitch black shed whispering their escape plans to one another.*

Reality jarred her awake. Berta was *not* crouched helplessly in the old shed with Ana. She w*as* lying in a stinking old room alone with a huge bump on her head and pain knifing through her shoulder. She wasn't whispering secret escape plans with her sister. In fact, she wasn't sure where Ana was or what she was doing. Surely she was safe at *Rita's Place* since Ana wasn't here with her now.

At the moment, her cotton-filled head could only conjure up two images, the face of Ana, snoring lightly in her bed.

And the face of Andrew, the one who promised his love to her and that he would one day rescue her from the life as a young prostitute.

Again, Berta tried to sit up. With a heavy hand, extreme pain and unconsciousness pushed her back onto the floor leaving her with one thought.

*Andrew, you were too late.*

*******************

Out in the gathering morning light, two lone figures stood smoking cigarettes and talking quietly.

"Did you get it delivered?"

"Of course. I told you I would hold up my end of the deal," the short stocky man snarled at his companion. "Worry about your part in this."

Rising to his full height, the man in black answered, "My part is done. I took Berta and delivered her to you to keep Andrew quiet. We don't need any more information leaked from him unless you want to see the stills shut down and your girl's visits come to a halt."

Nostrils flaring, the other responded, "You're not *threatening* me, now are you? You remember who has control here! You may be the one *with* the sources of booze and girls, but I am the one who can shut it all down with one word to the Alaska State Troopers. Understand?" By the end of his speech, the bulldog of a man was inches from the other's face. Cursing under his breath, he inhaled deeply from his cigarette.

The man in black knew he had no retort to those words. Turning his back on the other, he looked out into the early morning light creeping across the Alaskan sky. He took a long drag from the stubby cigarette causing the butt to glow brightly. Finishing the cigarette he flicked it to the ground and stomped it with the heel of his shoe. "What do we do with the girl?"

"*We* won't do anything with her, but *you* will sneak over here and check on her every few hours. Make sure she's alive, throw her some food and water, then when she's done eating, gag her again. We don't want anyone hearing her scream or cry for help, do we? When her little *boy*, Andrew, gets word about his precious Berta, that will keep his mouth shut about what he knows. She's our insurance in this deal. When he goes back to his house and finds that note, then we can rest assured he will stay quiet." Stretching his arms over his head and yawning, the man said, "I've got the weekend off from work so I plan on resting after all of this excitement. I'll be at the house if you need me for anything. You know your job, right, Peter? Keep an eye on the

8

girl. Make sure no one knows she's here or even comes around this place."

Clapping his Aleut companion on the shoulder, the short stocky man strutted off through the woods towards Seal Harbor and his house. He and Peter had just shut Andrew's mouth for good. Confident at how things were going, he quickened his pace towards home and his waiting bed. He knew the Aleutian could handle things from here with the girl. Now it was time for him to get some much needed rest and put this behind him. His stills were safe for a while longer and life would continue on as usual.

# CHAPTER 2

Ana's piercing scream awakened the entire house at *Rita's Place.*

Rita was the first to find the girl in hysterics. Flipping on the light, she raced to Ana's side and grabbed her shoulders. "Ana, what is the matter? You will wake the dead!"

Ana could only point. She covered her mouth with one hand and pointed to Berta's empty bed with the other.

Milly pushed into the room. She quickly surveyed everything and was filled with immediate dread. The open window and fluttering curtain. Berta's empty bed. Frozen in her tracks, Milly stood with mouth agape.

"Ana, where is Berta? Ana!" Rita shook the sobbing girl's shoulders until she had her attention.

"I don't know. I woke up freezing and noticed the window was completely open. I had only opened it a crack before bed.....and then I saw Berta was gone! She never leaves without telling me. She wouldn't open the window all the way and she would never leave me!" Knowing she was hardly making sense, Ana's words broke off in another sob.

"Someone came in and *took* Berta while you were sleeping?" Jocelyn asked. "That can't be true. Have you searched the house? Maybe she's in the bathroom or—or *something*."

"No, she's gone.....the window.....her coat and shoes are still here....I already checked the bathroom myself....she's gone—" Ana could only point to Berta's empty bed.

Scanning the tiny room Rita could see for herself that if Berta had left the house she was running around in the cold with no coat or shoes. Her robe and slippers were still in their rightful place. Something wasn't right with the whole scene.

Rita tossed her reddish, auburn curls over her shoulder, embraced the girl, and hugged Ana to her massive bosom. "Milly, go quickly search the house for Berta. Liza, you go phone the AST office if we don't find her. Oh wait, they aren't in the office yet…..Just go—go make us some tea while I think. Girls, all of you, to the kitchen."

Milly quickly shut the window and locked it. Following Rita's orders, the sock and slipper-clad girls all headed for the kitchen. Fear wrapped itself around each of their shoulders like a heavy robe.

Rita drew a shaky hand over her aging face and pushed her wayward, red curls back in place. Helping Ana to her feet, the two of them followed the entourage of scared girls to the kitchen.

*My poor girls…..Oh, God, what has happened to one of them? Where is Berta?* Knowing she had to be strong for the frightened young ladies, Rita drew in a shaky breath and tried to calm herself. Hysterics would help nothing.

Rita looked around the large kitchen with its green and white checked gingham curtains and matching table cloth spread out on the round oak table. The black, frying pan-shaped clock over the stove pointed to 4:25 in the morning. It was too early to phone for help. Rita looked up as all ten, no, nine of her girls, stood at attention awaiting her plan.

Rita began giving orders. "Felicity, go to each room and lock all windows and the front and back doors, and check the pool hall doors too." The girl raced out of the room to do Rita's bidding, grateful for something to do.

Looking across the kitchen table at Liza, her daughter, Rita's eyes threatened to tear up as she realized it could have been her own flesh and blood that was missing and not Berta. Standing out like a flaming red bush, Liza's hair matched her mother's red mop.

Clearing her throat, Rita continued, "Penny, you and Liza go get dressed. Liza will drive you two to town. *Freda's Diner* will be open at 5:00. Someone there will know where the Sergeant lives. We can't wait for him to open the trooper's office to get help. I want the Sergeant here now. One of my girls is gone." Having their way, tears pooled in Rita's eyes as she dropped to the nearest chair. Placing a trembling hand over her heart, Rita could only wait with the others until help arrived.

Uncertainty tried to creep in around the edges of her brain. Other thoughts vied for Rita's attention. *You can't just request for the Sergeant to show up and help you out. Not with the type of business you run with these girls. Rita, you could get in big trouble with the law snooping around.....No, he will only see that I run a pool hall, and nothing else. The girls and I have taken great pains to keep this place looking reputable and not like a....a.....*

After all of these years, Rita still had trouble admitting to herself that she indeed ran a brothel. Though her home began as an open door for wayward girls, all of whom sought her out, it had turned into more than a pool hall and bar. Most of her fifty plus years on earth had been spent selling her body, but that was her own choice. Forced to drop out of school as a young girl, Rita had little education. Her mother had insisted she learn to read but that was it. As she grew

13

older, Rita knew she had to make ends meet and take care of herself financially and selling her body was the quickest, easiest way she could make a few dollars.

Before coming to her, some of the girls she had under her roof had already chosen this same, sad path so it was easy for them to follow in her footsteps, while the others chose to work in the pool hall and help out in the house. Calling the law to her business to help her out both frightened her and comforted her at the same time. She *needed* help. Pushing all thoughts away except for Berta's safety, Rita looked up as she heard Milly's approach.

Milly burst into the kitchen, her pretty round face red with excitement. "She's not here. I checked the pool hall and every room. She's gone....." Overcome with emotion, tears traced wet trails down Milly's cheeks.

The announcement sent the entire room into fits of sobbing, hugs, and quiet exclamations. "No! Not Berta....Who would do something like that?.....I don't believe it...."

Ana became even more overcome with emotion as the truth stared her in the face. Berta was gone. Burying her face in her arms, Ana leaned over the table and wept openly. Coming to her side, Emily and Stasia comforted Ana as best they could.

Eyes tearless, Jocelyn turned to the stove and put the kettle on for tea. Straightening her shoulders, she began setting out the unmatched tea cups and saucers for the little group. Grabbing a handful of spoons and the tin canister of tea bags, she tapped her foot nervously waiting for the kettle to whistle.

White-faced and tight-lipped, Darcy gathered her long straight hair and quickly twisted it into a knot, pinning it out of her way.

Reaching for one of the loaves of bread Felicity had baked yesterday, she began slicing pieces for them all. It wouldn't do for them to be hungry right now. Felicity cooked their meals like clockwork, but right now at this early hour, they needed a bit of something to quell the raging emotions that were having their way with each stomach in the room. Stopping short at slicing the usual eleven pieces, Darcy felt her throat knot with anguish. Berta wasn't here to join them. An unnoticed tear splashed on the countertop beside the scarred cutting board.

Always nostalgic and thoughtful, Darcy looked at the uneven, broken slices of bread laced with tiny holes and thought of their little group of women. From the youngest, Ana, to the oldest, Miss Rita, they were all broken and uneven with jagged edges and holes throughout. Life had broken them. People had left holes in their hearts. Circumstances and choices had knocked off their smooth edges.

Darcy turned and leaned her heavy hip on the countertop letting her gaze travel over each face before her. She loved this mismatched bunch. They were her family and where she belonged, and they all had one common thread that bound them together, *Rita's Place*. All knew that Rita would not tolerate any judging or condemning attitudes between the girls. Each had their own story and their own reason for living and working at Rita's, whether they earned money selling their bodies, cooking the meals, sewing and washing the clothes, or cleaning the pool hall and house.

As Darcy's eyes flitted from face to face, her mind conjured up each girl's story and connection. A couple more tears rolled down Darcy's cheek as she looked at Ana, heart-broken and scared. Her older sister was her life, her anchor in this crazy world. No one knew

15

the sisters' story or how and why they arrived on Rita's doorstep. All she knew was that they were the first to arrive and would probably be the last to leave.

Years earlier, Rita had just completed the addition on her newly acquired house, pool hall, and bar when Berta and Ana appeared on Rita's doorstep one frozen dawn at ages twelve and thirteen. There was no telling what horrors they had run from. Needing food and shelter, they became Rita and Liza's helpers and quickly the foursome had *Rita's Place* up and running. A couple of years later the two also joined Rita in her side business, one that was shameful indeed, but a decent money-maker as they sold their young bodies along with Rita and her daughter to men in Seal Harbor. Darcy knew those two sisters were sadly the beginnings of Rita's brothel of girls. Yes, Ana felt completely alone in this old world with her sister missing.

The tea kettle whistled its loud shriek and startled everyone in the room as Penny and Liza dashed out the door in search of the Sergeant.

Jocelyn began filling tea cups and placing a tea bag in each. Getting to her feet, Felicity placed a comforting hand on each shoulder as she put a steaming cup before the girls seated at the table.

Swiping at another silent tear, Darcy looked at Stasia and Emily as they continued to comfort Ana. Stasia had simply "appeared" in their lives a year ago and she was one of the few who stayed. Bruised, battered, and unwilling to talk about where she came from, Rita gave her a few weeks to recover and she quickly turned to working for Rita as well. The only hint Stasia had ever given was that she needed to leave the place she was working prior to Rita's for her own safety and

16

during one of her nightly visits with a "customer", he had dropped a hint about *Rita's Place*. After seeing her busted lip and blackened eye, the man gave her a tip she would always appreciate. He knew Rita was a good woman and cared for her girls. The man gave her directions to Seal Harbor, a five dollar bill, and she left that very night in search of safety, at least as much as she could hope for in this line of work.

Emily's sweet spirit poured like a healing balm on Ana. The sobbing girl had quieted enough to sip her tea and force down a few bites of bread. Rubbing Ana's back, Emily was able to coax Ana to eat and drink some more.

Darcy knew sweet, gentle Emily couldn't "stomach" the work of selling her body. She tried it, but couldn't endure it after her first attempt. Rita never forced any of her girls, as she called them, to do what they couldn't so she put Emily to work as their housemaid and laundress, just like she had allowed Felicity to stay on as their cook and Penny as seamstress. Darcy suspected that Rita created jobs for the girls who couldn't handle the atmosphere of the bar and the demanding men just to keep them off the streets.

Felicity came to Rita very soon after the pool hall opened and applied as a cook for the then small group and for the pool hall. She never sold herself to any man, nor would she ever. Her skills were in the kitchen and not the bedroom. Darcy had talked long into the night with Felicity after arriving on Rita's step as well. The two became fast friends.

Engaged to be married, Felicity had met a handsome, poor, farmer who was ten years older than she was when Felicity was barely a teenager. They quickly fell in love, planned their future lives together and got engaged after two years. Without warning, her fiancé broke off their engagement and shattered her young heart to pieces. The very next week she saw him in town with another girl on his arm and Felicity knew she would do whatever it took to get away from him and the town. She took all of the money from her waitressing job she had saved for their new life and bought a one-way train ticket to Seal Harbor, Alaska. The small town offered no immediate job for her and she had no place to live after her money ran out within the week. The owner of the local diner told her of the pool hall called *Rita's Place* and sent her there to look for work. Rita did not turn her down.

Turning back to the broken bread, Darcy sliced off a couple more pieces. Breathing a deep sigh, she knew her own story fit oddly with the others, a heart-breaking tale of pain and neglect mixed with her own stubbornness to do and have things her way, to make life her own and live free from the pain of her past.

As a young teen, Darcy had fled the hurts and disappointments of life as she knew it and ended up at Miss Rita's like some of the other girls, cold, hungry, down-trodden, ready for a new start. But the fairy tale she had dreamed up during the long, lonely nights of childhood never matched up with life's stark reality. Darcy was well aware of one thing. In her plight to make life different, the tables had been turned on her, and now, life had made her very different. Desperate times had created desperate measures; survival became paramount over her dreams and fairy tales. And Darcy was like most of the others at Miss Rita's. Living a life she would never have dreamed for herself, caught in the never-ending state of wondering if she would wake up from the haunting dreams and recurring nightmares that had become her young life.

Rita's voice brought Darcy from her deep musings. "Girls, let's get dressed for the day. The Sergeant will be here soon and this crisis on our hands will not make the rest of the world stop spinning. Thank heavens it's Sunday and the pool hall and bar is closed! But still there's work to be done. Idle hands will drive us all crazy if we don't find something to do." Rita ended her little speech when her voice cracked and eyes misted with more tears.

The room erupted in a flurry of activity as the girls all scurried to do something, anything to distract them from the heartache they were all now bearing. One of them was missing. Now all that could be done was wait and cling to a sliver of hope that might be buried in any of their shattered hearts.

Within the hour Rita heard cars approaching as Liza and Penny returned followed by an Alaska State Trooper's vehicle. Finally they could get to the bottom of this and find their precious Berta. Nearly unable to restrain herself from pulling the Sergeant from his patrol car, Rita forced herself to calm down before she did something stupid from the insanity that threatened to overtake her.

Glancing around at the bright, lipstick red, two-story house with white shutters and front porch, Sergeant Will Walker emerged from his patrol car along with another officer. He knew of *Rita's Place* tucked in the hillside on the other end of Seal Harbor. This side of town was separated from the rest by a long wooden fence, the area being designated as simply "The Harbor." Known as the sleazy part of town tucked away into the coastal hillside, The Harbor was not Will's usual stomping grounds.

The newly formed Alaska State Troopers headquarters, or AST, was greatly under-manned and under-financed. So much happened out of his control on "the other side of the fence" that caused a great source of frustration for Sergeant Will Walker. Right now his main concerns were illegal booze and prostitution of young girls, so when he was called from his home this morning and found out where the incident had taken place, Will was surprised to have received a call from anyone in The Harbor. People on The Harbor side of town kept as far away from Seal Harbor as they could and as uninvolved with others not from their area.

Having only been employed for a year and a half as Sergeant with the AST, Will knew he simply couldn't do the work of four or five good lawmen to keep the inhabitants of Seal Harbor safe and to rid the town of the evil that lurked in the hills. He knew what kind of establishment *Rita's Place* was, but without the man-power in the AST office his hands were tied.

The two men stepped up onto the porch and greeted Rita. "I'm Sergeant Will Walker and this is Officer Brandon Hughes with the State Troopers department. I understand someone who lives here may be missing."

Tears instantly pooled in Rita's eyes as she showed the two men into the kitchen. Not knowing what else to do with herself, Felicity brewed a pot of fresh coffee for them while Ana endured the first round of questions from Sergeant Walker, then he asked Rita for information as well.

After going over all the details of their early morning discovery, Walker sent the girls with Hughes to make rounds of all of the bedrooms, for them to show Hughes all the outside windows on the first floor, and to make sure no clue was left unturned. With Hughes and the other girls out of the room, Will took advantage of the time and asked some questions of his own of Rita.

Clearing his throat, Will crossed his massive arms over his barrel chest and looked Rita in the eye. "Tell me how you came to have ten girls living with you, Miss Rita." Conscious of his body language, Will made himself take a more relaxed position. He wanted information from the lady sitting across from him. Deep in his gut Will had no doubt what kind of "house" Rita was running.

The familiar anger began stirring in his chest, knowing there was little he could do about the "greater crimes" he had begun to encounter. His daily job was mainly focused on dealing with the "lesser crimes" such as theft, burglaries, disputes, and traffic violations. He was even expected to do something about the wayward black bear that wandered into the residents' yards looking for a snack. He simply didn't have the men nor money to deal with much more.

But during this last month of employment with the AST, Will was beginning to see the clearer picture. Booze and prostitution were a real issue. And to make matters worse, as with most any small town, the longer he worked in Seal Harbor, the more he realized some of the people had the ability of looking the other way when it came to certain crimes, especially boot-legging and prostitution.

Reaching for his cup of coffee, Will took a sip and added extra sugar. Clearing his throat, Will brought Rita back to the present. Clearly she was distracted with the missing girl.

Rita topped off her own cup before responding to him. Drawing her black sweater over her ample bosom, Rita's green eyes flashed a warning in Will's direction. "What exactly does the number of girls living with me have to do with Berta being missing, Sergeant?" She tried but couldn't keep the edge from her voice.

Taking his time, Will looked her up and down a moment before answering. "Honestly, nothing. I'm just wondering how ten young ladies have found a home under this one roof." Will's eyes matched her gaze.

Fear wrapped icy fingers around Rita's heart. *How should I answer him?*

Unable to control the fear-induced defensiveness in her tone and words, she raised her chin a couple of inches and replied, "I'm not sure what you are thinking, but you will find nothing illegal going on here in this house today, Sergeant Walker. You may ask any of my girls if they would like to leave and I wouldn't stop them if they chose to. To answer your question, except for my own daughter, each girl came to me. They sought me out for work and shelter. I employ them to help run the pool hall and give them food and housing."

Rita raised a trembling hand to her face and brushed back her wayward flaming curls. Looking the Sergeant squarely in the eyes she asked in an acidic tone, "Are you so *duty-bound* that you would suggest the girls go live out in the streets where God only knows what would happen to them just for the sake of *Seal Harbor's appearance*?" Rita let her comment settle in around the Sergeant before continuing. "Or.....can they live here with the promise of a roof over their heads and food on the table? I *know* this is not a traditional arrangement, Sergeant, but this house and I are all these girls have."

Will knew he could do nothing at the moment without proof of any wrong doing. There were enough rumors around town to add to his suspicions. Glancing around the cozy kitchen, he had to admit it looked much like any other kitchen and nothing looked suspicious to his eye. But what did he expect the kitchen to look like in a suspected brothel?

Draining the last few drops of his coffee, Will stood to make his exit. "I will go speak to the girls again before leaving and make sure Officer Hughes is done with his questioning. If you think of anything else that would be pertinent to this investigation, please don't hesitate to call me. If I am not available you can leave any information with Officer Hughes or Patrolman Tom Dorne. My home and office numbers are on this card." Will withdrew a small white business card from his pocket and laid it on the gingham checked tablecloth. He touched the edge of his hat and left Rita at the table.

Taking one last sip of her coffee, she replaced the cup in its saucer. The trembling in her hands made the task difficult as the thin, china cup clinked against the small plate. Anxiety, worry, and fear from the last few hours of horror, and now the discussion with the Sergeant, set her hands to shaking slightly with nervousness. Reaching her hand to her unruly hair, Rita expelled a loud breath as she worked to calm herself. She needed to stay strong for the girls, *her* girls.

# CHAPTER 3

Edward Hamilton shut the door to his hotel room and headed for the twin bed that was calling his name. So much had happened in the past few days; it all seemed to be catching up with him at this very moment as his body demanded that he stop while his mind sought quiet reflection.

Who would have ever thought that the "short-term mission trip" he had agreed to would end up changing the course of his life? One moment the tall Texan was employed as assistant coach in Little River, Washington at the local high school and decided to enjoy a summer mission trip with his best buddy, Gabriel Parker, as they worked to help the Aleut people of Datka Island, Alaska. In what felt like the span of a breath, within the next few weeks he found himself now camped out in a hotel room in Seal Harbor, Alaska....waiting. Waiting to see what the next step was for his future.

Ed had come to the tiny Datka Island in the Aleutian Island chain with Gabe and his parents, Randall and Rebecca Parker, wanting to escape the humdrum of life as usual. There had been a deep stirring inside him for the past year that maybe coaching *wasn't* the call on his life. He loved to coach and enjoyed the students immensely, so when the stirring that was akin to an active beehive began in his chest, he was surprised.

After his own troubled years of being raised by parents who preferred partying over parenting, coupled with his personal bout with alcohol as a teen, Gabe and his family had introduced Ed to a new way of life. One that involved freedom from addictions to cover up the pain, one that meant loving others and helping them in their time of

25

need, and most importantly, he had given his life to Christ and had chosen to follow the path that God would direct him towards.

But Ed was still uncertain what that path looked like. He could see a little ways ahead but was unclear on what was around the bend.

Right now, instead of being in charge of a group of students, he was looking out for a twenty year old Aleut man who had only been released from jail two days ago. Upon his release from his Seal Harbor jail cell, Ed knew Andrew could not return to life as it was prior to his arrest, so they were in the process of determining the next step for the young man. Having gotten Andrew a hotel room adjacent to his so he could keep an eye on him for the next few days, Ed's heart went out to Andrew; the young man was the main reason Ed was still in Seal Harbor. Hoping to use his past experiences, Ed felt called to aid Andrew in any way he could. Remembering what it felt like right after deciding to make better choices in life, Ed knew the next few steps for Andrew were crucial to him staying out of trouble, and he was committed to see it through with the troubled young man.

At the moment, that was the direction this path was taking him. Ed had received the blessing of John Miller, one of the department heads of AMRA, Alaska Missionaries Relief Aid, to stay on and help Andrew get resettled into a new life.

Stationed in Fairbanks, AMRA was the springboard for all mission trips the Parkers had participated in over half of Rand and Becca Parker's married life. When their son Gabe was born, he naturally followed in his parents' footsteps and grew to love the Aleut people as much as they did. Then when Ed joined the small family, he too was introduced to mission work. Ed was eternally grateful for the

Parkers and AMRA knowing that without these two influences, his life would have taken a very different turn.

With Andrew only a few feet away in the next room, Ed could hear his loud snores filtering through the thin walls signaling the young man had settled in for a nap. Kicking off his cowboy boots, Ed shed the denim shirt he wore over a dark green t-shirt. Like a large tom cat stretching out in a patch of sun, Ed sprawled out on his hotel bed, interlocking his fingers and placing his hands behind his dark brown mop of hair. With little time for a haircut since arriving in Alaska nearly three months ago, Ed was feeling a bit shaggy. Maybe this week he would visit Seal Harbor's barber for a haircut. At least he didn't have to worry about what the women thought. A half-grin spread out over his face as he pictured the sight he must be. Several years back, he would have never let himself get this shaggy. He cared then what the women thought, but now, he knew he had more important things to worry about than catching a lady's eye.

Ed closed his tired eyes and instantly a beautiful brunette with gorgeous green eyes flashed in his mind. Snippets of his last conversation with Jade Miller, the only daughter of John and Jill Miller with AMRA, floated around his weary brain. She had stolen a part of his heart in three short months, and now she was stationed in Fairbanks with her parents working for AMRA as well. Between the laughter and jokes, the haughtiness and snide comments, that one stolen kiss and several arguments, there was no denying that Jade Miller had gotten under Ed Hamilton's skin. The two had forged a friendship that left them unsure of where their relationship would lead in the future. Jade had definitely stirred his emotions.

27

He placed an arm across his eyes in an effort to block her out, but to no avail.  Their last conversation assaulted him full force.  The two had been on Datka Island preparing to leave for separate destinations after the few months of working together with the rest of the mission team.  He could remember their exchange, word for word.


*"Hi, Tex." Jade looked across the crowd without making eye contact.*

*"I've missed you.  Did your dad tell you my plans for staying in Seal Harbor?"*

*"Yes—yes, he did." Jade looked very uncomfortable.*

*"Jade, I promise not to kiss you, okay?  Relax.  It's just me." Ed elbowed her gently in the ribs bringing a sad smile to her face.*

*Ed continued.  "I'm going to stay on and spend some time with Andrew until he's headed in the right direction, maybe help him some with his struggles with alcohol.  Then I want to connect with the other young men from Datka with the same struggles I had and see what God does.  I have AMRA's blessing on this little short-term venture and I really feel good about it.....so, maybe we will see each other soon in Fairbanks. I have to return there and have a meeting with the head-honchos in a couple of months and see what the future holds.  Things are a bit uncertain, but I don't really need more than light enough to see one step in front of me.  That's good enough."*

*Jade looked out into the trees awhile before speaking.  "How can you want to take on such a project as the young men, Ed?  Haven't you had enough of that in your life that you would want to stay away from those kinds of people?  Don't you want order and direction in your future and not just 'light for one step ahead?'......Ed, these young men have*

28

*made their choices, and now they need to deal with the consequences. What can you do for them?"*

*Ed didn't answer. Inside, he knew he didn't need to answer. Jade was obviously not in his immediate future. They saw things so differently. He needed to hear her say what she thought and she just did, very plainly.*

*"Jade, our fights usually go back to how differently you and I see things, don't they? Everyone's world can't be all order and perfect people. You will search the rest of your life if that's what you are really looking for. It's the inside that I care about with these guys, not the outside. Don't you see that?"*

*A humorless laugh escaped from Jade's lips. "Ed, you sound just like my dad."*

*"I will take that as a compliment then. My boat leaves in ten minutes, so I guess this is it. I will see you soon, Jade. Still friends?" Ed held out his hand to her.*

*"No matter our differences, Tex, we can do better than a handshake."*

Ed could still feel Jade in his arms as they shared one last hug before their paths took them separate ways for a few weeks. A deep sigh escaped from Ed's lips along with a whispered prayer that bounced around the walls of the tiny room.

"God, I don't have a clue what is in store for me and Jade, maybe nothing more than friendship. But whatever You have planned, that's what I want. Help me trust and walk close to You, to hear Your voice and know where You are leading me. I want to help Andrew and his buddies with their struggles and I *know* You want me to be here for them. I give You myself. Use me however and wherever You see fit. I trust You, God. Amen."

Leaning up on one elbow, Ed listened for more snoring coming from Andrew's room through the thin walls. Sure enough, he could still hear the young man sawing logs. Chuckling to himself, Ed decided a walk into town was what he needed. Lying around gave his mind too much freedom to wander and dwell on things he could do nothing about. Ed scribbled a note to let Andrew know he was headed into town, then pulling his boots and shirt back on, he slipped the note under Andrew's door and left.

Exiting the hotel on Seal Harbor's Main Street, Ed headed for *Freda's Diner* for a cup of coffee and slice of pie. He had a few items to purchase at *Smitty's Five and Dime* but his growling stomach signaled it was way past lunch time.

Nearing the AST office, Ed saw his newly acquired friend, Sergeant Will Walker enter the front door. Head down, Walker hadn't spotted Ed, so the young man decided to step in, say hello, and give the Sergeant an update on Andrew.

Ed reached the office and set the brass bell above the door to clanging as he entered. Turning from the constantly filled coffee pot, Sergeant Walker smiled as he looked up to see Ed.

"Hello, Ed. What brings you here?" Setting down his cup, Will extended his hand to Ed.

Ed firmly returned the handshake and answered, "Boredom, I guess. I should ask you the same since this is your off day. Andrew is getting in a Sunday nap at the hotel, and I couldn't settle down so I

30

went for a walk. Got too much still to resolve to relax. How's the family?"

"Good. Sophia took Lauren to church this morning. I was called to an investigation at 5:00 a.m. so didn't get to go with the girls. Coffee?" Will extended a clean cup in Ed's direction.

"Sure. I was headed to the diner for coffee and pie when I saw you. I can get pie later." Ed accepted the offered cup.

"Believe it or not, I have two slices of my wife's homemade apple pie she sent with me this morning. No time for breakfast so she shoved a sack lunch in my hand when I left. Sophia's afraid I will starve to death, I guess." Will rubbed his slightly plump belly. Still fit for his sixty-two years, the extra pieces of pie were starting to barely show.

"Great! I love apple pie. And this will give me a chance to run some ideas by you concerning Andrew."

Will retrieved two plates and forks from the office's little kitchen area and placed a man-sized pie slice on each then motioned Ed to the chair in front of his desk. "Mm-mmm. My Soph knows how to make a pie. So fill me in. What are you thinking?"

Around bites of delicious pie and coffee, the men discussed what might be best for Andrew and his future. They decided that it would be better for the young man to return to Datka Island and try to make amends with his family and community there than stay in Seal Harbor surrounded by the temptation to return to booze and his old ways and friends. Andrew had expressed a desire to return to the Island, but was afraid of how he would be received after stealing from his parents and from another inhabitant from his home place. It wouldn't be easy, but Ed was willing to return to Datka and stay with him until Andrew was settled back into a routine.

"When will you return to the Island?" the Sergeant asked Ed.

"First, Andrew said he needs to go to his house here at Seal Harbor and get some things, and then we will rent a boat for Datka if the weather holds out."

"Sounds like a great plan. So you are willing to stay in Alaska for some time? How will this affect your life in Washington to uproot for a time? That's a huge commitment, Ed." Will's face showed true concern for the man.

"You're right, it does affect my life in Washington. I've spent much time in prayer and discussion with the AMRA director that I am under. You remember John Miller. He is of course back in Fairbanks and has talked with the other heads of AMRA and they have given me their thumbs up to stay under the umbrella of AMRA while I work here on the Island with Andrew and the other young men struggling with the same issues. And AMRA thinks that if I can stay in touch with the people of Datka it will help the mission board keep its finger on the pulse of the Island. We still have several projects to complete there. I can help with those while I work with Andrew. I resigned from my coaching position for the first semester of this school year. The superintendent said I could have my old job back in January if I want. I feel like this is where I am supposed to be, but there are just so many loose ends." The tall Texan fumbled with his shirt tail as he talked giving away his trepidation over his future.

Noticing Ed's uneasiness, Will questioned him. "I know you believe you should work with Andrew and his friends, so why the anxiety? What loose ends are you dealing with?"

32

"Well, for one, housing. I will be provided a small monthly allowance by AMRA to help with expenses in exchange for my work here, but I have no idea where to even begin looking for a place to stay. Do I move to Datka? Should I stay in Seal Harbor? What about transportation to and from the Island? You know, all the usual questions. Who, what, when, where, how, and why?" His usual jovial demeanor appeared as a half-grin erupted across Ed's face.

Leaning back in his desk chair, Will laced his fingers behind his neck and frowned in concentration. "Hmmmm."

Ed let him absorb all of this information for a moment and sat in silence sipping the remainder of his coffee. He lifted his fork and pressed it into the last few crumbs on his plate then devoured those too.

Finally, Will spoke. Leaning forward with his elbows on his desk, he looked as if he had a plan. "I think I may have a solution for you, man. Obviously your work with the projects will have you back and forth between Seal Harbor and Datka Island. I am sure you can stay with a family on the Island, so your lodging here in Seal Harbor is the big issue. Let me talk it over with Sophia, but I already know she won't mind. I have a small hunting cabin at the back of our property that you are welcome to stay in for free and you can eat your evening meals at our house. I'm sure Soph's pie might convince you to do that. The cabin isn't much. It was already there when we bought the land and we built our house not far from it. It's basically just a one room cabin with a sleeping and kitchen area and a tiny bathroom. If you can handle living in a cracker box, it's yours for as long as you need it."

As Will talked, Ed felt hope swell in his chest once more. "That would be great, Sergeant! Talk to your wife and daughter first, and then we will discuss it again soon." Ed couldn't contain his excitement. "I better get back before Andrew wonders if I abandoned him."

Shaking hands with Will, Ed nearly floated out of the office. God definitely had His big hand on him and was working things out. Expectation rose inside of Ed along with a deep sense of knowing that he was in the middle of God's plan. Nothing was more fulfilling to him than that.

Knocking on Andrew's hotel door, Ed waited with his hands in his pockets anxious to tell his news to the younger man.

A sleepy Andrew answered the door. He was just buttoning his shirt when Ed arrived. Yawning, Andrew stretched his arms over his head and stepped back to let Ed enter. "Come in, Ed. I slept longer than I thought I would have. Now I am starving. Did you get a nap?"

Ed chuckled at his Aleut friend's jet black hair standing on end. "Nah. I couldn't sleep. You look like a bear waking from hibernation."

Andrew tried to smooth his coarse, black, hair back in place, but it was no use. He needed to get to his house, if you could call it that, and collect the remainder of his toiletries and clothing. "I am ready to go back to my place and get the rest of my belongings. What do you think, Ed? The weather looks like it will hold off on rain and wind for the next few days so this may be as good a chance as any to make the boat trip to the Island."

Clapping Andrew on the back, Ed agreed. "Let's do this if you are ready."

Enjoying the twenty minute walk to Andrew's small house, the two remained silent all the way to the front door. Andrew rode the waves of emotions, vacillating between hope and discouragement, fear and strength. He longed to see his messed up life change, yet wondered if he was capable of walking it out. Not only did he desire to be reunited with his mother, Natalia, and his sister, Rose, Andrew wanted to see his Datka community once again and live in peace among them. His many mistakes hounded him while the words of truth, forgiveness, and life from his friend Ed did their best to remain in the forefront of his mind. Andrew knew the road ahead would be a difficult and challenging path, but with Ed and his fledgling-faith in God, he believed he would make it.

Visions of a pretty face danced before him. Andrew still held onto the dream of wanting to free Berta, his girl. It was so very difficult to think of her in another man's arms. The last conversation they had, Andrew promised Berta as soon as he could earn the money he would take her away from *Rita's Place* and they would run off to start a new life together. But Berta couldn't see herself in any other way than what she was, a young, used, girl without hope of ever escaping the life she had chosen. No matter what Berta thought at the present, Andrew was determined to show her he could and would get her out. She needed and deserved a new life, just like he was on the brink of getting, and he would help her find it as soon as possible. Not only for his sake, but for Berta's, Andrew would work hard to make the necessary changes to live a free and good life.

Tucked back in the trees, the leaning shed of a house appeared before them. Startled at the condition of the place, Ed broke the silence. "Is this it? This is where you live?"

Embarrassment caused Andrew's face to turn bright red. "Yes. This is it. I know it isn't much, but at the time, I wanted to be free and this was the only way I could see to try to stand on my own, live alone, be a man. What a mistake!" Stopping in his tracks, with new eyes Andrew saw the place for what it was. Nothing more than a falling down, one room shack that looked more like a prison than freedom. Except for Patrolman Dorne and his constant intimidation and threats, the jail cell he had been locked up in at the AST office had been better than this place.

Slowly Andrew ascended the steps to the small, rotting porch. Withdrawing a key from his pocket, he unlocked the door and pushed it open. Mustiness, dust, and old empty booze bottles assaulted his and Ed's senses when they entered. Switching on the small lamp on the bedside table, the dim light illuminated the tiny room.

Grabbing a canvas bag from the floor, Andrew began stuffing it with his few belongings, clothes, a pair of shoes, a sheathed knife, a comb, the colorful blanket from the bed, and other assorted items. Looking under the bed, Andrew reached for the cedar club he had fashioned long ago with the help of his now dead father.

Remembering the last time he had laid eyes on the club, the day of his arrest seemed eons ago. That day, every fiber of his being had screamed at him to grab the club and use it on the face of Patrolman Dorne. Until his eye had fallen on the yellow satin ribbon that was lying on the floor beside the club. Berta's ribbon. The yellow ribbon had kept him from doing the unthinkable.

*Where is Berta's ribbon?* Andrew wondered to himself. He patted the fronts of his shirt pocket and then remembered tucking it in his inside coat pocket. Reaching inside his coat, Andrew withdrew the ribbon. A small, sad smile touched his lips.

Ed stood back and quietly took the scene in, allowing Andrew the time he needed to gather his things. He watched the varying emotions cross Andrew's face. "You okay, man?"

Startled from his thoughts, Andrew stuffed the ribbon back into its secret place. Clearing his throat, he reached for an empty box on the floor and headed towards the small cupboard on the opposite wall. With his back towards Ed, he answered, "Yes. I am fine. Let's hurry up and get out of here."

Andrew began filling the small box with a few dishes and canned goods. They weren't much, but they were his.

"Can I do anything to help?" Ed looked around the small room furnished with the bed, cupboard, small kitchen table, and one chair. "Is the furniture yours?"

"No. It belongs to the man who let me rent this place." Andrew cast his eyes around the room. Sitting down on the bed, momentary weariness engulfed him as the weight of his very recent past life set in. Booze, theft, girls....bitterness, lies, hatred. Unconsciously, Andrew reached for Berta's yellow ribbon again. Withdrawing it, he ran the silky strand between his fingers.

Ed waited. Silently he prayed for Andrew. *God help me to help him.*

*Ask.* Hearing the word deep in his soul, Ed took this as his cue. *Ask him.*

"Andrew, what's the story with the yellow ribbon?" Ed sat and waited. When he thought Andrew hadn't heard the question, the young man opened his mouth to speak.

A mirthless laugh escaped from Andrew. Still holding the ribbon, the Aleut man spilled the short, sad tale to his Texan friend. "I have told you about Peter bringing booze and girls to Datka and how my friends and I would pay Peter for both. What I didn't tell you is that I met a….a sweet, beautiful girl, and….she and I—we—she was the only girl……" Hanging his head, Andrew paused.

To ease the discomfort of the moment, Ed filled in the blanks for Andrew. "You and this girl were a pair?"

"Yes, and she was the only girl I was ever with. My friends did not care what girl they had, only that they were with a girl. The girls did not care either. Except for Berta." Again, Andrew paused.

"Berta was your girl? A *special* girl to you, Andrew?" Ed's frown deepened as he tried to understand what Andrew was implying.

Rubbing his hand over his eyes, Andrew sniffed loudly. Taking a deep breath, he answered, "Yes, she was. I mean, still is. At least before I was in jail. I saw her that week of my arrest and told her that I love her and want to help her escape from where she lives. Berta lives with a woman across town who runs a pool hall and houses girls willing to—to—"

Slowly Andrew shook his head. Between gritted teeth, he ground out the next words. "I want her out of there!"

Andrew stood from the bed and paced the room like a caged animal. Something caught his eye as he walked by the small table. Retrieving a scrap of paper, he unfolded it and immediately blanched as he read the words. Dropping the paper, Andrew fell into the chair beside him. Placing his head in his hands, a low moan escaped from his throat.

Ed quickly snatched the bit of paper from the dirty floor. Quietly he read.

*Your girl is in our hands.*
*Keep your mouth shut or*
*you will never see her pretty face again.*

"Andrew, what does this mean?" Ed shook Andrew's shoulder.

Pushing back from his chair, Andrew's face was a mask of pain, utter hatred, and deep fear. "He took her! I know he did! Berta's gone......." Trailing off again, Andrew sunk to his knees on the floor. Bending at the waist, he fell face down on the filthy wood. "Nooooo! No! No! Not Berta....."

Stunned, Ed could only stand and watch the grieving man before him. Walking to the front porch of the shack, Ed looked to the spot of sky in the tall evergreens and breathed a prayer heavenward. "Help us, God. Help Berta wherever she is."

Fear constricted Ed's chest. It felt as if all the forces of evil in the world has descended on the tiny shack, and he was left to defend Andrew, himself, and an unknown girl.

# CHAPTER 4

The short airplane ride from Alaska to Washington allowed for one of two things, quiet reflection or a quick nap. Rebecca Parker would have preferred the latter, but her mind overrode her tired body this time.

Looking across the aisle of the small aircraft, Becca smiled sweetly at her son and husband as they both snored quietly. Pride swelled in her heart as she watched Gabe and Rand sleep knowing both were equally exhausted. The end of an eventful mission trip always did this to them. She would have to sleep later though.

Graying at his temples, her handsome husband, Randall, or Rand as she affectionately started calling him when they were dating, was ready to return to their home in Little River, Washington and to their teaching jobs. Rand and Becca both worked for the same school district in their town, he as a high school teacher and she as a kindergarten teacher. Rand loved these mission trips as much as she did, but he loved teaching his students too.

Believing that men had a way of returning to normal much more quickly than women, Becca pushed aside her envy for the moment and sighed deeply. Trying for a different position in the small seat, Becca resettled herself for the remainder of the trip.

Turning towards the foggy window, Becca wiped the condensation from the glass as she looked below at the changing landscape before her eyes. So much had changed, just like this view. Only six months ago she wondered aloud to Rand if they were through with mission trips, especially the arduous, difficult ones on the

Aleutian Islands. Both fifty years of age, she questioned their wisdom in future trips.

But the very week she wondered if they would return, the couple had received a phone call from AMRA that their beloved Aleut people of Datka Island had survived a fire that damaged homes, fishing boats, and the school. That was all it took for she, Rand, and Gabe to respond to the call to go. Gabe had headed up the team and invited his best friend, Ed Hamilton as well. They had just ended their time on the Island, and after several months of hard work, forged relationships, trials, and triumphs, Becca knew her mind and body were still processing all that had happened.

*Oh, a quick nap would be so wonderful right now. I envy my two men.* Brushing a strand of lightly gray-streaked, blond hair from her face, Becca let her musings have their way.

One emotion after another vied for position. Momentarily she felt her throat constrict as she pictured the precious Aleut people, her other family, as they stood on the shoreline of Datka and waved good-bye to them. Their characteristic dark brown eyes, black hair, dark skin, and giant smiles would stay in her memory forever. Becca could still feel the small hands of the children holding hers as she walked with them looking for special rocks. She could feel the brush of the weathered hands of the older women as they cooked together in the large kitchen preparing lunches for the hard-working men as they rebuilt the homes and repaired the school. A tear trickled down her cheek unchecked.

In the place of bittersweet sadness, a touch of anxiety surfaced. One particular Aleut face crossed her mind's eye. Sweet Rose. Physically unlike her Aleut people in several ways, the tall, hazel-eyed girl had stolen her son's heart, and now what would happen? Becca was concerned about Gabe and Rose and how their future would play out. No doubt, the two loved each other, only Becca kept hoping they would see clearly how it couldn't possibly work out. Oh, she loved Rose as well, but what would that mean for her son? Would he leave home for Alaska? Becca always knew Gabe held a very fond and special place in his heart, like she and Rand, for the Aleut people, but to consider a relationship with an Aleut girl? The second tear found its way down her face. Becca quickly swiped it and that particular train of thought away before anyone saw her distress.

Hitting her square in the gut, Becca knew she very possibly had one short month before Gabe might go back to AMRA. When they made the return trip to Fairbanks and AMRA headquarters last week, Gabe learned that the position he had filled in for as team leader was now open. The man who previously had the job needed to move to New York to care for his aging mother, so Gabe had been asked to consider the position in light of his logistics degree and the success of the recent mission trip to Datka. He had asked for one week to consider it before answering.

Deep down, Becca suspected he would accept. Before this mission trip, Gabe had been job-hunting and this was right up his alley with his passion and education.

And it was closer to Rose.

Her mother's heart was also torn with Edward Hamilton's decision to stay in Seal Harbor. She wanted Ed to follow God and His leading as much as she wanted her own son Gabe to. But Ed had been like a member of their family since he entered their world as a hurting,

43

broken, lonely teen. Could she stand having both the boys living far away? Ed's future plans were in limbo, as were Gabe's.

Feeling the air pressure in the small cabin of the plane change, Becca knew they were nearing Washington and the airport. She reached for her purse and sought a piece of gum. Digging around, Becca withdrew an unusual piece of paper. Frowning, she didn't recognize the paper nor the handwriting. Forgetting the gum, Becca's attention was on this strange page she held. Slowly she unfolded the paper and glanced at the top that read, *Dear Ms. Becca.* Her curiosity had the best of her now. Who snuck a letter into her purse without her knowledge? Glancing at the bottom, the feminine script read, *Forever grateful, Rose.*

A strange sensation gripped her stomach, a mixture of uncertainty and curiosity. Folding the paper in half, Becca glanced across the aisle to Rand and Gabe before continuing. Yes, both were still asleep. Turning her back to them, Becca opened the paper once again and read its contents.

*Dear Ms. Becca,*

*Words are difficult for me to find so I chose to think about what was in my heart and write you a letter instead of having a hurried conversation before you and your family left Datka. There are several things on my heart that I would like to tell you.*

*First, I am thankful to God that He brought you and Mr. Randall and Gabriel into my world and onto my Island. Your love for the Aleut people is very precious to me. I have known you since I was a little girl when you first came as missionaries to Datka. I am very grateful that*

*you brought God to our Island and to me. Without Him, I do not know*
*where I would be today.*

Becca looked up from the letter as a vision flashed before her
of a small group of young Aleut children sitting around her knees many
years ago while she taught the little ones stories and songs about God
and His Son, Jesus. Rose was among that group along with her son,
Gabriel. He began traveling to Datka Island when he was a boy of
about six and had been around the Aleut people for several weeks to a
few months every year of his young life. Yes, he and Rose had known
each other, had played together, but so had Gabe and many other Aleut
children. *Never* did Becca dream that her son would fall in love with
someone from the Island. Shaking her head, she returned to the letter.

*Second, I am thankful for the man you raised your son to be.*
*Most importantly, like you, Gabriel has also shown me the love of God*
*who saved my soul. And your son rescued me from drowning. He saved*
*my life so that I can know the love of God! I have never thanked you for*
*Gabriel's actions. Today, I say "thank you" for the son you raised.*
*And last, I am thankful for the friendship and love Gabriel has*
*shown me. Always he has been my friend since the first day he came to*
*Datka with you when he and I were children. But now, a deeper love has*
*grown in our hearts, a love that I did not expect to ever have. Gabriel*
*said that he told you and Mr. Randall of his words of love to me. I, in*
*return, love him.*

Mixed emotions toyed with Becca. She should be happy for her son. And Rose was a very beautiful, sweet, delightful girl. So why the turmoil?

*Gabe and I have talked about how our relationship might affect you and Mr. Rand. I know this must seem strange to you. I am an Aleut girl. I am not American, like the three of you, and we have so many differences.*

It was like Rose was reading Becca's mind. Their differences were great and that was part of what troubled her. Glancing back down at the paper in her hands, she read on.

*Ms. Becca, there are so many questions in my heart and Gabriel's but I know that God will lead us. I wanted to tell you that I do not take your son's confession of love for me lightly, but with great seriousness and joy. For now, I ask that you please pray for us.*
*Forever grateful,*
*Rose*

Quickly, Becca put the letter back in her purse. She had about ten minutes before they landed, and she needed to wake the sleeping guys. But before she did, Becca breathed a quick prayer. *God help me trust You with Gabe and Rose. I don't think this is the best for them. They come from two different worlds.*

Reaching for the piece of gum, Becca heard words whisper across her heart. *You have prayed for Gabe's future wife since he was a young boy.*

Becca hung her head as the truth became clear. Yes, she had prayed since he was born. But in her daydreams about her son's future wife, the face she saw was not at all like the face of Sweet Rose. She saw Gabe with a darling, God-fearing, girl who was *American*, for goodness sake! Not an *Aleut* beauty! Oh, how she had missed this one!

But what if he had made a mistake? What if Rose wasn't the one for him?

And what if she was?

Eight short hours later, Rand and Becca sat at their kitchen table in Little River, Washington enjoying the mountain's display out the picture window. Exhausted but satisfied with the last few months spent in Alaska, the couple reminisced and enjoyed the much needed alone time. Both sipped a cup of hot tea and reflected on their favorite moments with their precious Aleut people.

Rand's carbon copy, Gabe, entered the room. Father and son looked much alike except Gabe had Becca's clear blue eyes. Carrying a pair of worn sneakers in one hand and a sweatshirt in the other, Becca knew where he was headed.

Pulling out a chair opposite his parents, Gabe began putting on his shoes. He had missed his favorite jogging trail. "What are you two up to?"

"Just reminiscing about our time on Datka. And trying to decide who gets to go to the grocery store. There's absolutely nothing to eat in this house. What do you want for dinner, Son? I am craving a juicy steak." Rand watched Gabe as he finished tying his shoes.

"Steak sounds great! I've missed your cooking, Mom. I'm just headed out for a run, but I'll help with dinner when I get back. I need to run off some tension and pray through some things. I really missed running when we were gone." Gabe pulled his gray hooded sweatshirt over his blond head.

Becca reached across the table and laid a hand on Gabe's arm. "What's got you so tense, honey?"

A deep frown creased his brow. Gabe sighed deeply before answering. "I don't know.....the future, the offer to work for AMRA.....the Aleut people...." His words trailed off as he stood to retrieve a glass from the cabinet and get a drink of water.

"You will know what God wants you to do about the job offer. Dad and I are praying too." Becca hesitated a moment, wanting to ask a question, but unsure how to word it. "Gabe, what about you and Rose?"

"What do you mean? What *about* me and Rose?" Not like Gabe, his tone of voice held a hint of agitation at the question.

Her mind flashed back to the letter she found in her purse from Rose. "Well, we haven't exactly discussed your relationship with her. There was so much going on during the mission trip, we hardly had a chance to talk to you, much less ask any questions. From what Dad and I observed and heard, you and Rose have grown to like each other very much." Trying to keep her voice even, Becca smiled sweetly at the end of her little speech.

"Mom, you *know* how I feel about Rose. No, I haven't discussed it with you and Dad, but I have come to care for her very much. Yes, I declared my love to her and she said she loves me as well. I'm sorry, but I didn't realize I needed to *discuss* my feelings with you in advance." Gabe hated how he sounded to his mother. This was not like him at all. What was wrong with him?

Taken aback, Becca sputtered a retort. "Gabe, that's not what I meant—"

Always the peacemaker, Rand intervened. "Okay, you two. We are all exhausted and tense from the flight and trip." He stood and placed a hand on Gabe's shoulder. "Gabe, go enjoy your run. Mom and I will head to the store and maybe the three of us can talk later."

"You're right. We should talk later." Becca sipped her tea as she felt a tightening in her throat. Nothing grieved her more than being at odds with one of her guys.

Nodding at his father, Gabe exited the house, now even more in need of the run.

Becca hung her head after Gabe left the house. Tears threatened to spill over, but she would not allow them to. "Oh, Randall. Me and my big mouth."

Sitting down across from Becca, Rand took her hands in his. "Look at me, Becca. We are all tired and anxious and feeling every other emotion that can be felt right now, especially after a trip like the one we just finished. It was wonderful and difficult. I know how hard it was for you to leave, but still you wanted to come home to our normal routine." He gave her hands a gentle squeeze and continued. "Gabe will know what to do. He's at a threshold in his life and only he can make these decisions. You aren't helping him pick out his school clothes anymore, Becca. We have to let him process things and, like always, Gabe will talk to us when he's ready. Don't push him. I want to do the same, but now's not the time. We *have* to trust God with our son. We have prayed for him since the day he was born that Gabe would follow God's path for his life. Deal?" Rand smiled at his wife encouragingly.

Laughing quietly, Becca looked into his eyes. "Deal. I know you are right. It's just hard sometimes to let go......I need to show you something. I'll be right back."

Becca rose from the table and got her purse. Withdrawing a slip of paper, she handed it to her husband. "You need to read this. I found it in my purse when we were on the airplane coming home. It's from Rose."

Within minutes, Gabe was focusing on the gorgeous Washington scenery surrounding him. He forced himself to take deep breaths as he began a slow jog. The tall evergreen trees mixing with the stately birches seemed to touch the blue sky overhead. Before long, fall would be upon them in full force with its cooler days and cold nights. He loved this corner of the world, having lived here his entire life. How would he handle leaving this place he treasured so very much if he chose to move to Fairbanks, Alaska?

His mind replayed the exchange in the kitchen with his mother. His little family had always been close to each other and had shared what was going on in their lives and hearts freely. So why was he upset at her questions? His parents had every right to know what he felt and thought about his future and what his plans might be.

Thinking back over his time on Datka, Gabe realized he had been so very busy heading up the team of workers for the last three months that most of his time with his parents was spent working. There had been little to no time for quiet talks. Without wanting to admit it, the truth stared him in the face. He had intentionally created space between the three of them when he saw his heart being pulled toward Rose. Down deep, Gabe knew this would be a topic he normally would have wanted to discuss with them, but with the circumstances and obvious differences surrounding his and Rose's relationship, Gabe secretly feared that they would not approve. Thus, the distance between them.

As his feet picked up speed and pounded out a rhythm on the trail before him, Gabe's thoughts turned to Rose. There was absolutely no question in his mind that he loved her and she, in return, loved him. He knew the promise he made to her to return and never leave her was true. Rose had stated that she believed Gabe's words and they both committed their hearts and lives to God and His plan for their future. Gabe felt a deep ache in his heart to be with Rose.

The frustrating part was the logistics of their relationship. The one thing he knew how to handle and deal with. What he had gotten a college degree in. But he could not, for the life of him, figure out the logistics of his and Rose's future. Knowing he had sounded confident in his love and commitment to her the last time they were together, Gabe still believed it was not *impossible* for them to have a future together, but how was it *possible*?

The one link was this job offer with AMRA to take over the future organization of the missions work. Just before leaving for Datka this past summer, he had been job hunting, looking for some way to use his degree. And now here it was right before him. The man who used to hold this position had to retire and move to New York and the door stood wide open for him to enter.

One short week. That had been his request from the AMRA board. He needed one week to pray and think about the huge changes that would happen in his life if he said yes to the job. Seven days to hear and know that he had made the right decision that would

51

influence the course of his life forever. Gabe had been given a week to decide and one month to make arrangements to make the big move if he chose to work for AMRA.

One bonus to taking the position was he would be closer to Rose in proximity, but still not close enough. Would the position limit how much he would be able to see her? Laughing quietly to himself, Gabe knew that was a silly thought. How much more would he see her if he remained in Washington? If he took the position with AMRA, it would definitely benefit his relationship with Rose. But he knew the decision must be based on what was best for him and the mission board, not on his love for Rose. It all seemed so confusing.

All of that aside, how would he handle leaving his home, parents, and his best bud, Ed? Home, family, and friends were on the top of Gabe's list of important things in life. Could he just *leave* all he held dear and start anew in a strange place, with a strange job, and a handful of people he knew?

Gabe needed someone else's input on this. Almost always seeking his parents' counsel first, Gabe wanted to talk to them and knew he owed them an explanation about his distance and attitude on the Island and earlier in the kitchen. But would they be the best ones to help him since his decisions would be difficult for his parents?

Gabe knew just who he would call. Pastor Greg.

# CHAPTER 5

Slamming the door a bit too hard, Jade Miller stalked into the front office of the AMRA headquarters, her long, dark, unruly hair escaping from its usual ponytail. Tugging her sweatshirt off, Jade headed for the office's kitchen in search of lunch and a drink. She was exhausted from running errands and helping her parents move into their new home. Today had been like all the others in the last week. Unending boxes and trash. Mountains of things to find a place for. Furniture to arrange. Cabinets to stock. *I feel more like forty years old than twenty,* the green-eyed girl grumbled to herself.

Jade entered AMRA's kitchen and opened the refrigerator looking for yesterday's left-over salad. Scrounging around in the kitchen, Jade finally found a fork and plate. She dumped the salad onto the plate and poured some dressing over the top. Next she found a bottle of root beer in the back of the refrigerator and a bottle opener then settled herself at the tiny table.

*Why am I so grouchy? That's not like me,* Jade mused. She felt the frown line that creased the spot between her eyes and willed herself to relax. Thoughts began tumbling in on each other as she hungrily ate her left-overs.

*Maybe this week has worn me out. New house. New environment. New job for Mom and Dad. I'm not adjusting as quickly as I thought I would. I miss the people from Datka but we will go back soon. I was excited to settle in Fairbanks and work with the mission board. It's what I have enjoyed all my life. So why the sour attitude?*

Immediately a tall, dark-haired man with an accent as big as Texas flashed to mind. Ed Hamilton, or "Tex," as she called him. She missed hearing his cute nickname he had for her. No one else called her "Little Lady." But it was obvious to Jade that they came from two very different worlds. She and Ed had shared an exciting mission trip together and were inseparable every day on Datka for three months. And how could she not be attracted to the handsome guy that oozed charm? They either got along really well or they acted like a brother and sister who fought constantly about everything.

And then there was that kiss. Jade felt her cheeks flame to life at the thought of their one, unexpected, unplanned kiss.

But it was all wrong. Ed wasn't her type; that was certain. She wanted a man who had been pure like her, saved himself for his future wife, had the same values and morals as hers, and was on the same level spiritually as she was.

No. Ed Hamilton would never fit those requirements.

Guilt swirled in the pit of her stomach as she remembered that Ed *was* on the same level as her spiritually. He had given his life to Christ about four years ago if she remembered correctly but had lived a very wild and crazy life before that. Jade had her standards and she was determined to stick by them and hold out for the perfect guy.

Even if her dad didn't think that was fair or right.

*Enough about Ed, Jade. That will do you no good thinking about him.* But Jade truly missed him. Was that why she had been so grumpy? Because she was letting Edward Hamilton get to her?

Dumping the remainder of her salad in the trash, Jade was quickly startled when she turned around. She hadn't seen her mother, Jill Miller, enter the small kitchen. Letting out a little squeal, Jade put her hand over her heart to still it.

54

"Mom! You scared me!" Jade spoke a bit too harshly to her mother.

"I'm sorry, honey. You looked deep in thought when I came in here. What has you so distracted?" Jill hugged her daughter.

"I don't know, Mom. Maybe I am just tired from the moving and unpacking." The girl's jade-green eyes matched her mother's. Both were short and athletically built with dark, wavy hair, only Jill's was cut in a shorter style more fitting to her fifty-something years.

Jill looked into her daughter's eyes. She reached a thumb to smooth away the frown line on Jade's forehead. "Honey, I understand. It always hits me hard when we end a mission trip. Remember after our Guatemala stay how sad I was for months? And on top of the trip being over, you are having to adjust to a new home and new jobs for all of us. Things are *different*, yet *good*. Change is always hard. Give yourself time."

"You're right. I really do miss the Aleut people and look forward to going back," Jade said.

Jill winked at Jade and replied, "Maybe you will see Ed since he's staying at Seal Harbor and visiting Datka frequently."

"Mom—Ed has nothing to do with how I feel right now." Jade's frown returned.

Leaving the kitchen, Jill said over her shoulder in a teasing voice, "I wouldn't be so sure."

"Ugh!" Jade stalked out of the kitchen and headed toward her father's office. She found him sitting at his desk eating a sandwich and looking over some paperwork.

"Hi, my green-eyed doll!" John always could coax a smile out of Jade even on her worst days.

"Hey, Daddy." She plopped down in the chair in front of him as the phone jangled on his desk.

Holding up one finger to Jade, he answered the phone. "AMRA Headquarters, John Miller."

Jade could tell the voice on the other end of the line was male.

"Hi, Ed! How's Seal Harbor treating you?" John listened for a response.

*Good grief! I can't even get away from Ed here,* Jade fumed. Shifting in her seat, Jade decided to listen in on the conversation a minute.

"How is Andrew? Did you get him settled on Datka yet?" Again John paused.

"What?......Oh, no!....Yes, we will be praying.....I'm meeting with the new pastor and his family for the Datka church tomorrow and will schedule a trip to the Island for next week, if not sooner. Keep me posted on Andrew. I will call you in a day or two. Let me get your phone number for the Sergeant's place......" John scribbled down the number and ended the call with Ed.

"What's wrong, Daddy? That didn't sound good." Jade was curious now. Removing her ponytail holder, she shook out her wavy hair and tried to tame it again.

"Run get your Mom and I will fill you both in. I'm going to call Rand and Becca to get them praying too." John lifted the phone's receiver as Jade went in search of her mother.

The two women returned to John's office just as he hung up from talking to Rand.

"Honey, what's wrong? Jade said there was an emergency based on your talk with Ed." Concern colored Jill's face.

"In a nutshell, Ed took Andrew back to his house to get the remainder of Andrew's belongings to move him back to the Island. They found a note on Andrew's table saying that a girl Andrew was in a relationship with had been kidnapped! Ed can't get any details out of Andrew except that the girl was someone he used to see before going to jail. Andrew has clammed up and won't tell him anything else. He is very upset. Ed asked us to pray. He said Andrew won't listen to him about going to the AST for help. This just doesn't make sense. Why would someone take a girl that Andrew knows and leave him a threatening note?" John shook his head in confusion.

"Oh, my goodness." Jill put a hand to her heart. "That's crazy!"

"Daddy, what can we do? Is she a resident of Datka?" Jade was concerned too.

"Jade, I don't know any more than what Ed said. I am meeting with the new pastor tomorrow for lunch and will plan to go to the Island as soon as possible. What a way for the man to start his position! Coming on the scene during a possible kidnapping? Girls, we need to pray."

The three did what came very natural for them. They formed a tight circle and lifted the situation to the One who could handle things best.


After returning to her new home in Fairbanks and having dinner with her family, Jade went to her bedroom to think. Shoving aside a stack of books that occupied the center of her bed, Jade plopped down with her favorite pink pillow. She hugged it to her chest and stared at the empty wall across from her that awaited her decorative pictures and favorite photos of old friends and past mission trips.

*What a predicament Ed is in,* she thought. *Having to deal with a man right out of jail and getting him settled back into his community, and now the man's girlfriend has been kidnapped! Who would do such a thing to a girl? I can't imagine who Andrew's girlfriend is. Surely not someone from Datka. I met all of the girls there and none of them ever spoke of Andrew. Maybe someone from his past in Seal Harbor? God, please be with this girl whoever she is. And help Ed know how to deal with Andrew.*

Jade shifted her position and stretched out on her bed, her mind engaged in its own private conversation. *I tried to get Ed to see that this wasn't smart taking on a project like Andrew. And now it's causing him grief. He should have listened. I wish I could talk to him......Silly, you would only end up fighting because Ed doesn't see the truth that people have to suffer the consequences of their choices. I just don't get how Ed would* want *to help a man like Andrew.* Slowly shaking her head, Jade just couldn't grasp *why* Ed insisted on the fact that God *wanted* him to help someone who was a known drunk and thief. It seemed to Jade, that with Ed's past life, he would do whatever it took to stay away from the likes of Andrew.

The face of the man she enjoyed being with, but knew would never be compatible with her, flitted before her. *Oh, Ed. If only you could see things the way I do. We might could have had a future together if you had lived a better life.*

Jade recalled a moment right before leaving Datka; her father had found her sitting alone and crying. He had hugged her tightly to himself and listened to Jade pour out her heart.  Their conversation flashed in her mind.

*"Dad, why would God send us here and then I meet this wonderful guy who has absolutely no interest in me who would be the perfect guy for me, and then I get to know this other guy who is the most imperfect guy for me and my heart and emotions and mind get all confused?  Nothing makes sense right now, nothing, Dad.  I know Gabe has only feelings of friendship for me, and I have come to terms with that.  Ed has feelings for me, strong feelings, actually.  I like him and then the next minute I can't stand him......He either makes me laugh or makes me mad.  And before we know it, we will all go our separate ways and live separate lives.....like I said, how can I talk about this, Dad?"  Jade huffed an exasperated sigh.*

*John chuckled.  "Sounds like you are doing a pretty good job of talking about it to me, honey.  Jade, none of us know what the future holds, what God has in store for each of us.  All we can do is take it one day at a time and when we do hear God's voice or feel Him leading us to go here or do this, like when we knew we were supposed to leave Guatemala and move to Alaska, then we do what we believe He is telling us.  In the meantime when we don't know exactly what to do or what to think, that's when we trust.  Simple quiet trust.  We are still on the inside, and trust.  And wait.  Fretting and worrying leads to nothing good, Jade. It only clouds and darkens our mind and our ability to hear God......As for the perfect and imperfect guys, what is determining if they are perfect or imperfect? Your standards and ideals?  Your judgment?  Yes, we are to be smart and choose our mates wisely, but you will shut out some really great men, Jade, if you are too harsh and critical in your opinion of them. It's a person's heart that matters, not their past."*

Frustrated, Jade rolled to her stomach and buried her face in her arms. *But why can't I see beyond Ed's past to his heart like Dad says? Maybe if I could, then there would be a future for us. He loves God, wants to serve Him, enjoys missions work, has a great sense of humor, is handsome.....But he doesn't fit the image of who my future mate should be. Maybe I need to give him another chance and see if something happens between us, something more than a few laughs and one stupid kiss.*

Jade flopped around on the bed a while longer and pondered writing Ed a letter, maybe telling him of her desire to get to know him better and see what happened with their friendship. She definitely liked Edward Hamilton; there were just some things that tripped her up when she saw him in her future. Things that could make or break a relationship as far as she was concerned. His past would never go away, even though he had changed. She just couldn't see herself with someone who had been as wild as a bucking bronco and she had been the polar opposite.

Grabbing her notebook and pen, Jade started a letter.

*Hey Tex,*

*How have you been? I'm still adjusting to my new surroundings, but I feel sure I will settle in great in Fairbanks.*

*I've really missed you.*

Jade stopped and chewed on her pen thinking. Placing pen to paper she continued to write her letter to Ed, ready to do something she had never done.

Expose her heart to the man she couldn't get off her mind.

# CHAPTER 6

With lunch time nearly over, Sergeant Will Walker's stomach reminded him of its neglect. It had been six hours since he had eaten Sophia's wonderful blueberry pancakes, maple syrup, and elk sausage early that morning. Deciding he would head over to *Freda's Diner* for a club sandwich, Will began stacking his paperwork to complete later.

The Alaska State Trooper's office door jangled loudly as the bell swung back and forth from its brass hook. Will looked up to see his patrolman, Tom Dorne, enter.

"Whoo-weee, you stink, Dorne." Will waved a hand over his nose at the offensive cigarette smell wafting off his patrolman and emitted a loud sneeze.

"Sorry, Sarge. Should have aired out a bit before coming in here. Nasty habit I picked up in high school." Dorne removed his hat and hung it on the hook after attempting to clear the air with it first.

Will enjoyed their easy banter. "How was lunch?"

"Good, Sarge. Had the special at *Freda's*. She cooks a mean pot roast and potatoes." Dorne sat down in his desk chair and leaned back, propping his feet on the desk.

"I was just about to head over for a sandwich, but pot roast sounds better. Hey, I've been meaning to ask you. Where were you Sunday morning? Hughes and I swung by your place to get you for the investigation on the missing girl at *Rita's Place*. Your car was gone. That was probably about 5:00 a.m. That's early for you to be out on a Sunday morning. Sunrise church service?" Will knew Dorne didn't attend church, but he liked to tease him from time to time.

"Yeah, that was it, Sarge. Sunrise service." Dorne laughed, but evaded the question.

Waiting for an answer, Will stood watching Dorne stretch and yawn. "Well....."

Immediately shifting his relaxed position, Dorne tensed up at the question. "Uh—my sister's boy had a birthday--and I completely forgot about it until Saturday morning, so I made a mad dash to their house. Her husband and I got too involved in a little card game after the boy's party and I didn't want to drive home that late Saturday night......so I came home Sunday afternoon."

"Oh, that reminds me. I've been meaning to call them about the car they had for sale. I really need to get something better for Soph and it sounds like what I want by the way you described it." Will put his cap on his head. "Leave her phone number on my desk again. I seem to have misplaced it. Gotta run. That pot roast is calling my name." Will donned his sergeant's hat and left the office.

Cursing under his breath, Dorne expelled a deep sigh along with the offensive words. He ran his hands through his crew cut, snatched up a section of the newspaper from his desk and wadded it in a tight ball. Throwing as hard as he could, Dorne sent the paper sailing across the room. It bounced off the wall and rolled across the floor.

The stress was taking its toll on him as he tried to uphold the perfect patrolman's image in the office and control his emotions at the same time. Jumping up from his chair, Dorne paced the floor from one end of the office to the other. His mind raced with tangled thoughts.

*I can't give Sarge my sister's number. Why on earth did I use her as an excuse for where I was Sunday morning? Maybe he will forget about the stupid car. I can't risk him calling her!* His brain had too

64

much to keep straight. The lies were closing in around him and were more numerous than he could keep track of. Dorne's breath quickened as he paced a while longer. Consciously slowing down, Dorne sat at his desk again and focused on the work at hand. He had to get some things accomplished and this wasn't helping matters.

A half hour later, the doorbell announced Will's return from lunch.

"How was the pot roast, Sarge?"

"Perfect as usual. The only thing that Freda could have added to it was a place to take a nap after eating such a fine meal. I know better than to stuff my belly and have to return to work." Will let out a loud yawn. He ran a hand over his face and started another pot of coffee.

Dorne looked up from his desk and tried to sound casual. "Hey, Sarge. Any developments on the kidnapping at *Rita's Place*? I haven't heard you mention anything in a couple of days."

"No, nothing. I think I will send Hughes back over this weekend to investigate some more and question the girls and Rita again. See if they remember any other details. Likely, the missing girl's a runaway and she just wanted to disappear. That's my best guess. Still, I want to see if Rita or the others have come up with anything else."

"I agree. She probably just ran away. Not much more to investigate if you ask me. Just a waste of time if she's a run-away. I say let her be," Dorne replied wanting to encourage the Sergeant's run away theory.

A deep frown creased Will's forehead showing his complete displeasure at Dorne's comment. "That's *not* what I mean at all, Dorne.

Any missing person is *not* a waste of this department's time! I will expect you to remember that in the future."

"Sorry, Sarge.....That came out all wrong." Dorne mentally chided himself for not watching his words better. Looking for a reason to get out of the office, Dorne asked, "Want me to go over to the elementary school and see what Mrs. Parkins called about? Sounds like a bear probably messing with the trash behind the building and not vandals snooping around."

"Yes, Dorne. Why don't you check on that this afternoon?" Will fought to keep the frustration out of his voice.

Making a hasty exit, Dorne grabbed his hat and jacket. He was ready to get out of there for a while.

Will shoved back his chair and headed for the coffee pot. Wide awake now after Dorne's display, Will was still fuming silently at his patrolman's words. *What has gotten into Dorne?*

Stirring the usual three spoons of sugar into the hot brew, Will sat back down at his desk. *Where did I put his sister's phone number? It's got to be here somewhere.* Never having been called a neat person, Will shuffled papers around on his desk top and then rummaged through its four drawers. He lifted the large desk calendar and peeked underneath. A yellow slip of paper caught his eye, one he didn't readily recognize. *Maybe that's her number.*

Will unfolded the paper and saw it was a note instead. Silently he read the words.

*Sgt. Will,*

*Call me when you have a moment to talk privately. Have a few things to discuss with you. Will be on vacation a week from tomorrow for ten days. Hopefully we can talk before I leave town.*

*Hughes*


Remembering seeing this note before, Will tried to recall when Hughes had left it. Finally, he knew. After Andrew had been arrested by Hughes and Dorne for stealing traps, Will had found the note when he returned to the office after being sick with the flu. Unable to work for several days, Dorne and Hughes had handled things for him while he recovered.

The last several weeks had been taken up with Hughes' vacation and with the kidnapping investigation. With Hughes only in the AST office on weekends, there had been little time for Hughes to bring up whatever was on his mind. Will stuck the note in his shirt pocket, his interest heightened. He would have to find out what Hughes had needed to discuss with him that had been so urgent.

Continuing his search for Dorne's sister's number, he located it under the edge of his telephone after going through his entire desk. He would call Tammy later and see if their car was still for sale. Stuffing the other slip of paper in his shirt pocket, Will shook his head at his absent-mindedness. *Mental note, Will: Call Tammy and Hughes.*

Hanging the *"Out of Office"* sign on the AST door, Will headed toward home. He had plenty to work out in his brain that couldn't possibly be accomplished in the stuffy office.

Catching his eye, Will noticed two half-smoked cigarette butts lying right by the front door of the office, one of the double green striped butts still smoldering. *Dorne. He knows I hate for him to drop his butts by the door. Expensive cigs to smoke only half of them.* Will ground out the cigarette with his heel and kicked the two offending butts away from the door then headed towards the comforts of home.

*******************

Stiffening at the soreness in her limbs, Berta slowly rose to a seated position. She had lost track of the number of days the sun had peeked through the cracks in the walls then disappeared once again. Her mind had turned to cotton, her body to mush, her spirit to utter despair. Time meant nothing. Thoughts of survival had waned after the first few days.

Treated like nothing more than a caged animal who received the barest of necessities, she looked forward to her food and water rations. Three times a day she would receive a jug of water and a small container with bread, jerky, cheese, and occasionally a piece of fruit. A larger bucket with a lid was left in the corner of the shed and removed each evening. This was her toilet. Berta had given up on any semblance of hygiene.

After her kidnapping when she had been brought to the dark, cold, cramped shed, Berta had torn a section from the bottom of her navy-blue, flowered, nightgown and used it to dip in the water then wash her wounds. Forcing herself to move around when she wasn't eating or sleeping, Berta was feeling less sore each day, though she still felt very weak. After what was probably the passing of two days, her tears had all but dried up. There were none left to cry. No longer thinking of herself, Berta's mind was consumed only with two thoughts. Ana's well-being and Andrew.

68

As with the past few consecutive days, her tiny visitor had now arrived. The little mouse seemed to know when food would be brought to the shed and would sniff around in the corners waiting for Berta to drop the smallest of crumbs for it to eat. At first, she detested the creature's presence, but now Berta watched for him to arrive and purposefully left crumbs for the mouse to gather. They had become fast friends, both dependent upon the other. Berta needed the distraction and companionship; the mouse needed the food.

Today had started out the same as the last. She awoke to the stream of sunlight and then very soon heard the approach of footsteps signaling the arrival of her food and water. Soon after Berta had been discarded in the horrible shed, she discovered the men meant no harm to her. They could have each had their way with her or beaten and tortured her, but all they ever did was speak quietly among themselves out of her earshot, bring her food, and remove her waste bucket. Some days, one or both came, but they were always dressed in black and wore a face mask.

Every time one of the men entered the shed, Berta scooted as far away as possible and remained quiet. She simply waited for their next move. Her past experience had taught her to never question her captor or draw any unwanted attention, but that it was always better to remain silent and wait. And that's just what she was doing. Waiting for the right moment to......to what? That was where Berta's mind always stopped. *What* exactly did she think she could say or do to change the situation? *Why* had she been kidnapped in the first place? They weren't abusing her or punishing her. The two men were simply holding her prisoner. But for no apparent reason.

If she let her mind wander too far, panic overwhelmed her. Then sheer panic pushed her to the brink of insanity, making her believe she would die in this God-forsaken shed and never see Ana again. In those moments, Berta's body began pouring sweat despite the cold temperatures. She would jump up and pace the small shed trying in desperation to plan an escape. Her pacing would turn to searching. Searching for a crack in the walls. Screaming her lungs out, hoping to be heard by someone, anyone. Hoping to be rescued and returned to her sister. But as the days went by and her screams weren't heard, she gave up on being rescued.

Berta was able to discern that she was in a shed tucked among trees. That much was obvious since she could hear leaves rustle when the winds picked up. It sounded like a lot of trees at times. Occasionally when it was still outside, she thought she could hear the faint sound of a nearby stream. Wondering if her mind was playing tricks on her, Berta focused on the reality of her surroundings. The graying wooden walls. The dust that floated in the streams of sunlight peeking through the cracks. The crumbling chinking between the walls.

And the constant sense of being totally forgotten and alone.

Lately, in her desperation Berta had turned to quietly talking to herself. Trying to stay calm and not go crazy. Then yesterday, Berta noticed what she was saying repeatedly, over and over, like a chant or rhyme or song.

*God, if You can hear me, please help me.*
*God, if You can hear me, please help me.*
*Please help me.*
*Please.*

It almost struck Berta as funny. She had never prayed a day in her life before yesterday. So why now? Why plead to a God she didn't know or even believe knew her? Why did her talking turn to praying?

She did notice one thing. It brought a semblance of calm and peace when her mind threatened to close in on itself and leave her an empty shell on the floor of the filthy shed.

So she continued the little prayer.

*God, if You can hear me, please help me.*

*God, if You can hear me, please help me.*

*Please help me.*

*Please.*

And then night fell.


The next morning before the sound of footsteps reached the shed's door, Berta heard two men talking quietly. She tried to make out their words, but could not even distinguish who was speaking. Berta assumed it was the two who had kidnapped her.

Intensity and anger filled one of the men's voices. The other man's voice rose to match the intensity of the first, and soon the two were arguing.

Fear crawled up her spine as Berta wanted away from the two angry men, but her gut told her to pay attention and listen to what was being said.

*God, if You can hear me.....please.*

Scooting as closely to the door as possible, Berta pressed her ear near a crack and strained to hear. Snatches of the heated conversation floated through to her.

"…..long do we keep her here?.....tired of playing the prison guard to a……."

"…..you want to lose your booze supply…..having that idiot kid turn us in…….keep him quiet this way."

"You are not having to empty the girl's bucket…..I am doing it all…..you are off with your women and booze…..stuck here…..done with this!"

Berta heard the crack of one man's fist come in contact with the other's body. Not sure what was happening, she knew a scuffle had ensued. The voices continued.

"……your buddy Andrew who will end what I have worked hard to……this girl will keep his mouth shut!…..you dare threaten me or tell me you are done……shut you down faster than your Aleutian head can……"

Grunts of pain followed the man's words. "…..give you a few more days and we need a new plan…..cannot keep her here in the same spot…..will find out." Berta could tell that obviously the one man who was sick of guarding her was trying to change the other's mind about things.

"…..give her the food and get out of here a while. Take a break and think things through. She's the only way to protect the…..do your job." Berta heard a set of footsteps retreating.

Silence surrounded her a minute longer. Then the sound of the other man cursing under his breath reached her ears. She could hear him pacing and cursing, trying to calm down after the altercation. His voice was plain enough to reach her ears. Berta froze in place, her breathing stopped as awareness settled in around her like a thick fog. She *knew* that voice! She knew who one of her captors was!

72

It was Peter.

Knowing who the man was only caused fear to tighten in her gut even more. Berta knew what Peter was capable of. She had seen him in action. A mean streak as wide as a stripe on a skunk, Berta had seen how Peter treated Andrew and his friends. Fear and intimidation were how he controlled everyone around him.

Berta and some of the girls from *Rita's Place* had been the ones traveling to and from Datka Island, with Peter as their escort. She had been Andrew's girl from the start of these little trips. The few Datka men had been a small source of income for Berta and her friends. Berta knew Peter was simply the delivery man for these Aleutian men, she and her friends from *Rita's Place* the goods. He had arranged the time, place, and women and had earned money off the boys as well. They were willing to pay, and Peter was willing to deliver.

But why was she the one they had targeted? What had they meant by her being the only way to protect something? Protect what? And what did Andrew have to play in this? What could he possibly end for these two men?

Berta's foggy brain couldn't make things fit together. She had some of the pieces to the puzzle, but the picture was still unclear. What was their connection, and what was Andrew's part?

At that moment the door to the shed came open and the black clothed, hooded man entered. Yes, she knew now, without a doubt, that it was Peter from his build and how he carried himself. In her state of distress, she had missed the similarities. Did she dare talk to him or address him?

Fear kept her silent as she watched him leave her food and water. Once again the lock clicked back in place on the shed door, leaving Berta trapped and very, very afraid.

# CHAPTER 7

Having arrived at the diner fifteen minutes early, Gabe had plenty of time to collect his scattered thoughts. He arranged a meeting with his Pastor the day before and desperately needed an outsider to help bring some sanity to his madness. Before, Gabe would have talked to his parents, spent hours jogging his favorite trails talking to God, and eventually things would have sorted themselves out. But not this time around.

Remembering a time as a young boy, Gabe recalled a day he had been chasing a squirrel through the Washington woods behind his family's home. The squirrel remained two or three trees ahead of him. Young Gabe kept his eyes fixed on the gray animal, its silver body flashing among the green leaves of the tall trees. Trying to remain quiet yet quick, Gabe continued to follow the little creature from tree to tree. Unable to see the massive spider web ahead, Gabe ran head first into the offending web. Not knowing which way to move to free himself, Gabe found he was getting even more tangled in the transparent net. His young imagination quickly took over and by the time he was free from the web, Gabe's mind had conjured up a spider at least the size of a large tarantula complete with hairy legs and fangs ready to grab him as soon as he was fully caught in its web. Gabe screamed in horror and ran as quickly toward home as he could all the while swiping at the web that clung to his face and arms.

That was how he felt at this very moment. Caught in a web of indecision and unseen consequences that would eventually end up entangling him in a mess of sticky, clingy, events that somewhere down this path would lead to a larger than life creature ready to attack. Confusion, indecision, and the unseen did that to a person, and Gabe seemed to be trapped with no clear way out.

Thus his meeting with Pastor Greg.

The sound of a chair scraping across the linoleum floor brought Gabe back to the present. Quickly he stood and extended his hand to his Pastor. "Hey, Pastor Greg. It's good of you to meet me."

Pastor Greg returned the hand shake and patted Gabe on the shoulder. "Great to see you, Gabe! I'm glad we get to have lunch together."

The two sat and picked up menus. Within a couple of minutes the waitress arrived with two glasses of water and her notepad ready to take their orders. After requesting hamburgers and onion rings, Pastor Greg looked up at Gabe.

"So, what's up, Gabe? You looked as if you had seen a ghost when I walked into the diner and first saw you." Pastor Greg leaned his elbows on the table and looked intently at his young friend.

Uttering a mirthless chuckle, Gabe returned the look. "No ghosts, just spider webs."

"Spider webs? I've never counseled anyone with a fear of spiders before." Pastor Greg reached for his glass of water and took a sip waiting for Gabe's explanation. He could see Gabe was deeply troubled about whatever was on his mind.

"Sorry. I was speaking metaphorically. I guess that did sound a bit weird……What I mean is I feel caught, trapped by the invisible. Without knowing it, I have found myself in a web of confusion and indecision and don't know the way out."

Pastor Greg remained silent allowing Gabe time to collect his thoughts.

"Maybe I need to back up and explain some things before we get our food. You know my family's involvement with AMRA and all the years of mission work we have done. You also know about my education and that I hadn't yet found a job before we left for this last trip to Datka. So here's the deal…..I have a job offer and I don't know what to do about it."

"That doesn't sound like a sticky situation to me. Is it a job that interests you? What does this job offer entail?"

"One of the big issues with it is location. AMRA has offered me a job as Missions Coordinator. The man who previously held the position had to move to New York and the position is open immediately. AMRA had me lead the last mission trip to Datka Island which allowed me to use my logistics degree and abilities, and they were pleased with the success of the trip. My parents and I worked with a newly hired AMRA director and his family. All went extremely well, plus I will be under this director if I take the job. I enjoyed working with him very much and could see us being able to work well together." Gabe came up for air as the waitress delivered their plates.

"If you two need anything else, let me know, gentlemen." With that, the waitress breezed off to care for other patrons.

Pastor Greg prayed over their meal then continued the conversation. "Let's eat while these babies are hot and get a few words in between bites."

Gabe grunted his muffled agreement around bites of the juicy burger. He had skipped breakfast for a morning run and was definitely hungry. Snatching a few onion rings and dipping them in ketchup, he chewed contentedly a moment then continued the conversation.

"Back to where I left off. I think the job would be great, and it combines the two things I am passionate about and skilled to do. So I asked AMRA for a week to consider the offer and I now have four days left to make up my mind. They told me that if I decided to take the job I had one month to arrange for the move to Fairbanks."

"So where do the creepy spiders come in? I am missing something in this picture. What are you hesitant about if the job seems like a great fit?" Pastor Greg spoke around bites and did one of the things Gabe appreciated about him; he listened.

"Well.....I guess—I don't know.....It just seems to me that—" Frustrated at his inability to put his thoughts into words, Gabe shook his head and sighed.

Pastor Greg eased Gabe back into the conversation. "Okay, let's talk about the pros and cons of the job offer. I've heard you mention a few of the pros: great boss, excellent opportunity to do what you love and use your skills, wonderful organization to be a part of. What are the cons?"

Gabe's brow furrowed with thought. "I will be away from my family and friends. I'll miss Washington......but—"

Pastor Greg stuffed an onion ring in his mouth. Around his food, he prodded Gabe. "But?"

"But I will be doing the one thing I love and will be closer to some very special people." A slight blush tinted Gabe's cheeks and he squirmed in his chair.

Pastor Greg hadn't missed Gabe's discomfort or blush. "Special people, huh? Want to talk about these very special people? They seem to cause the scales to tip a bit."

Gabe laughed softly. "You noticed, did you? To put it mildly, you could say that."

"So what's her name?" A huge grin broke out over Pastor Greg's face.

Gabe had taken a sip of his soda and nearly choked on it as he tried to swallow. "What gives you that idea?" he sputtered. Grabbing a napkin, Gabe wiped his face, hoping to erase the reddening he could feel creeping back in place.

Laughing good-naturedly, Pastor Greg responded. "Look, Gabe. I've been in the business of people for quite some time now. Long enough to read if there might be someone of the opposite sex in the picture or not. Let's just say, you gave it away." His smile slipped away as he continued. "No wonder you feel caught in a spider's web. Women can do that to you."

Gabe snorted a reply, but none came out. After a moment, he continued. "Okay, you nailed it. There is a woman in the picture. Her name is Rose.....and—and we have both professed our love for each other. So yes, that does complicate things, but not in the way you may imagine."

Pastor Greg cocked his head and waited for Gabe to go on.

"She's Aleut. Rose lives on Datka Island." There. He had said it.

Leaning back in his chair, Pastor Greg now looked as if he understood. "Ahhhh. Now I see."

Gabe sat silently, deep in thought.

"Where is AMRA located? I don't recall where the headquarters are."

"Fairbanks. An easy flight to Datka. AMRA is still in connection with Datka through some continued future projects that I would head up if I take the job. When we work with the people of Datka, we get all of our resources from Seal Harbor and are stationed there as well. It's about an hour's boat trip from Seal Harbor to Datka if the weather is good, so my buddy, Ed Hamilton, is currently working for AMRA short term and is in Seal Harbor and commuting to Datka when needed. It's a long story, but it gives you an idea of my whereabouts in relationship with the Island and AMRA headquarters. So, yes, I will be in contact with Datka for some time as we finish up projects there."

Pastor Greg finished for Gabe. "And you will have the ability to see this very special person frequently, which seems to tip the scales in favor of the job with AMRA."

"You got it."

"So then, what is holding you back from taking the job? I don't get that part."

"My parents aren't exactly thrilled with the idea of my being in love with an Aleut woman. And did I mention she's young? Bear in mind that compared to American young women, Aleut young women are more mature and act several years older than they really are. Life sort of demands it. Aleut childhood ends way earlier that American childhood. Don't get me wrong, Pastor Greg. My parents love the people of Datka as much, if not more, than I do. But it came as a shock to them that on this last trip, Rose and I had developed a close relationship. I don't think they have had time to process this yet. I didn't exactly do anything to prepare them for this news. In their defense, I was very busy and distant when we were on Datka and didn't talk to them much about anything other than the mission work. All the while, Rose and I were falling in love."

"I see." Pastor Greg stroked his chin thoughtfully for a moment.

The two returned to their meal in silence for a bit. When Pastor Greg was finished eating, he pushed his plate away and leaned his elbows on the table again. Looking at Gabe, he said, "Well, it seems pretty easy to me.....Don't take the job, keep your parents' minds at peace, stay home and don't rock the boat while you look for another job. You know there are plenty more out there." Pastor Greg watched the expected emotions cross Gabe's face, first confusion, then a hint of anger, and next, complete surprise. He continued with his speech. "That way you will still be close to your parents and Ed when he returns from Alaska and all will remain the way it should be in your world. Rose will get over things and so will you. At least you will have smooth sailing from here on out if you do what your parents want and expect."

"Wait—wait a minute.....Who says I *want* things to stay the same.....and that the boat shouldn't be rocked a bit.....and Rose, that's not fair!.....I can't just break her heart by telling her that things have to stay the way they are for everyone else's peace of mind.....I don't think I agree with you, Pastor—" A smile slowly spread across Gabe's face as reality dawned in place of confusion and turmoil.

Pastor Greg folded his arms across his chest and leaned back in his chair remaining silent and giving Gabe a little more time to process things. Eventually, he spoke to Gabe again. "It looks to me that you already have your answer. I think the real problem is openness, honesty, and trust with your folks, and most importantly, trusting God to handle their emotions with their son leaving home and loving a woman that may not have been their ideal choice for you. Would you rather follow their leading and expectations for your life and be miserable at the same time, or would you rather follow God's leading and trust Him to work out the things you can't do anything about anyway and be happy and fulfilled in your choices? Gabe, I see God's hand all over things. Do you?"

Gabe's smile covered his face. "Yes, Pastor Greg. I do. Today, right now, I finally do."

*******************

About two thousand miles away a similar conversation was taking place on Datka Island, a tiny plot of land in the Aleutian Island Chain. Two girlish heads were bent towards each other, one head full of jet black, straight, shoulder-length hair, the other head a rich, dark brown mane, the two whispering their confidences to one another. They had been best friends since their births and for the most part of their lives had been inseparable.

"Oh, Luka! I miss him so much....what if he doesn't return? What if I never see Gabriel again as long as I live? What if he changed his mind when he returned to Washington and his home?" Rose reached an olive-toned hand out to her beloved Malamute dog, Stormy, and scratched the dog's ears. Rose's constant companion and protector, Stormy sat contently at her master's feet while the two girls talked.

"Silly friend!" Luka scolded. "You *know* Gabe will return. You have to trust him and what he has told you. Like my Yuri says, 'The man's heart is good. He will be good for Rose and her future.' If Yuri sees the good in Gabe and believes he will come back to the Island for you, then Rose, you have to believe too. Gabe loves you, Rose. You have to know that." Luka pushed her long black tresses away from her face.

Rose raised her hazel-green eyes to meet Luka's black-brown ones. "I *do* believe him, Luka. It is just very difficult to do so as the sun continues to rise and set with no word from Gabriel. It's easy for you. At least you and Yuri live on the same Island. Gabe and I are hundreds of miles away from each other with no definite time of his return."

Sympathy filled Luka's face. "I would feel the same as you if the roles were reversed. It must be very difficult to wait and hope."

Rose gave Luka a playful shove on her arm. "Especially with you and Yuri around all the time! I have to watch the two of you together and it makes me miss Gabriel even more." Luka giggled at Rose's pretended aggravation, knowing down deep Rose was truly happy for Luka and Yuri.

Rose sighed deeply. "Enough of my troubles. When will you and Yuri marry? Have you set a date?"

Luka blushed furiously. "Well, actually, yes. As of last night, we decided to marry in three weeks!"

"What?!?! So soon?" Rose was shocked at the news.

Again Luka giggled and blushed. "Yes. Why *should* we wait to get married? Yuri already has a house large enough for us, complete with a family too." Luka beamed with pride.

"What do you mean, complete with a family?" Rose frowned at her friend.

"Michael, Lydia, Ola, and little Lillian will stay. I could not think of them having to start over just because Yuri and I were getting married." Luka looked at Rose as if the explanation was obvious.

Luka was referring to the tragedy that struck Datka Island several months ago. A fire had destroyed homes and fishing boats and part of the school. Michael and his wife, Lydia, along with their daughter, Lillian, and Lydia's aged mother, Ola, had moved in with Yuri right after the fire had destroyed their home. Yuri had lost his parents and sister to illness several years earlier and had a large enough home to include the little destitute family. Time together had drawn them all very close, and neither Yuri nor Luka could see any reason their newly found love and upcoming marriage should change the way things were. Yuri had decided to ask the family to continue to live with him instead of starting over and rebuilding a new home for themselves. He had more room than he needed and had grown to love the family as his own. God had used another's loss to fill a deep need and void left in his life after losing his parents and sister. Yuri did not intend to lose another family if he could help it and they were willing to stay.

Luka continued. "Yuri and I will talk this over with them tonight and make them know we *want* them to stay and be part of our new life. So why should we wait to marry? There is no reason, Rose. We love each other and want to begin our lives together."

"I understand, friend. I am really very happy for you and Yuri. Please don't think otherwise." Rose hugged Luka close and the two continued to discuss the upcoming wedding for Yuri and Luka.

# CHAPTER 8

The past few days passed quickly amidst a flurry of activity. Ed Hamilton pulled on his customary denim shirt and closed the snaps with deft movements. He had just finished unpacking some of his meager belongings at Sergeant Will Walker's hunting cabin. Ed had accepted Will's offer of the small hunting cabin to serve as one of his homes while in Alaska. Now he was throwing a few things in another bag for the scheduled trip to Datka Island.

He and Andrew had decided it was past time for Andrew to try to re-adjust to life back on Datka. The road ahead looked very tenuous for Andrew.

The young Aleut man was justifiably concerned about how his little family of his mother and sister would receive him and how Yuri would accept his presence again on the Island. Having taken money from his mother and now deceased father, and stealing traps from Yuri to sell in Seal Harbor for booze, Andrew had served his time in jail and was now seeking to live a better life. The hard part was that he knew the "better life" would not be had unless he faced his mistakes back at home and make amends with those he loved. Maybe then he could be the man he wanted to be, a good man, like his father. Sadly after his father, Ivan had died, Andrew could see how good of a man he had been and he wanted to live his life as one his father would have been proud of, something Andrew had not done the last few years of Ivan's life.

But that is what Ed had stayed on in Alaska for. To help the young, struggling man get back on track. Ed's own past mistakes had taught him many valuable lessons, ones that he hoped would influence

Andrew and hopefully other young Aleut men with the same struggles with alcohol and misguided futures. Thankfully he had met up with Andrew before the man had become a full-blown alcoholic and unwilling or unable to change. And more than that, Ed was so very grateful he had led Andrew to Jesus not so very long ago.

Days like these, Ed was grateful for his past. Only because he could use his mistakes and mess-ups to help someone else through their own.

But like a pesky fly, a thought flitted in front of his face and buzzed in his ear. *Yeah, but your past sure screwed up your future.* He shoved the thought away as he would have an annoying insect. Today, Ed knew he didn't have one second to waste on any regrets that would try to distract him from what he needed to do. Any thoughts of what he may have had with Jade Miller, yet had to forfeit due to his past mistakes, were not going to get under his skin.

Ed felt the now familiar churning of regret and willed himself to not give it any attention. Yes, he regretted his past, but was thankful God could use it in someone else's future to help them out. And obviously, he regretted the huge, unmovable wedge it had driven between him and the beautiful Jade. If only he had been like his best bud, Gabe, been raised in a great family, and at an early age had turned his life over to Christ, it would have greatly altered the course of his days. He would have been acceptable and approved by Jade and probably would have had a future with her, one that would have begun very soon. But that's not how things had played out.

Instantly, the pesky fly of a thought was transformed. Like a beautiful butterfly, another thought entirely different brushed across his mind. A simple, yet profoundly truthful verse he had read last night before bed.

*And we know that God causes all things to work together for good to those who love God, to those who are called according to His purpose.*

Ed breathed a silent prayer for the simple reminder from Romans 8:28. *Thank You, God, that You use ALL things, the good, the bad, and the ugly, in my life for Your good.*

Breathing deeply, Ed forced his past and Jade out of his mind. This was getting him nowhere. Dumping the contents from the bag he had just stuffed, Ed started over. Only this time he paid attention to what he was packing. Looking at the contents he had haphazardly stuffed in the bag, Ed chuckled at himself. No, he didn't need a hammer, a red ball point pen, and one blue sock for the Datka trip. Those items he tossed on the table and instead chose items that would be beneficial instead.

Besides, he could hear Andrew pacing on the small porch waiting for him to finish grabbing his things and be on their way. Anxiety was now Andrew's constant companion and he let it out by pacing.

Grabbing his coat and bag, Ed locked the door of the hunting cabin. "Ready, Andrew? Let's go pay a visit to Sergeant Will before we catch our boat to Datka."

Andrew nodded in agreement and followed Ed silently down the short walk to Will and Sophia's house. Will had come home from the office for lunch and told the two to drop by the house for the lunch Sophia had packed for their boat trip.

Before Ed could knock on the front door, Sophia opened it and started talking. "Come in, guys. I was just headed out to run errands. Will's in the kitchen. I left your lunch packed in a basket on the table. Now be careful and don't be gone too long. Oh, Lauren said to tell you both good-bye before she left for school."

Ed grabbed Sophia by the shoulders for a quick hug. "Thanks, Miss Sophia for the food! Tell your daughter that I will see her soon and to keep studying math more than the boys." Ed chuckled. "She will know what I mean."

"I'm sure she will, Ed. Bye, Andrew. You have our prayers. Take care." Sophia patted Andrew on the shoulder and headed to her car.

Once inside, the two men found Will finishing up his lunch. Will carried his dishes to the sink and rinsed them off. "I hope you have rented a cargo ship to take you to Datka. Soph packed enough food for you to travel around the world and back. That woman." Will chuckled to himself.

Will turned to see Ed pouring himself a cup of coffee and Andrew pacing the room like a caged animal and glancing out the window. "Andrew. Sit, son. You're about to wear a hole through the floor. Are you that worried about seeing your family? Maybe we should wait a little longer until you are more comfortable with this. They have already been notified about your return and the people have had time to consider it."

"No, Sergeant Will. I don't need to delay this. I need to see them and make things right if I can." Andrew slowed his pacing.

"Then what is it? What's got you so tense?"

"Nothing for you to be concerned about."

88

Ed had reached his limit. He didn't want to betray Andrew's trust, but at the same time, he couldn't sit by any longer and watch fear and worry destroy Andrew. Standing a good head taller than his friend, Ed walked over to Andrew and firmly placed a hand on his shoulder. "Andrew, enough! We are here to help you in any way we can. You need to talk to the Sergeant. Now."

Ed watch Andrew's nostrils flare and face redden. If he had to tell Will what was going on, he would, but first Ed wanted to give Andrew one more chance to talk.

Andrew cast an angry glare at Ed and looked over at Will who was the picture of patience.

Without beating around the bush, Andrew blurted out, "I know the girl who was kidnapped."

Instantly, Will was on his feet. "What? How?"

Gaining courage, Andrew stood facing the man and breathed deeply. "She is a friend. I have known her for some time."

Ed knew this would be like pulling teeth so he settled at the kitchen table with his coffee and watched the match between Sergeant Will and Andrew.

"Where do you know her from?" Will queried.

"From around. Datka. Seal Harbor."

"You are helping no one by being vague, Andrew. Remember, I am here to help you." Will forced himself to remain calm when all he wanted to do was shake the man in front of him until he had answers. A girl's life could be at stake. *Calm yourself, Will.* Taking an even breath, Will steadied his nerves.

Ed watched Andrew's Adam's apple bob up and down in his throat. Silently, he prayed for Andrew. *God, give him the words to say and the ability to say them. He needs Will.*

Shutting his eyes tightly, Andrew ran his hands through his short-cropped, black hair. The Aleut man's struggle was obvious. "If I tell you, she will be killed. I cannot say much more. Trust me, Sergeant Will."

"Sit, Andrew." Will sat in the chair next to Ed and pointed to one of the remaining chairs. Andrew did as he was told.

Placing his face in his hands, Andrew searched for the words. "Her name is Berta. She works for Rita."

This much Will knew. "Yes. Go on. How exactly do you know Berta?"

Saying her name made it all the more real to Andrew. "Berta is my girl."

"Your girl?" This confused what Will suspected of what was going on at *Rita's Place.* He ran a hand over his face. *Maybe she is Andrew's girl. Maybe she worked in the pool hall and not as I suspected for Rita.* He needed clarity. "What do you mean, Andrew?"

"She is my girlfriend......I love her." His face screwed tightly with unshed tears, the heartache apparent.

Will felt sorry for the man's pain. "Look, Andrew. I know this is difficult for you, but if you don't tell me anything, I can't help you or her."

Andrew looked up. "All I can say is this. I know Berta was kidnapped. She did not run away. A very evil man—" Andrew paused to regain is composure. "Someone very evil took her."

"Do you know who did this?" Will pressed.

90

Andrew shifted his eyes to the left. "No."

Clearly he was lying. Will stood abruptly from his chair, slamming it against the kitchen wall, the noise startling Ed and Andrew. Bending over the table, Will moved his face within inches of Andrew's and shouted. "Don't lie to me! Any information you withhold only hurts *your girl!* Berta! If she means that much to you then you would help me out here, Andrew!"

Andrew stood to match Will's stance and volume. "That's exactly *why* I can't tell you, Sergeant! It will hurt her *if* I tell!"

Nose to nose the two men eyed each other. "You know her kidnapper, don't you? Why can't I know? Who is threatening you, Andrew? Someone is threatening you that they will bring her harm if you talk, right?"

Nostrils flaring again, Andrew spun on his heel and headed for the front door. Will took a step towards Andrew and gripped his shoulder tightly causing him to stop. "The longer they keep her, the more likely she will suffer harm anyway. You can stop this! I know it. Why wouldn't you tell me *who* it is?"

Before he could say another word, Andrew was out the door. Ed looked at Will and shook his head. "Figure it out, Sergeant Will. I know you can do this!" As quickly as Andrew left, Ed knew he had to follow the man to keep track of him.

Ed broke off into a run and caught up with Andrew. Hollering his name, Ed placed a hand on Andrew's arm with an iron-like grasp and stopped him.

Through gritted teeth, Andrew said, "Have you told him anything?"

91

"How can I, Andrew? You haven't exactly told me anything either, so how could I have given any other information to him? Look, if you don't know by now that you can trust me, then you never will. We are here to help you, Andrew. Even if you won't talk. But you can mark my word, Sergeant Will is smart enough to figure things out on his own."

Ed stood amazed at the amount of fear that clouded Andrew's face. He placed both hands on Andrew's shoulders giving them a shake and said, "Who are you so afraid of? Who wrote that note, Andrew?"

Silence filled the space between the two men.

Frustration marked Ed's next words. "If you won't talk, the least we can do for now is get you back home and get some things resolved there. *That* I can help you do."

Watching the two men leave his porch, Will returned indoors breathing a prayer heavenward.

He decided to call Tammy about the car while he had a moment. Dialing the number, Will waited for an answer.

Finally she picked up. "Hello?"

"Hi, Tammy. Sergeant Walker with the AST. Your brother told me a few weeks ago that you had a car for sale.....Oh, I hate to hear that. I missed buying it by a day, huh?.....No problem.....How old are those boys now? Dorne said one of them had a birthday last weekend and he came for the party.....Oh. Hmmm. Maybe I misunderstood him......It's next week, okay. Well, tell the little guy I said 'happy birthday' and stop in the office the next time you and the family are in Seal Harbor......Thanks, Tammy. Bye."

The gnawing sense of anger and mistrust started up again in Will's gut. He *knew* Dorne had told him a day ago he was at Tammy's the weekend of the kidnapping for a nephew's birthday. *Why is he lying about where he was? Something's not right. This is not the first time I've suspected Dorne wasn't being truthful.....God, give me wisdom.*

It was time for some things to come to the light. Will remembered the note he had found from Hughes and determined to speak with him privately as soon as he could.

*******************

The boat ride to Datka was silent for the most part for Ed and Andrew, both caught up in their own thoughts and the steady rhythm of the gentle waves pushing against the small watercraft. Their boatman had said little as well, limiting the small talk on the one hour trip.

Seeing the distant shoreline brought both men to attention. Andrew's face was an unreadable mask. Ed didn't blame him for being nervous and gave him the space he needed to process what was about to happen. Meeting his family and community wouldn't be easy.

A lone figure stood on the shoreline. Unable to tell who it was, Ed knew it was one of the local men. Giving a huge wave in that direction, Ed saw the man return the wave and disappear out of view. He was headed to alert the others of their arrival.

Thankfully, John Miller, the head director with AMRA had contacted Ed several days before their trip to the Island and had told him of his letter to Natalia and Rose and one he had written to Elder Dan as well. John felt it would be best to prepare the family and the community's respected leader of Ed's and Andrew's arrival and of Andrew's intentions to make peace and begin his life anew at his home.

John had also announced in a letter the anticipated arrival of the Hudson family: Stan, Elaine, and daughter, Lindy. Stan was to be the new pastor at the church on Datka. Many years earlier the little Island's church became all but non-existent after the church leader's untimely death. No one had taken the previous leader's place, resulting in the Island having church services only when the missionaries could come for an extended stay which was usually once or twice a year. Occasionally during a special event on the Island, such as a birth, wedding, or death, one of the older generation of Datka men would recite some scripture tucked in their memories from long ago. Now with the commitment of the new pastor and his family, secured and overseen by AMRA, there was hope for the Island to see their church doors open once again.

Ed and Andrew's arrival fell on the day after the Hudson's arrival. Like the inhabitants of Datka, Ed was excited to meet the new pastor and see Rose's dream of the church re-opening come to life. Knowing the importance of church and God in his own life, Ed knew this was one of the best things that could possibly happen for the tiny Island.

Knowing their arrival was expected, Ed's face filled with his half-grin. A deep chuckle sounded in his throat as he turned to Andrew. "Do you see that crowd? Your family is the first to come meet you. And look at all the others! See, you have nothing to worry about. I'm not saying it will be easy, but I don't think moving home will be as difficult as you think, buddy."

Andrew's eyes grazed the small group as their boat drew closer to the rocky shore. There they were. His mother and sister. Natalia and Rose had never looked better to him. And he saw Luka and Yuri, Michael and Lydia, Aggie and James. Elder Dan stood on the edge of the group, his face stern but open. Andrew didn't know what to think. He deserved to arrive with no one to greet him; that much he knew. Tears threatened to sting his eyes, but he refused them. Now was not the time to cry. He wanted to see each face that awaited him on the shore. As he and Ed disembarked from the small craft and unloaded their belongings, Andrew searched the faces again. There was no hostility. No anger. He did see some reservation in their eyes. But that was okay. Trust had been broken and trust would need to be earned. With God and Ed's help, he believed he could do this.

Glancing at Ed, Andrew felt his friend's hand grip his shoulder in reassurance. Ed gave him a little nod of encouragement. As if his feet had a mind of their own, Andrew began walking towards mother and sister. Natalia and Rose reached for each other's hand and ran towards him. Engulfed in their embrace, Andrew knew he was finally home.

Back at the hub of the small Island's community, Ed felt like he had indeed reached a friendly and familiar place. It felt like walking through the door of a beloved friend's home and feeling the welcoming arms of friendship and love. He had missed these people, had missed their friendship, and missed sharing a project with them.

Ed had spent his entire summer's vacation here with these Aleut friends, with Rand, Becca, and Gabe Parker, with John, Jill, and Jade Miller, all working to restore the fire's damage to their lives.

95

Working together for weeks on end seemed to forge relationships that lasted for an eternity.

At least most relationships. Ed had one that hadn't survived that test. He and Jade.

Casting that thought aside so not to spoil this sweet reunion, Ed enjoyed the easy banter and conversations that flowed around him. It was so good to be back. His heart had really longed for Datka, more than he had realized. Any lingering doubts vanished like the Aleutian fogs when the sun shone brightly through. Ed *knew* he had made the right decision to stay on at Seal Harbor and Datka to help out in whatever ways God saw fit to use him.

Glancing up to the heavens, Ed nodded and whispered a quiet *Thank You* to his Maker.

Looking around at the precious faces, Ed saw Michael and Yuri talking. He decided to go visit with them a while. Before Ed reached the two men, he stopped dead in his tracks, his breath caught in his throat.

*Jade!* There she was not twenty feet from him. Ed had no idea the Millers were coming to Datka this soon. Last he had heard, it would be next week. And there she was.

Ed let his eyes linger on her short, petite, athletic frame. Her long dark hair hung down her back in waves over her red sweatshirt that he just knew said *Guatemala Matters* across the front. She was speaking with a couple he had never met before. With her back to him, Ed took his time before he approached her. Curiosity was getting the better of him.

When Ed was five feet away from Jade, her name escaped from his lips, "Jade." Instantly, she flipped her long dark hair back away

96

from her face and turned in his direction. Now face to face, and eye to eye with Ed, she let her hair drop back in place.

But before it did, Ed saw the side of her face and gasped aloud. That was not Jade! Now that he could see her, it wasn't her at all. This girl had an angry red scar on her left cheek and on the side of her neck that was quite noticeable. Nor did she have Jade's telltale green eyes. This girl had sapphire blue orbs that could light up any room.

Ed's discomfort colored his face instantly. Unconsciously, he reached a hand up to his head and grabbed a mess of brown hair.

The unknown man the girl had been speaking with stepped his direction and extended a hand to Ed and spoke, "Hi! I'm Stan Hudson, the new pastor here on Datka. This is my wife, Elaine and daughter, Lindy."

Ed released his grip on his head of hair and shook hands with Stan. "Edward Hamilton. Nice to meet you, Sir. Mrs. Hudson. Lindy. Good to meet you, too."

# CHAPTER 9

Discomfort buzzed in the air around them. Ed had just made a fool out of himself and the young lady was as uncomfortable as he was with the introductions.

Turning her face to the ground, Lindy cleared her throat and said quietly, "Excuse me, but I think I will go get my jacket. Um, nice to meet you, Edward."

"Ed's fine. That's what most people call me." He nodded his head at the retreating girl. Looking at Stan and Elaine, he replied, "Sorry about that. I thought Lindy was someone else I knew. Didn't mean to make her uncomfortable. So, you are the new pastor on the Island?"

"Don't worry about Lindy; she's fine, just a bit shy. Yes. We just accepted the position and arrived yesterday. We're really enjoying getting to know the people. They have all been very welcoming and receptive to us." Stan placed an arm around his wife's shoulders as he talked.

"They have been wonderful to us! Such hospitable people." To Ed, Elaine looked to be in her late forties to early fifties. She smiled easily and made Ed feel comfortable instantly. "They have been telling us stories of the reconstruction team. I heard your name mentioned many times. I'm glad to finally meet the famous Ed."

"Well, don't believe everything you hear, ma'am." Ed shot the couple his half-grin and ducked his head in embarrassment. "I know the Island is very glad you are here. And that's an understatement. It seems you arrived at an eventful time. There's a lot going on here on Datka. But I am sure you will be up to the task."

Stan frowned his concern. "I think John Miller has filled me in on most everything, but I would appreciate any insight you might have."

Ed laughed at Stan's statement. "Sir, as you saw earlier, I am not the best with words and insight. I tend to stick my size ten cowboy boot in my mouth regularly. John will be your best source of Island information. I am great with a hammer and pretty good with the young man who arrived with me. I'm hoping God can use my past to help his future. We will definitely talk more, Pastor Stan." With that, Ed made his exit.

Elaine eyed Stan. "Well, he's an intriguing young man, isn't he? I haven't seen Lindy react to another guy like that either. She took off quickly."

"Honey, you know how uncomfortable Lindy is around people she doesn't know. This whole experience will hopefully do her some good and help bring her out of her self-made shell. She will grow used to the people here and return to her old self soon. As for Ed, having an attractive man approach her did set her teeth on edge. This might get interesting."

Lindy stared in her small hand mirror for the thousandth time. Long ago, she had grown accustomed to the fact that this was how she would look for the rest of her life. Deformed. Disfigured. Unattractive. Always able to emit a gasp or encourage a stare from a stranger. She hated the left side of her face!

Looking again in the mirror, Lindy turned so she could see only the right side, the normal side of her twenty year old face. It still looked the same, only she smiled less than she used to. *You would think that after fifteen years, I would be used to this kind of reaction. And here I am twenty years old and it still bothers me when someone is surprised by my face. Grow up, Lindy!*

Troubled by what had triggered her nasty reaction earlier, Lindy thought back to a few moments ago. While she had been talking with her parents, the tall, attractive, denim-clad man approached them and had taken her completely aback. He had done nothing wrong, just simply walked up.

Lindy had quickly felt welcome and accepted when she and her parents had been introduced the day before to the Aleut people of Datka. She felt comfortable with them because she and her parents were already "different" since they were the only Caucasian, American people around. So her "differences" were not marred by her physical abnormalities but by her overall difference in ethnicity that easily overshadowed the discomfort of her scars.

Only today, when another Caucasian, tall-dark-and-handsome, male appeared, she was reminded that she was "different" due to her noticeable scars. Anger crept its way in as she replayed the scene in her mind once more. *How dare he act so put off at my appearance? So rude!*

*And,* Lindy thought, *I know I heard him say the name 'Jade' when he walked toward us and looked at me. That was strange! He definitely could use some manners.*

Knowing that anger would only lead to other unhealthy emotions, Lindy did her best to bring her emotions to the One who could help her. Breathing deeply, she utter a silent prayer for help.

Reaching a hand up to her face, Lindy traced the four-inch long patch of reddish skin down her left cheek and the equally long strip down her neck. Underneath her shirt, she knew the scarred place was there that brushed the top of her left shoulder. Frustration pushed its way in and she shook her head at her own reflection then laid the hand mirror down. Time, a loving family, great friends, and finding out that her true beauty was from *within* had brought Lindy to a place of emotional healing, especially after the empty years of being a teenager and having only one date in her lifetime. She felt frustrated because she believed she had come so far, so very, very, far in accepting who she was and her appearance. But after tonight's emotional upheaval, which she usually was a master at hiding, she wondered how far she had truly come. Lindy did her best to hide her emotionally-charged moments even from her parents, but they could read her like a book.

Sighing deeply, she reached for her jacket knowing she couldn't take much longer in getting it before one of her parents came in search of her. Stepping out of her family's new house, she lingered at the door and smelled the crisp scent of burning firewood from the small bonfire where people were still gathered. Lindy pulled her jacket tighter around her shoulders. This environment would definitely take some getting used, but she felt she was up to the challenge.

Watching the dark-skinned, black-haired people around her, Lindy felt a peace settle in her chest again. Yes, she knew down deep she was where she should be. Tucked away on a tiny Island in the Aleutian chain with plenty to do, at least for a season. Here, she could immerse herself in helping others and get lost in the little sea of people where her abnormality wouldn't matter. She wouldn't be surrounded by other twenty-something's and their relationships and dates and career plans.  She could just be herself, Lindy Jane Hudson, and not worry about those things she had shoved way down deep in her heart.

Spotting the young ladies she had met yesterday, Rose and Luka, both close to her age, she headed their direction.  Looking around for the tall man she had just met, Lindy saw him walking away from the group with another couple.  *Good.  I don't have to worry about staying at a distance from him for the rest of the day.*

Rose and Luka looked up as Lindy approached them.  "Hi, girls.  I would love an Island tour before it gets dark if you two aren't busy.  Maybe you could introduce me to some others, too.  I want to settle in as quickly as possible and get to know everyone."

Luka spoke first.  "Sure, Lindy.  We would love to!"

Rose linked her arm through Lindy's and led her off to start their tour.

As the three walked, they chatted away like school girls.  Lindy was full of questions and bounced them off both Luka and Rose.  "First tell me about each of you."

Rose started first.  "Well, I turned eighteen a few days ago.  The last year has been full of difficulties for my family.  I do not mean to sound selfish; it is just the truth.  But it will explain a little of why Datka is in the shape it is right now."  Rose emitted a soft chuckle.  "Hopefully you will not want to leave after we tell you about some of us.  But if you and your family are to live here, you need to know some things.  My dear father passed away not long ago, leaving me and my mother…..And my brother, Andrew.  Sadly, Andrew made some wrong, horrible choices and as you saw earlier, he returned to Datka with Ed today.  Andrew was in jail for stealing and being caught with illegal booze in his possession.  Lindy, our parents did not raise us this way.

103

He just chose to live his own life, and it has caused much trouble. A few months ago, you have probably heard, there was a fire on the Island and homes were destroyed. No lives were lost, but our school and some fishing boats were damaged." Rose hated to tell the rest, but knew she had to. "My brother and a few friends caused the fire. So now, the missionaries from AMRA have spent the last few months helping us rebuild and start over. Ed Hamilton has decided to stay here a while and help my brother who has struggled with alcohol and.....other things. We are very blessed to have you and your family here. Our community needs our church reopened and a full-time pastor. God is good to send you to us. I guess that is all about me. Now, Luka, it's your turn." Rose turned to her friend and gave Luka a chance to talk.

Laughter bubbled out of Luka and both girls looked at her strangely. "That is *not* all about you, Rose! Shall I finish or will you?"

Blushing furiously, Rose ducked her head.

Luka took over. "Fine. I will tell our new friend the rest of Rose's story." Luka relished the moment. "Lindy, Rose has hidden something from you. She has a man in her life. She is a woman in love."

"Luka!" Rose shook her head good-naturedly at her friend.

"Oh, this is getting good! Carry on, Luka." Lindy nudged Rose gently in the shoulder.

"Gladly. Rose is in love with and awaiting the return of Gabriel Parker, a missionary to Datka. An *American* man. From the States, not the Island," Luka added with emphasis.

Lindy placed her hand over her chest, truly surprised. "Rose! Wow! That is incredible. What do you mean 'awaiting'?"

"Gabriel's family has come to Datka for many years. They would stay here on our Island for several weeks to a couple of months since he was very young. Now he has confessed his love for Rose and she is awaiting his return from the States and his promise to come for her."

"What a story, Rose! How exciting! I am amazed that you are in love and looking to marry at such a young age. You are eighteen and I am twenty with no prospects yet." Longing filled Lindy's chest as she thought of having a man to love her in return.

A cloud passed across Rose's pretty face. "We may seem young to you, but inside we are much older than we look." Silence settled around the girls for a moment. "Enough of that! Luka, tell about yourself now." Rose shut down the direction of the discussion.

"I too am a woman in love, and I am not too shy to admit it, unlike someone else we know." Luka playfully shoved Rose. "I am committed to marry the handsome Yuri. I know you met him yesterday when you arrived. He showed you and your family your new home. And I do mean new. It was originally being rebuilt for Michael, Lydia, and their little family, but Yuri wanted them to continue to live with him and they were happy to do so. Michael and Lydia lost their home in the fire, and Yuri lost his parents and sister to illness years ago, leaving him alone. So when he took the family into his large home, he hated to see them leave. He loves their little girl, Lillian, so very much and Yuri and Michael are great friends. So you and your parents received the home for Michael and Lydia which would still be empty if you hadn't arrived."

"That is such a wonderful story. Sad, yet wonderful. So you and Yuri will marry soon? Will you move out of his house?" Lindy waited for Luka to continue.

"Oh no! I am just another addition to the family. I am glad for the arrangement with Michael and Lydia. I love them very much as well. With your father as pastor on Datka, I think Yuri and I will be his first wedding ceremony to perform here." Luka looked starry-eyed a moment before continuing.

"Now back to my story. My brother, Markus, is one of Rose's brother's best friends, who also was in the midst of the trouble with the fire and illegal booze. He was not arrested. Actually, I do not know where he is. It grieves my family and me so much. I hope he will return as Andrew and another of the boys have and make things right. They became friends with an evil, man who is a few years older than them from Datka who has led them down the wrong path. So much has happened because of this one man. He no longer lives on the Island, but his influence still remains in some of our young men."

"I am sorry to hear that, Luka. Datka has suffered greatly. I'm glad you have AMRA to help and that God sent us here too. Some of what I have seen makes sense now. I have a question.....Who is Edward? I met him briefly when he arrived with Rose's brother."

Rose answered Lindy's question. "He is Gabriel's best friend. Ed has decided to stay and help out however he can. He has been most helpful with my brother and will continue to live in Seal Harbor and come here frequently to the Island and oversee a few unfinished projects. The school is not quite finished with its repairs so after that, I guess he will return to the States and his life there."

"I see," Lindy responded. "You both are a wealth of information. I believe we will be friends for life."

The newly arrived Amerian girl, having forgotten the things that hold her back in life, linked arms with the two Aleut girls, and continued on her Island tour with new-found friends. Lindy felt as if God's big hands were on her and guiding her steps. Looking forward to what the future held on this Island adventure, Lindy breathed a little easier than she had an hour ago.

# CHAPTER 10

Swiping the damp dishrag across the small wooden tables, Rita surveyed her pool hall. Men and women alike gathered in clusters all around the large room, a typical Saturday. At this afternoon hour, the noise level was already rising as the patrons requested refills of the amber liquid. Several couples lingered at tables, and a group of four gathered around the pool table awaiting the winner of the game. Pool balls clinked along with glasses, smoke filled the room, laughter and raucous behavior everywhere she looked. Saturdays were her busiest day, the time of day unimportant to the patrons of *Rita's Place.*

Rita did her usual check of her girls. Strangely, Jocelyn, Stasia, Darcy and her own Liza were all in the pool hall laughing and talking with the male patrons. Usually the girls were gone with one of the men or up in their room with one. But not today.

Without checking, Rita knew that Felicity, Emily, and Penny would all be gathered in the kitchen over steaming cups of tea either mending torn clothing, making bread for the next day, or washing dishes, mopping floors, and changing bed sheets. The work never ended.

And Ana, poor soul, would be shut away in her bedroom, except for mealtime, grieving over Berta with Milly trying to coax her out. Ana had not entered the pool hall since the night of Berta's disappearance. She claimed her heart was not in the work, though Rita knew that wasn't possible with this line of work.

Years had taught Rita that a girl's heart *never* would be involved in this "career," nor could it. One chose to sell her body and eventually her soul, if any was left, to the men willing to pay for a few moments of pleasure just for survival. Broken lives always led to broken choices. Whether the girls suffered abuse or neglect or a young, broken heart, the choice almost always came down to one thing. Survival.

Like having a veil lifted from her tired eyes, Rita could see it clearly. Maybe Berta's disappearance had something to do with it, but she knew that these girls all still had a fragment of heart left. They all grieved deeply for the loss of Berta, every one of them. And each girl walked around with fear-filled, haunted eyes. Rita could only imagine what they were thinking. *Who did this? Why did someone take Berta? Will one of us be next? Will we ever see her again? Is she dead?*

They did have hearts; they all felt deeply her disappearance.

Rita's unspoken thoughts tormented her as she washed the same tables over and over without realizing it. *I should have never allowed these girls to follow in my footsteps. I only wanted to help them. If they had chosen to come to me to clean, or cook, or wait the tables, that would have been fine. Safer even. But I expected more from the girls. More money. I made them to be like me, a whore.*

Unaccustomed to crying, a tear splashed on the table top. Quickly swiping it away, Rita thought, *I guess I too have a little heart left.*

Tossing the dishrag behind the counter into the pan of soap, Rita walked up to Liza and spoke quietly to her. "Honey, I have a headache and need to go lie down. Can you and Jocelyn close up later? Or you can wake me and I will help with shutting the place down."

"Sure. Go rest. We can do this." Liza gave her mother a sad smile. Their matching, unruly red heads came together in a brief hug as masses of auburn curls fell together. "Love you, Mom."

110

Rita's high-heels clomped up the staircase and down the hall to her bedroom while she noticed the marked difference in the atmosphere of the place. The girls were clearly under the spell of the deep sadness that lurked in the hallways and rooms of the establishment since their friend's disappearance. The girls were purposefully staying busy with other things in the house and less attentive to the male patrons coming around. Berta's disappearance had changed some things and Rita suspected this was one of them. But honestly, right now in that moment, Rita didn't care if the patrons were happy or not. Her emotions were too spent.

Flopping down on her large bed with its many pillows, Rita kicked off her shoes. Her feet and back ached from standing and serving people in the pool hall the first half of the day.

A dark, cold chill settled around Rita's shoulders like an icy cloak. Shivering, she quickly stripped from the thin blood-red, low-cut, dress and grabbed a warm flannel gown from the bottom of her dresser drawer. She hadn't worn this particular nightgown in years, but tonight, she needed its comfort and warmth surrounding her.

A small emerald green book caught her eye as she retrieved the gown from the depths of the drawer. Rita quickly placed the little book on top of her dresser and donned her gown and thick robe. Though the sun was still high in the sky, she threw back her bed covers, she slipped under the sheets with the green book.

Instantly a scene from years ago made her eyes water. Rita's young heart had been shattered into pieces and she couldn't bear to live in the same vicinity with the man who had destroyed her life. Never heeding her mother and grandmother's warnings about men and their carelessness with a woman's heart, Rita knew she had to

111

leave and start her life over somewhere far away from the man she now despised.

Having formulated a plan, Rita entered the back door of her mother and grandmother's home, determined to never return. She had to move on. Her mother, Lorena, knew instantly that Rita was leaving just from the look on her daughter's face. Expecting this to happen, mother hid all emotion from daughter and simply handed her an emerald green book as a parting gift. Without looking inside, Rita said a quick good-bye to her mother and stuffed the book in her travel bag.

And today, more than twenty-five years later, Rita was face-to-face with the little book.

Already knowing what it contained, Rita pulled the covers more tightly around her and opened the worn book. The first thing she saw brought a sad smile to Rita's lips.

*Marguerita Lorena Liza Holbrook.* Her full name was scrawled across the first page. She had been simply "Rita" for so long the name caught her off guard. Named after mother and grandmother, Rita had passed on part of the name to her own daughter, Liza Ann Holbrook.

Oh, she wished life had taken a different turn for Liza. But, by Rita's own hand, she had directly influenced the path her daughter had taken and had broken the whispered vow she made the night Liza was born.

A single tear made its way down Rita's worn cheek. She could remember her whispered words like she had spoken them just a moment ago after Liza's birth. *"Little Liza Ann, your mommy promises to give you a better chance at life than she had. You won't be like me or your grandmother or your great-grandmother. I promise. Life will be good for you, sweet innocent one."*

But as a single mother with no help or support, Rita re-entered the world of prostitution for survival, one she hoped she could be rid of forever after Liza was born. After years of no hope for change in Rita's world, Liza became what her mother never wanted for her, a shadow of the three women who had lived before her.

Tears splashed on the blanket on Rita's lap. Using the corner, she wiped them away and returned to the book.

Turning to the next page, attached in the corners with tiny black triangles, Rita saw the yellowed, old photo of a woman with hair much like Rita's, only longer, and swept up in shiny combs. Loose tendrils of curls escaped down around the woman's face, a face much like Rita's too. Her mother. Lorena. Another shadow of the woman Rita knew would be in the older photo on the next page.

Carefully flipping the next page over, Rita stared down at her grandmother, Liza. Same auburn hair, same unruly curls, same sad smile. Now there were four generations of sad, red-haired women doing the same type of work. The only difference was their surroundings.

A deep, gloomy, disappointment engulfed Rita as she stared at the two pictures before her. Disappointment in herself, as a mother. She had failed her daughter and the vow she had made the tiny baby. What if she had tried harder, kept looking for work other than what she had been brought up in? What if she had.....? It was too late. What was done couldn't be undone.

The next page of the emerald book contained a strip of yellowed tape that barely clung to the page. Rita knew what had been behind the tape. A twenty dollar bill. Long ago, when she was afraid she would starve to death, Rita had slipped her fingernail underneath the tape and used the bill for food and housing. It was all her mother could spare at the time she left home and never looked back. Knowing the money had probably saved her young life, Rita was grateful for her mother's sacrifice.

The next few pages of the book contained her mother's handwriting. One-line quotes that must have been favorites of Lorena's were the last words Rita would have that were her mother's. She flipped through several pages of the meaningless words and stopped on one that she liked.

*"Change the past. Change the future."*

This one always puzzled Rita. It was simply six words that at one time seemed important enough for her mother to scrawl in the book for her daughter. Rita never put much thought into these quotes her mother had written, but tonight this one jumped out at her.

She re-read the two small sentences. *"Change the past. Change the future."*

What was she supposed to get from these words? Her eyes and mind seemed magically, mysteriously drawn to them. What hidden message was she missing?

And suddenly, like a light being turned on in a dark room, Rita was blinded at first by the message, but then instantly grateful for the meaning of the words. Sitting straight up in her bed, Rita *knew*. She got it! Rita hugged the little emerald book to her large chest and released one more tear.

Grabbing a pad of paper and a pen, Rita began writing as quickly as she could before she lost the meaning and the moment. A pivotal time in her aging life, a moment of change and redirection. It was time for her to change her past so the future too could be changed. For her. For Liza. For her other girls.

*******************

Pulling into the parking space of the bright red building, Officer Brandon Hughes glanced around at the place. Taking in the other cars in the parking lot, he was surprised at the number of patrons in the early afternoon.

Opening the door to the pool hall's entrance, Hughes eyes adjusting to the dim light, he saw one of the girls he had met the night of the initial investigation. He remembered she was the owner's daughter.

*What was her name, Lily? No—Liza. Pay attention, Hughes. This is your job and you are good at it, good with details.*

The flaming red-head was standing very close to a man in a dirty looking plaid flannel shirt. Not having noticed him enter, Hughes took the moment to take in the scene. Liza was giggling and talking quietly to the man who wore a grin and blush so big and bright they covered his face. Running her hand down the man's arm, Hughes could tell she was flirting and toying with him.

Looking up, the girl spotted Hughes. Her motions stopping in mid-air, she cleared her throat nervously. "Uh, can I help you, Officer Hughes?" As she spoke, her pale face blanched ever whiter.

Taking his cue, the man in plaid made a hasty exit out the door Hughes had just entered.

Hughes looked her up and down. "Liza, right?"

"Uh—yes, yes, it's Liza. What can I do for you, sir?" A nervous habit she had inherited from her mother, Liza tried desperately to rearrange her impossible hair with her hand but to no avail. "Can I get mother, uh, Miss Rita for you? How about a cup of coffee? It's cold out there today. Come into the kitchen and warm up if you'd like."

Nervously, Liza led Hughes to the brightly lit, warm kitchen. There he found three other young ladies, each attentive to some task. They all looked up as he entered and mumbled quick *hellos.*

"Ladies." Hughes touched the brim of his AST hat and accepted the offered cup of coffee.

Felicity quickly reached for a spoon and the creamer and sugar set as she directed Hughes where to sit. Placing a plate of cookies before him, the girl took over. "What brings you here today, Officer Hughes? Any news on Berta?"

"Sorry to say, but no. Not yet anyway. I am here to ask a few more questions and look around again. It never hurts to investigate the scene multiple times. Something may turn up or come to mind that wasn't seen or mentioned during the initial investigation. Is Miss Rita available to join us?"

The girl Hughes knew was the missing person's sister stood and said, "I will go get her for you." He didn't miss the glimmer of tears in her eyes before she turned her back and left.

Momentarily, Rita and Ana returned. Rita extended her hand to Hughes, saying, "Well, hello, Officer Hughes. How can I help?"

"I would like to ask you all a few more questions and have another look around outside and in the area surrounding the building. You never know if something else has come to mind or if another clue

116

is found. Would that be okay?" Hughes took a sip of his coffee, and to be polite, ate a cookie.

He was intrigued by the dynamics of these young ladies. Never before had he seen a group so close and so sad looking in all his life. Hughes wondered if their sadness and hollow eyes were the result of the life they lived or because one of them was missing; these desperate eyes would haunt his dreams for nights to come. Hughes retrieved his notepad and pen from his shirt pocket and began the questions.

Twenty minutes later, Officer Hughes stood to take his leave. His heart had expanded enough in these last few minutes of hearing bits and pieces from the girls that he knew he was, now more than ever, determined to find Berta. This girl hadn't just disappeared or run away. *Someone* had kidnapped her. He felt it in the pit of his gut and knew there were answers out there. The commitment and love the girls had for each other and for Miss Rita was obvious. Berta wouldn't have just up and left them. That much was obvious.

With a final word of goodbye and a promise that he and Sergeant Walker would keep them updated, Hughes exited the front of *Rita's Place* and grabbed his work bag from the patrol car. Always prepared, he brought gloves, plastic bags for evidence, a few tools, a small hand shovel, flashlight, and various other items that would be handy for this sort of outdoor investigation. The day of the initial disappearance of Berta, he and Sergeant Will had spent more time questioning the girls than making a thorough search of the surrounding area. When they had done a detailed search in the house and around its immediate vicinity, not much had turned up. The ground wasn't soft enough to yield any footprints in the yard.

Knowing there had to be clues out there, Hughes wanted to spend some time on the outer reaches of *Rita's Place.*

Walking around the back of the tall red building, Hughes entered through the backyard's rusting gate. Stopping just inside the gate's opening, Hughes tried to imagine what might have taken place the night of the girl's disappearance. One thing they did know was that the bedroom window was found open much farther than Berta and Ana had left it the night in question.

Thoughts began to tumble over each as the officer stood surveying the scene before him.

*Bottom window to the left of the kitchen is the room of the two sisters. So.....did Berta run away or did she find herself in the hands of an abductor? My gut says she was taken....she wouldn't desert her sister or the others if I am guessing correctly.*

Walking slowly towards her window as he was thinking things through, Hughes just couldn't wrap his mind around the girl leaving on her own free will, without a note, without shutting the window back how it was, or even sneaking out of the bedroom she shared with her sister. *No, that would have been too loud, too risky if she was running away. She would have snuck out the back door of the kitchen or the pool hall entry. Just doesn't add up.*

Visually scouring the ground of the backyard and underneath the window, Hughes turned up with nothing. No clue to help him. *But what if she was abducted? How would that possibly have played out?*

Walking back to the gate, Hughes surveyed the area again, thinking and trying to envision the scene that might have happened that night. His brain whirred with thoughts. *If she was abducted, it appears she was taken from the bedroom and the abductor didn't take the time to shut the window back how it was. And according to the sister it was definitely left open enough for someone to exit the window easily. Okay.....so the abductor would have had to enter this back gate to reach the window. But where would he have been hiding and waiting before making his move? He didn't just appear in the backyard. There would have been a spot where he would have waited and watched for the right time.*

Exiting the small yard, Hughes stood stock-still and perused the surrounding area. The little backyard bumped up against a grove of taller trees which sloped gently upwards into a wooded hillside. *Easy place for someone to hide and watch the house.*

Walking slowly and observantly towards the grove of trees, Hughes tried to take in each detail, each tree, leaf, rock, and fallen branch to see if there was anything willing to offer up some clue of what might have happened. Wandering slowly around in the trees, his boots crunched over the fallen leaves as he purposefully looked for a spot to hide and wait. He saw two places that could have been an abductor's chosen spot to watch. Approaching a large, lichen-covered, boulder, Hughes crouched down behind it in several places and looked towards the house. *No, this wouldn't be the spot. There's no clear line of sight to the back of the house.*

Undaunted in his work, Hughes looked around for any other possible place. Not ten yards away was another smaller boulder. Again Hughes repeated the same process of sitting in different positions, looking towards the house, trying to imagine someone plotting to kidnap a young woman. *Perfect! If a kidnapper was waiting in these trees, he had an excellent view of the backyard and entire house, and he would be completely hidden from the house. This would be it.*

119

Scratching around in the fallen leaves to see if anything caught his eye, Hughes spotted several man-sized shoe prints and rounded deeper impressions of where maybe someone had knelt down or even sat on the soft ground. *Good.....good.*

Getting out his new Kodak camera, Hughes checked the film and made sure it was ready to go. He snapped a few shots of the surrounding area and of the house from this spot. Getting a few photos of the footprints and indentions on the ground, he took out ruler and paper and measured each impression and made notes. Finally satisfied with his findings, Hughes gathered his things and slung his bag over his shoulder. He needed a few more hours of daylight to satisfy his curiosity about the rest of the area, but for now, Hughes needed to talk to Sergeant Walker about his discovery and suspicions.

Two heads were always better than one.

# CHAPTER 11

Approaching the small cluster of girls, Liza whispered closely, "Girls, we need to have a meeting tonight after Mom has gone to sleep. Spread the word to the others. See you later. I have a *meeting* with someone in a bit." Liza drew quotation marks in the air with her crimson-painted fingernails as she spoke the word *meeting*. With that, she pulled a bright lipstick from her pocket and smeared some across her young lips, donned her coat and disappeared into the night.

Jocelyn was the first to speak. "Well, that was mysterious. I wonder what kind of meeting she has in mind, especially one that doesn't include Miss Rita."

"Beats me, but Liza has been pretty quiet these past few days. You could almost see the wheels turning in that pretty red head of hers." Emily laughed to herself.

Placing a plump hand on her hips, Milly eyed the group. "I have a *meeting* to get to myself. Can't keep Tom, ummm, men waiting can we?" Rushing out the door, Milly exited the kitchen to cover the slip of her tongue before the girls could ask questions.

"Tom? So that's who Milly's secret rendezvous is with.....okay, who's Tom anyway," questioned Emily.

Saying nothing, Darcy's face noticeably turned as pale as a ghost as reality hit her square in the chest. One of her closest friends among all the girls, Milly and Darcy had been the two who shared their secrets and bared their wounded souls to each other. Darcy knew of Milly's secret guy, but her friend had never spoken his name, not even to her.

Until today.

121

*Surely not! Surely Milly is smarter than this....how could she put us all in such danger? Tom?* Fear wrapped itself around Darcy's shoulders as she put her coat on. Stepping out into the cold night, she too had somewhere to be. But first she needed to confirm her suspicions.

Milly couldn't be that far ahead of her. Often curiosity had gotten the best of Darcy, and she had watched out the window as Milly left for her secret meetings with her secret guy. She knew just which direction to follow.

*******************

The Alaska morning sun was just peeking over the horizon when Officer Brandon Hughes reached the Alaska State Troopers headquarters in Seal Harbor. Adjusting his Trooper's hat, Hughes entered the office in preparation for his meeting with Sergeant Will Walker.

Two days ago Walker had phoned Hughes requesting this Saturday morning meeting. Will had apologized for not making time to talk with Hughes and admitted he had misplaced the note Hughes had left requesting the private meeting.

So today was the day. Hughes wasn't fond of speaking against another co-worker, but he felt there was no other choice in the matter. Having lost nights of sleep over this issue, Hughes was ready to spill the beans and let Walker figure things out from here. He was ready to wash his hands of the entire matter and return to his weekend shifts at the station without any further drama and complications. Thank goodness, he wasn't the Sergeant; the position of officer was enough for him.

Within fifteen minutes Will arrived with a thermos of coffee and a covered plate of something cinnamon-smelling that set Hughes' mouth to watering. "Good morning, Hughes. Sophia sent a plate of cinnamon rolls for us to share. You know how she is...always afraid I will miss a meal." Rubbing his stomach, Will uncovered the plate and grabbed two coffee cups from the station's cupboard.

"If you weren't married to Sophia, I would marry the woman simply for her cinnamon rolls. I'll pour the coffee if you get plates and forks. Mmm-mmm." Hughes sniffed appreciatively of the rolls.

After the two men were settled and had eaten one apiece, Will spoke up. "Okay, man. I've been in suspense for too long now over the note you left. What is so important that you need to talk to me about? I'm sorry for the delay, but with the girl's disappearance we both have been occupied. I can't wait another weekend to talk."

Taking a deep breath, Brandon rubbed his scruffy chin before speaking, trying to gather the words and courage to say what he needed to say. Knowing there was no easy way around this, he decided to plunge in. "Since there's no way to sugar-coat this, I'll just say it. I think your Patrolman is a menace and danger to this office and community."

Surprised at Hughes' admission, Walker pursed his lips in concentration as he ran those simple words over in his mind. "That's a pretty serious accusation, Hughes. I hope you can explain yourself."

"I understand that and wouldn't have said it if I couldn't. Let me start from the beginning." Hughes reached for another roll and frowned. Taking a bite, he chewed slowly, gathering his thoughts again.

Will waited patiently for Brandon to continue as he refilled his cup with coffee and sugar. Stirring quietly, Will propped his hip on the counter behind him.

Hughes began. "When you were sick and Dorne and I had to investigate the tip about the Aleut man suspected of stealing and selling traps and having possession of illegal booze....I think his name was Andrew....I began noticing things that disturbed me about Dorne. He was sure the man was guilty of the crime before we talked to him, called him names like 'scum bag,' and referred to him as 'boy.' He was rough with him when there was no call for it. Later the young man's sister came in to see if her brother had been arrested and Dorne was acting even worse. He wouldn't deny nor confirm that it was her brother and called him.....a 'filthy Aleutian'.......I know this sounds petty, even to my own ears, but there's something just not right with Dorne and I felt it strongly enough that I believe you need to keep an eye on your Patrolman."

Will remained silent through Brandon Hughes' speech, the vein in his forehead beginning to pulse noticeably as he clenched and unclenched his jaw. One thing he wouldn't tolerate was disrespect, and Dorne had crossed the line if these things were true.

Brandon continued. "That day the sister came into the office, they left determined to speak with you on Monday. I followed her outside and apologized for Dorne's behavior and told her the name of the man we had in custody. I may have been out of line, but Dorne's attitude was completely unacceptable. I noticed how he treated the prisoner and how he spoke to him, and his tone and complete

124

disrespect for the man when talking to me was completely out of line. I can't stand by any longer and watch it. Dorne's got an attitude problem and a huge chip on his shoulder. Forgive me if I am stepping out of turn, but...." Hughes trailed off.

Will held up a hand to stop the Officer. "Hughes, I'm not surprised at what you are telling me, just very disappointed. Honestly, I have noticed some things that are troubling me about Dorne and this only confirms what I have already seen the past few months. Thank you for telling me this; I know it wasn't easy to do so. And, no, you didn't over step any bounds by showing concern for others. Let's keep this between the two of us for now and promise me you will report any further concerns to me as soon as possible."

"I will." Brandon breathed a huge sigh of relief that the conversation was over for now. "Enough of that, Sergeant. Do we have time to go over my findings from *Rita's Place*?"

"Sure. Fill me in while we finish this coffee and the rest of these rolls."

The two men looked at Hughes' notes and pictures and decided to head over to the woods behind *Rita's Place* for further investigation.

When the men arrived there and told Rita and the girls they would be in the back of the property, it didn't take long for Hughes to find the spot he had photographed. Sharing his ideas that this very spot they stood on could be where the possible abductor had hidden, watched, and waited for his moment, Walker couldn't help but agree with Hughes' thoughts on the matter.

"Good eye, Hughes. I see why you think this might be where it went down. The main question now is, where is the girl?" Turning full circle, Walker began looking around them and walked a few feet further back into the trees. "Let's each take a different section of these woods and look around for where the abductor may have taken the girl after he kidnapped her. We know he wouldn't have gone back through town or around the front of the house so the only option is back through the woods. There's got to be something here that we are missing."

Walker pointed out the directions they would each take and when to meet back if nothing turned up. "Blow your whistle if you find anything, and I mean any little thing. I'll do the same if I see something."

"Got it, Sergeant." Hughes took off in his assigned direction.

An hour and a half into their searching, Hughes turned up nothing. He headed towards Will's area and began following his Sergeant's footsteps. Soon he thought he heard the faint sound of a whistle. Walking towards the area he thought Walker to be in, he heard the noise again. Tweeting his own whistle, Hughes signaled to Walker that he was on his way.

Will had spotted a small lean-to, not much bigger than one of the jail cells. He wanted Hughes to check it out with him so Walker signaled the alert. After reconnecting, Will led Hughes back to the shed.

"I didn't go in, but it is obvious there has been someone around the shed lately. Lots of footprints through the leaves and the area looks disturbed recently. I don't want to check it out alone though." Pointing ahead, Will showed Hughes where the lean-to stood, barely visible through the trees. Lowering his voice, Will continued. "I will go in first to make sure we are alone. You watch the surrounding area."

"Got it." Hughes slowly withdrew his weapon and quietly followed Walker to the shed until the Sergeant motioned for him to stop.

Hearing nothing coming from inside the shed, Walker crept closer. Hiding behind a fallen tree, he crouched down to listen before moving on. Instantly, his stomach clutched at the sight before him at his feet.

Four green-striped cigarette butts lay on the ground beside the fallen, rotting tree.

Without another moment's hesitation, Will retrieved his handkerchief from his pants pocket and picked up the butts, tucking them into the cloth. Returning them to his pocket, Will was even more determined to find out what was going on. Deciding to keep his find quiet, Will continued to look for more clues around the shed.

There were obviously fresh human prints in the leaves and soft ground surrounding the area. But that was about it. Slowly approaching the shed's door, Will listened before moving again. Gun ready, he eased the door open and looked inside. No movement or sound came from the dark interior

Empty.

Walking around the exterior of the shed, Will saw nothing amiss so he motioned for Hughes to join him.

"Find anything?" Hughes asked when he reached Walker's side.

"Nothing but an empty shed and footprints in the leaves. Obvious someone has been here recently. I don't have a flashlight with me. Do you?"

Hughes removed a small flashlight from his pocket and gave it to Walker.

"Let's look inside."

A rusty lock hung precariously from the door's latch. The two men were aghast as they looked around. A covered bucket of human waste sat in the far corner. Clearly from the smell, someone had been kept here not so very long ago. Strips of navy blue cloth with a flowered print lay in the opposite corner, maybe torn from a woman's shirt or dress. A cast-off, thin, blanket was piled on the floor. There were evidences that water had been brought to the little shed from the few bottles that were lying near one wall. A tin plate was lying on the floor as well with bits of dried food on it. Scurrying across the dirty floor, a little mouse was in search of some crumbs. Someone had definitely been here.

Will broke the silence. "She was here."

The men quickly gathered the evidence before them, the lock, plate, bottles, scraps of fabric, and old blanket. Surely they were getting closer to solving this. There were two, evident, gut-wrenching facts.

The shed was empty, and they had been a mere few hours to a day late of possibly rescuing the girl.


Not twenty-four hours earlier, the little shed tucked way back in the woods witnessed an entirely different scene play out......

The scared, hungry woman huddled in the corner of the stinking lean-to rehearsed her plan. Now that she knew her kidnapper, things were different. For several nights, though Berta had no idea how many, she planned her move.

Yesterday dawned as the others had, with the morning sun easing itself into the cracks of the shed bringing her out of the constant nightmares. Or was this reality instead?

She heard the usual sounds of footsteps alerting her to breakfast, if you could call it that, a bottle of water, and an emptied waste pot. Her little mouse-friend scurried to his corner waiting for crumbs Berta would leave for him.

*Click.* Berta heard the key turn in the lock as her heart rate increased to pounding drums within her head and chest. She was ready. Gathering all of her courage, she waited.

The black-clothed man quickly changed out her waste bucket, laid her food and water in the door way and was almost out the door before she made a move.

*Speak, Berta,* she silently willed herself.

Opening cracked lips, she spoke. "Peter."

The man froze.

Before he could leave, she croaked his name again. "Peter! I know it's you."

Fear enveloped her in waves as he turned to look at her. She recognized those same beady, evil, black-brown eyes right before he would silence her friends, even Andrew, months ago on her trips to Datka Island with the others.

Seemingly eons ago, her exhausted mind flashed back to trips she, her sister Ana, Liza, and Darcy would take to the small Island. Peter would load the girls in a tiny boat and take them to Datka to spend the weekend on the far side of the Island in an old hunting cabin that had been Peter's father's. From the beginning, Berta and Andrew were always together, and poor Ana was stuck with Peter. Andrew,

Markus, Joshua, and Peter would spend the late evenings playing cards, drinking, and having their way with the girls until Peter dictated that their time was up, depending on how much money the boys paid him in advance for the weekend. Peter left no doubt in their minds that he was in control of these weekends, and without him, they wouldn't happen. The three boys feared Peter as much as the girls did; he was prone to slap or punch one of them silly if needed. Fear was his greatest weapon and Peter knew how to skillfully wield it. But truthfully, Berta and the other girls enjoyed this short-lived arrangement that took them from their usual life at *Rita's Place* and some unknown men they would have to be with.

And truthfully, Berta had fallen for sweet, innocent Andrew. He was different.

Peter's face was now inches from Berta's, bringing her instantly back to the present and what she needed to do.

Grabbing Berta by the throat, Peter tightened his hand around her neck just enough to nearly make her abandon the plan. But due to the living conditions she had endured, the endless thoughts of Ana, Rita, the girls, and Andrew, his hand around her neck only fueled her determination.

Only able to whisper, Berta did just that. "Peter, I know it is you. You kidnapped me. Why? What did I do?"

Momentarily, his hand tightened around her throat and Berta thought she would pass out any moment. Easing off a bit on her neck, she continued while the chance presented itself. "Who is making you feed me and carry my wastes around like a slave? I heard you arguing with someone the other day. This is not all your idea is it?"

Berta had rehearsed her words over and over in her mind, knowing Peter always wanted to be the one in control, knowing too that in this situation, he clearly wasn't. So she played on that fact. Watching something shift in his eyes, Berta knew she was playing her cards well, so she continued. "Who is behind this, Peter? You are nothing but a slave to this other man. I heard your conversation." Though Berta had caught only snatches of it, she hoped Peter would believe she knew more than she did.

She had Peter's attention. Flaring his nostrils, Peter didn't loosen his grip on Berta.

"Andrew was your friend. What has he done to you? Why did you kidnap me? You can't live the rest of your days afraid of the other man and what he will do…..Let me go, Peter. Please." Gasping for air, Peter loosened his hold but still held onto her throat. Again Berta took advantage of the ability to speak. "I won't say a word to anyone and we can both be free of all of this. You know Andrew won't talk. He is too scared. You can have your secrets and I can be free. Let me go and you run away from here as fast as you can, away from this life, from that man who is controlling you, making you clean up after a whore's waste bucket…."

Again his hand tightened around her neck. Afraid she had said too much, Berta sat still and silent.

Roughly shoving her away, Peter stood quiet for a moment then began pacing the small shed. After three rounds around the tiny room, he bent close to Berta and said, "I will be back."

With that, he left the shed and locked the door again.

Berta melted in a heap on the hard floor and gave in to the torrent of tears that shook her frame. Her mind raced through her gasps for air. *Surely I messed this all up. Peter will come back and kill me now! Why didn't I just shut up and wait it out?*

Terror like she had never known before almost swallowed the girl whole as she lie still, unable to move on the dirty floor. With thoughts as horrible as her worst nightmares swirling around her, Berta gave into fitful sleep.

Unknown to Berta how much time had passed, she awakened to the sound of the key in the rusty lock. Returning in full force, fear kept her silent as she waited for someone to enter.

It was Peter. He carried a small bag slung over his shoulder. Quickly kneeling down in front of Berta, he spoke in a whisper.

Berta could feel the heat emanating from Peter's body and see the utter hatred aflame in his eyes. He threw the bag at her feet.

"You have one chance to leave. I will leave the lock off the door when I go. You have money in the bag, enough for a few days then you are on your own. There are directions in the bag to get you to Markus' house outside of The Harbor. Stay there one night, then he will tell you where to go. If you don't leave the area, you will only bring harm to yourself, your sister, and friends."

Grabbing her roughly by the front of what was left of her dark blue dress, Peter spat the next words in her face. "I swear I will hunt you down and kill you if you ever mention my name about any of this. It is not what I wanted, but I had no choice. Understand?"

Tears coursed down her cold, dirty cheeks as Berta spoke around trembling lips. "Yes. I understand."

"Leave at dark. Markus is expecting you tonight." Peter stood and looked around the shed, then cursed under his breath. Pausing but a second, Peter's next words were barely audible. "I never wanted this to happen."

Overcoming her fears, Berta blurted, "Peter, why are you doing this? Why are you letting me go?"

Shaking his head slowly, Peter looked at the girl over his shoulder and answered almost imperceptibly. "For my own reasons......and for your sister."

With those last words, the black shrouded man left the ramshackle shed in the back woods of The Harbor and disappeared into the trees, never to been seen again.

# CHAPTER 12

As soon as the perfect moment presented itself and she was assured her mother was sound asleep, Liza gathered her tight-knit family of mismatched girls into her room for their meeting. Not one to beat around the bush, Liza dove right in with her concerns and worries.

Tucking her feet underneath her for warmth, Liza surveyed the eight faces gathered around her. "Girls, we have a problem; actually, several problems. There's been too much snooping around *Rita's Place* for my comfort. With the Sergeant and Officer Hughes dropping by unannounced for their investigation, it is making me uncomfortable. What if they discover that this is more than a pool hall? Mama could lose this entire place and we would all be torn apart, sent out on our own to fend for ourselves, or worse, put in jail." Liza knew fear was getting the best of her and she wasn't making much sense.

Ana spoke up first. "Liza, the Sergeant and Hughes *have* to come here. If they don't, then Berta will never be found." Her voice cracking, Ana placed a hand to her mouth to stifle the sob wanting to escape.

Liza reached a hand out and patted Ana's knee. "Honey, that's not what I meant. Yes, they have to come here. But during Hughes' last visit, he walked into the pool hall as I was about to escort a customer upstairs. That encounter very possibly raised his suspicions even more. The Sergeant has already been questioning Mama about how all of us came to live here. I think he knows Mama runs more than a pool hall."

Felicity tucked a stray strand of hair back into the knot on top of her blond head. "Wait, this doesn't make sense, Liza. *Rita's Place* has never been questioned before so why now? I am a cook, not a....."

Liza stood to her full height and faced Felicity. "Oh just say it. A whore? No, you are not like me or Milly or Stasia or—"

"Stop it, girls! This is not the time for our differences to get the best of us." Always the sensible, sweet-spirited one, Emily did her best to calm the beginnings of a storm that had brewed just underneath the surface between the girls that "didn't" and the girls that "did."

Darcy took over. "Stasia's right. Now is not the time for this. We are all still upset about Berta and we can't take it out on those we love most. Our personal choices can't interfere in this crisis. Now, Liza, what are you thinking?"

Taking a deep breath, Liza ran her hands through her red mop. She untied the green ribbon and retied it to secure her wayward hair. "We need a plan. That's why I called this meeting. We have to put our heads together and figure this out. With the investigation, the AST will be here again and we can't risk Mama losing this place or us. It would kill her. She's worked so hard her whole life and she loves us." For a moment, Liza let her ever-present guard down and the others saw a side of her that was not often on display.

Liza loved her mother. She had always envied other little girls and their mothers who went to the ice cream parlor for a double-dipped cone or who strolled hand in hand through the park. Liza grew up in a bar and she would probably live out the rest of her days in one. Liza believed Rita was a good mother, or at least as good as she knew to be. Oh, Rita had told her the story of her own childhood and how she was raised by Lorena and her grandmother. Much the same as

136

Liza's own upbringing. Sadly struggling through the days to make ends meet and keep a roof over their heads, clothes on their backs, and food on the table. All at the grave expense of their hearts and bodies.

Penny, the in-house seamstress, and practical to a fault, spoke next. "What if we turned this place into a restaurant? Just changed the entire place into a respectable business. There's enough of us to run it."

Liza's tough exterior was back in place. "Oh, Penny. A restaurant? The Harbor has enough of those already. We could never make a go at it. *Rita's Place* is known for two things, a place to have fun and play some pool, and a place for the men in this town to get what they can't at home."

"Really, Liza. You don't have to be cruel to Penny." Jocelyn had been quiet for most of the conversation until now.

Liza wasn't ready to be silent just yet. "You know what they say. 'Once a whore, always a whore.' Why would you think any of us could be anyone other than who we are? If you want more, there's the door to the big old world just full of opportunities for girls like us."

Penny looked down at her hands in her lap. A lone tear trickled down her young cheek.

"Liza, stop it!" Jocelyn had heard enough. "This is not helping. No, the world isn't knocking on any of our doors with new opportunities. So we have to do what we can at the moment. Protect this place and each other. Okay, what about this? Emily, Penny, Felicity, and Ana, you girls can be sort of look-outs for the rest of us. If you see that anyone from the AST even comes near this place, then alert the rest of us. We have to let them do their job and find Berta, and we have to protect ourselves. This place is strictly a pool hall first and foremost. That's what they need to see and *all* they will see."

Felicity nodded her head in agreement. "That sounds like a good plan for now. But I don't think we should give up on Penny's idea of a restaurant."

Liza glared at Felicity for siding with Penny's idea. "For now, let's forget about the stupid restaurant and think about watching our backs. We all need to get some sleep."

Liza's unspoken signal that the meeting was over sent everyone to their respective rooms. With everyone on high alert and scraps of a plan in place, the girls dispersed for the night to sleep.


While sleep hung heavily over *Rita's Place* in the wee hours of the morning, it evaded Sergeant Will Walker on the other side of Seal Harbor. Fluffing his pillow a bit too roughly, the man's tossing and turning awakened his wife, Sophia.

Rolling over onto her side to face her husband, Sophia pulled the navy blue and red log cabin-patterned quilt tightly under her chin. Knowing the hour was late and Will was still awake troubled her from her sound sleep.

Will's back was to Sophia, so she gently reached a hand to his shoulders and began rubbing. "Want to talk since we both are awake?" She tickled his ribs teasingly.

Turning to face Sophia, Will remarked, "Sorry, Soph. I didn't mean to wake you."

Laughing quietly, she teased him. "Honey, the only way you wouldn't have awakened me was if I were dead, and I am obviously not." Playfully she kissed Will's neck and snuggled into him. "So talk. I'm all ears."

Kissing the top of her head, Will teased back. "I completely disagree with that statement. You are definitely more than all ears, my Soph." He wrapped both arms around his wife and lay silent a moment.

After a minute it began to spill from him. "I just don't get it. Nothing is making sense. It's like someone has taken a dozen jigsaw puzzles, dumped them all out on one table, and then I am expected to make sense out of the pieces and put them all back together."

"That sounds pretty complicated, Will. I wish I could help."

"I know, Soph. All I can figure out is this.....each different puzzle has some of the same pieces. There are commonalities in the whole big mess. I can see part of the pictures, but not enough. Sounds silly even to my own ears." Laughing quietly to himself, Will hugged Sophia again. "I wish I could discuss the case with you and get your input, but you and I both know I can't. I would appreciate your wisdom on this one."

"Will, I can't help you much, but we both know from past experience since you have been in law enforcement that God can shed some light on things that man can't even possibly begin to understand. Have you spent much time praying about the case?" Slowly rubbing his neck, Sophia felt some of the tension ease from Will.

"Honestly, not enough. But you're right. I do need to pray more about this one, because if it turns out like I think it might, there will be big trouble down the road."

"That sounds ominous. Have you talked to Dorne about the details and tried to get his perspective? He knows about the case and can maybe shed some light on things."

Before answering her question, Will stayed silent awhile. "That just may be part of the whole problem. I don't trust my patrolman's perspective nor input any longer."

"Really? I know Tom Dorne's pretty rough and gruff but he means well and is a good patrolman for the AST."

"Yes, he is. But something's not right there, Sophia. Just pray that I don't act without all the facts or act too quickly. That could backfire on me and the AST."

Kissing her husband on the cheek, Sophia threw the covers back and put on her slippers and robe. "How about I start a pot of coffee? Your alarm goes off in less than an hour."

Rolling to his back, Will watched her retreating figure. Before rising from the bed and heading to the shower, he took Sophia's advice, the best advice he could have gotten from anywhere.

He prayed about the case.

Thirty minutes later, with the smell of bacon and coffee drawing Will to the kitchen, he embraced Sophia from behind as she stood at the stove stirring a skillet of scrambled eggs.

"Feel better?" Sophia asked. She turned and placed a quick kiss on his freshly shaved cheek.

"Yes, I do. But it was more from the praying than the shower. Thanks for reminding me of what I should have done days ago." Will began taking breakfast dishes from the cupboard and setting the table. "Should I go wake Lauren for school?"

"She's got another half hour to sleep so let her stay in bed a little longer," Sophia answered.

"Orange juice?" Will asked.

"No, thanks. Just coffee for me." Sophia brought heaping plates of eggs, bacon, and buttered toast to the table.

The two bowed over their plates and thanked God for his provision.

Around mouthfuls of breakfast, Will laid out his plan that came to him after praying and showering. "So, here's my thoughts on things. I promised Gabriel Parker and Ed that I would make a trip to Datka Island to meet the new pastor and his family. They are a little younger than us, but I am sure they could use some new friends. What do you say about going with me? It would be fun. You have never been to the Island, and I can be spared in the office for a day." Like an expectant schoolboy, Will awaited her answer.

Thinking it through, Sophia remained silent a moment. "That actually sounds like a great idea. I could use a change of scenery and an adventure." Sophia gathered their finished breakfast things and continued. "Can I meet you in about two hours at the AST office after I drop Lauren off at school? That will give me time to run an errand too."

A huge smile broke out over Will's face. "I was hoping you would say 'yes.' It gives us a little time together and it will be fun. I really believe we need to connect with this new pastor and his family." Will kissed Sophia on the cheek and grabbed his coat. "See you in a bit."

"Can't wait." Sophia quickly went to get dressed for the day and the adventure that awaited her.

With the unusual gentle breeze surrounding them, Will and Sophia prepared to disembark from the small boat he had rented in Seal Harbor for their trip to Datka.

Sophia had thoroughly enjoyed the landscape, the boat ride, the chilly air, and now the gorgeous Aleutian Island they were about to set foot on. Since no one knew of their arrival, they landed on the lonely, rocky shoreline and took the trail that led to the center of the tiny village. Will knew the path well, so he guided Sophia towards the close knit community.

Ptarmigan mothers called to their baby chicks as the couple came upon a little flock of the birds. Lavender-blue lupines waved from the side of the trail as they walked by. The sound of the shore behind them and the village noise increasing ahead as the couple drew closer captivated Sophia instantly.

Reaching for Will's hand she stopped him in his tracks. "Thank you for bringing me with you, Will....I mean Sergeant Walker." She giggled at his quick grin.

Placing a kiss on her nose, Will squeezed Sophia's hand and then instantly switched from husband back to Sergeant. She loved this game he played with her. Clearing his throat, Will took on an air of importance. "Now, if you'll excuse me, Miss. I have some important work to attend to." Giving her a quick wink, Will continued on down the path before her.

# CHAPTER 13

Time seemed to stand still. What seemed like weeks had been only a few hours. Berta listened for any noises outside the dark shed as she lie frozen in place, arms around the small bag afraid to believe it even existed.

She had heard the latch being put in place on the door, but she never heard him attach the lock and click it shut. Just as he said. Berta replayed snatches of Peter's words over and over in her foggy mind.

*One chance to leave.....lock off the door.....money in the bag..... you are on your own.....Markus' house.....he will tell you where to go..... I will hunt you down and kill you..... for your sister.*

Her fearful thoughts kept Berta frozen in place.

*Is he watching me, waiting for me to leave so he can kill me? Is this a trick or a trap? Why would I consider trusting a man like Peter? If this is real, why is he giving me a chance to escape?*

*Will he kill Ana when I leave?*

Knowing her thinking was completely confused, Berta tried to focus, tried to concentrate. *Check the bag.*

Releasing her grasp on the bag, Berta began digging through its contents. Darkness was now upon her. Her time to run. But she had to know if Peter had followed through on his part. Digging around, she felt like what must be a small flashlight. Clicking it on, Berta tried to shield the small beam from anyone who might see it. What if the other man was nearby?

Quickly she rummaged through the bag and found a small wad of cash, a piece of paper with directions scribbled on it, a container of water, a pair of shoes and socks, and a thin blanket.

Berta removed the blanket and placed it around her already shaking body. The fear, cold, and anxiety were taking its toll on her. Unscrewing the cap off the water, Berta drank a small amount. There was no food as she hoped to find. Next, she placed the socks and shoes on her dirty feet, for once grateful that she had been born with large feet for a girl. Returning all but the precious blanket to the bag, Berta sat back down and listened.

She heard the hoot of an owl looking for its own evening dinner. Berta's mind shot to her little mouse friend. Momentary sadness welled up in her chest. The little mouse would be confused and hungry come tomorrow. Who would feed it now? Would it feel deserted too, like Ana must feel with her gone?

A quiet, mirthless laugh escaped Berta's lips. *I must be losing my mind. My chance to leave this God-forsaken shed is here, and I am worrying about a mouse's feelings.*

No, definitely not God-forsaken. Before making another move, Berta dropped to her knees and prayed a simple prayer.

*God, if You can hear me.....*She stopped mid-sentence as something dawned her, like the morning's new sun coming up from its horizon-bed. Slowly, blindingly, bright.

A lone tear trickled down Berta's cheek. She began her prayer again.

*God, I know You do hear me. Thank You for answering my prayer. Watch over me now. Please help me. Please.*

The same newfound peace settled her down again. During her stay in the shed, Berta had become slowly aware of the peace that calmed her anxious mind and emotions every time she prayed. She could not do without that peace, especially now.

Rising to her feet, she knew it was time to go, time to flee this dreadful place. Fear tried to paralyze her again and make her stay put, afraid for her life if she left. But, no. Everything was as Peter said it would be with the lock and the bag. She had to try.

Quickly she dug out the flashlight and clicked it on. Next she read the scrap of paper with directions to Markus' house over and over so she wouldn't waste precious time getting there.

Throwing the bag over her shoulder, Berta eased the door open, the latch coming loose without much effort on her part.

Berta had sat free the past few hours awaiting the cover of dark. This irony struck her full force. She had been free to leave but was too afraid to not follow Peter's instructions to a tee.

Stepping silently from the stinking shed, Berta stood for a moment getting her bearings. Peter had instructed her to leave from the back of the shed and go further up into the woods. A road would be at the very top of the hill and she was to take it until she came upon the far edge of The Harbor. From there finding Markus' house was easy.

Berta had gone a short ways upwards and her legs began trembling with the exertion. She knew she had grown weak staying in the shed for so long but hadn't realized until her body was taxed just how weak she was. Berta felt like a new-born kitten only days old trying to walk. But she had to press on.

Fear and desperation fueled her exhausted muscles. Adrenaline coursed through her body until Berta thought she would surely collapse if she didn't reach the road soon. She needed to walk on flat ground and be done with the uphill climb. Knowing it was taking her way too long, Berta pushed on until the hill gradually came

145

to an abrupt stop. Within twenty feet of the top of the woody hill, a road was visible in the moonlight. Berta almost cried for joy when she saw the road. Pausing for a breath and a drink, Berta leaned against a large, cool boulder and rested a bit. Afraid to sit down, she remained standing, forcing her legs to stop quivering.

*Oh, Thank You. You are with me, God. Please help me get to Markus.*

Taking a deep breath, she continued on down the long road afraid the rising sun would reveal her location and shine a spotlight on her whereabouts. Fear still gripped her. Would the other man return and realize she was gone and come after her? Would he go to *Rita's Place* and bring harm to her sister or the others? Afraid she would go crazy if she continued with these thoughts, Berta focused on each step, each second that brought her closer to safety, at least for now.

Finally, she reached Markus' small house. Not much more than the shed, she stood in the trees and looked around as far as the cover of the early morning darkness would allow. Was Markus home? Was he really expecting her? She knew the Aleut man from the months she, Ana, and the others visited the boys on Datka, when Peter would take them there. Markus was always quiet and friendly. Maybe he would help her. This was her only option.

Tentatively she approached the house. Berta could tell that a small lamp was on from the warm glow it yielded. After weeks trapped in darkness, the only light she had received had come through the cracks in the walls or when the door was opened for Peter to leave her food. The warm lamp light beckoned her forward.

Climbing the steps as quietly as possible, the front door opened a crack and she caught a glimpse of Markus. "Berta? Is that you?"

Without answering, she nearly threw herself in the small house. Instantly she dissolved in a heap in the floor, a shaking puddle of tears. Her emotions and body overrode her mind. She couldn't hold them in another second. Utter exhaustion claimed her.

Markus bent down beside her and lifted her dirty, matted hair away from her face. Quietly he spoke, "Berta, you are safe now. You are going to be fine. You are safe here."

Sitting in the floor beside her, Markus pulled her to him and Berta placed her head in his lap and sobbed her heart out.

"I am so sorry, Berta. Are you hurt anywhere? Please tell me what you need. What can I do?" Markus stroked her back as her sobs ebbed.

Berta's thoughts turned back to the present. She realized how completely stinking, dirty, helpless, and shameful she must appear. A mirror hadn't been a luxury in the cramped shed and she knew she was a mess. Embarrassment colored her actions and she lifted her head off of Markus' lap, forcing herself to regain control.

"Markus, thank you for helping me. I can't believe I am finally free! I miss Ana so much and the other girls. And no, I am not hurt. I am just very, very tired and hungry.....and dirty." Tears sprang to her eyes as she remembered the beauty she once had been, how proud she always was to be able to turn a man's head. Now none of that mattered to her anymore. When the safety of your life and the simple things like food and water become the only essentials in your day, when you wonder if you will ever see the ones you love again, when a little mouse becomes your only friend.......

When God takes you by the hand in a cramped, shed.......what seemed important before fades forever like the drifting fog across the ocean.

"What did Peter tell you? I must know what he said." Berta brushed away the tears, too tired to rise from the floor just yet.

Markus sat in silence beside her. Varying emotions flickered across his dark brown face. Finally he spoke. "I always knew Peter could be evil. Driven by his own wants and desires, but this....this...." He couldn't finish.

Swiping a hand across his face, Markus continued. "He told me he was forced to kidnap you and lock you in a shed. After a while he could not stand it anymore and said you recognized him. He did not know what else to do so he came to me and told me I had to take you in or you would die. Either the man who forced him to kidnap you would kill you or you would die in the shed with the barest of provisions......Berta, I am so, so sorry. What can I do?" His voice broke with these last words.

"Did he tell you *why*?" Tears made their way down her cheeks again leaving smudges in the dirt on her pretty face.

"No." Markus stood and lifted Berta like a little girl and placed her on a nearby chair at a table. "Now, let's get you some food and water......and a bath." He gave a low chuckle and lifted a strand of her dirty hair.

Slowly she shook her head and let out a low moan. "Oh, Markus. It feels so good to be in a house, with someone watching over me. Helping me."

Quickly Markus got her a cup of cold water and placed it before her. He handed her two aspirin and Berta quickly drank the cold

148

liquid grateful for the medicine to hopefully relieve the pain in her taxed body. He made her a cold sandwich and placed it on a plate before her.

"I know this isn't a feast, but it is what I have."

A large smile spread across her tear-streaked face. "You have no idea what this means to me." Berta made herself eat slowly and enjoy each bite. The salty ham, hard cheese, creamy butter, and the dark brown bread were heaven to her.

Markus sat across the table from Berta keeping an eye on her. He noticed her eyelids began drooping and gave her a little nudge. "How about a hot bath and a warm bed?"

A look flashed across Berta's face and she quickly hid it behind her hand as she turned to survey the room.

Markus took her chin in his rough hand ever so gently. "Berta, I am here as a friend. Nothing more. I only expect you to get your strength back. You have a long way to travel to get away from Seal Harbor. We cannot risk Peter's friend finding you, *ever*! This is just your stopping off place. Trust me." Sincerity blazed in his eyes as he released her chin.

"A bath and bed sounds wonderful. And Markus, I do trust you. I will only ask for one other thing. I need paper and a pencil."

As soon as Berta towel-dried her hair, she grabbed up the paper and pencil Markus had left on the table for her. She quickly wrote the letter to Ana she had composed in her head while she soaked the layers of dirt off in the bathtub. Berta needed her to know that she was alive and well and would come back as soon as she knew it was safe.

But for now, she had to do the hardest thing she had ever done in her life.

Let her sister go one more time.

For her safety and for Ana's.

# CHAPTER 14

Rounding the bend in the path, Will and Sophia Walker came upon a cheerful, vibrant scene. A large group of people were scurrying like ants around the Island's church, each contributing to one task or another. Hammers, saws, paintbrushes, and brooms were all in action. There was one head that stood above all the rest, that of their friend Edward Hamilton.

Glad to see a familiar face, Will approached Ed as he was giving instructions to a group of young Aleut men and women. Respect and admiration shone on their faces as the young people gave Ed their full attention. A few American faces dotted the crowd. Will assumed they must be the new pastor and his family, part of the reason for his excursion to Datka.

When Ed had finished talking, he looked up and spotted Will and Sophia. A look of pleasant shock lit his tanned face. "Well, hello, you two! You caught me by complete surprise. I had no idea you were coming."

Shaking hands with his friend, Will said, "Sophia and I were in need of a long overdue date so we decided to come here and try out the place."

A quick half-smile flashed across Ed's face. Reaching for a hug from Sophia, he said, "Let me introduce you to some people. You haven't met the pastor, his wife, and daughter."

"Great! That's one reason I am here. I would also like to get to talk to Andrew again later if that can be worked out."

"Sure thing, Sergeant." Ed gave Will a quick salute and grin. "Let me get the Hudsons so you can meet them."

While Will and Sophia waited for Ed's return, several of the Aleut men that he had met on previous trips to Datka came up and spoke to them. Introducing each person to his wife, Sophia gave them a smile and warm greeting. Just another reason Will loved her so much. She had a way with people, even those she had just met.

Finally Ed returned with the Hudsons. "Pastor Stan, Elaine, and Lindy Hudson, I would like for you to meet my good friends Sergeant Will Walker and his lovely wife Sophia. The Walkers also have a daughter who is in high school. Sergeant Walker works for the Alaska State Troopers department and oversees Datka as well. The Hudsons have just arrived on the Island and have taken over the position as Pastor."

Handshakes and friendly greetings went around the small circle of people. Elaine spoke up next. "We were just about to break for lunch. Why don't you join us at our house and we can visit over a meal? Ed, you too."

"You know I never turn down food that I don't have to prepare. I will be right over after I tell the guys when to meet me back at the church." With that, Ed turned and went to speak to the group he had been working with.

Will quickly accepted the invitation for him and Sophia. "Sounds great! Actually Sophia and I were hoping to visit with you if time allowed. This will be perfect." Placing an arm around his wife's shoulders, Will and Sophia followed the family to their house that was settled in the trees very near to the church.

Inside the quaint home, Elaine turned to her daughter and asked her to help set the table while she took out cold meats and cheeses for their meal.

Sophia jumped right in the middle of the action in the cozy kitchen. "What can I do, ladies?"

"Maybe slice the bread for sandwiches if you don't mind?" Elaine liked the warm and friendly demeanor she saw in Sophia. She handed Sophia a knife and the loaf of dark bread.

While she sliced, Sophia looked toward Lindy who was washing some berries. "Lindy, I love your name. It is so beautiful."

Blushing, Lindy ducked behind her hair and laughed softly. "My name actually means *Beautiful.*"

"Very fitting for you then." Sophia returned to her bread, a small frown creasing her forehead. Finally she blurted, "I know! It has puzzled me since I first met you. You look just like someone who I have seen before. Jade Miller. Her family was in the area and served as missionaries to Datka over the summer. There is a striking resemblance between the two of you."

Dawning crossed Lindy's face. *That name again. Jade. This is the second person who thought we looked alike.*

Sophia continued. "I didn't get to spend much time with her. Only around her a couple of times. Sweet family though. How old are you, Lindy?"

"Almost twenty-one. And you aren't the first person who thought I was someone named Jade."

Elaine caught the discomfort in her daughter's voice. She knew how much Lindy hated for the attention to be on her. "So tell me what brings you and the Sergeant here today, Sophia?"

"He really wanted to meet the new pastor and his family and also speak with one of the men on the Island, so he invited me to tag along. I've never been here before. I'm glad I got to come." Sophia

153

finished the bread and placed it on the table with the rest of their lunch.

Elaine called the men to the table. "Lunch is ready. Anyone hungry?"

Everyone seated themselves around the circular table leaving Lindy and Ed to choose the last two chairs that were side by side. Slight blushes were exchanged by each as they both reached for the same chair. Ed quickly recovered and pulled the chair out and offered it to Lindy.

Giving him a quick smile, Lindy lowered herself in the seat next to Ed's as he sat down beside her.

"Ed will you offer thanks for this meal?" Pastor Stan asked.

Bringing Ed out of the embarrassing moment with Lindy, he bowed his head and spoke with the assurance and confidence of one very accustomed of talking with their Maker. "Father God, I just want to thank You for this incredible food, especially for the fact that I didn't have to prepare it. I thank You for these new friends and the ones I have grown to know and love over this past summer. Please bless this food and give our bodies the strength for this day's task. In Your precious Son's name I pray, Amen."

*Amens* quietly went around the table. Lindy was struck with the ease that Ed spoke to God. She liked that about him. Most people would have been uncomfortable if a preacher had asked them to pray. Not Edward Hamilton.

Easy conversations flowed making the food taste all the better. Ed even engaged Lindy in chatting about her past experiences as he filled in the blanks about his own. The two were amazed at how easily they carried on a conversation with each other.

Ed didn't miss the fact that his life's story was not judged or critiqued by Lindy as it had been by Jade. Looks was about the only thing Lindy Hudson and Jade Miller had in common. He had to work to get Lindy to start talking, but finally she seemed comfortable enough to do so. Jade would have been gushing about herself and her accomplishments. Lindy was a tad insecure, whereas Jade was very self-assured. Their differences didn't go unnoticed.

The adults were engaged in their own dialogue.

Will asked how Stan and Elaine had met and how they ended up in the ministry. Stan glanced at Elaine since his mouth was full and nodded for her to answer for them.

"Well......Stan was raised in church. He was a preacher's kid, though not your typical p. k. He didn't live the rebellious preacher's kid's lifestyle, thank goodness." Chuckling softly Elaine shot a sweet glance at her husband. "Probably because God saved him for me, knowing I would one day need this man." She reached a hand over and patted Stan on the arm.

Sophia instantly loved this woman before her. She admired her open devotion to her husband and her easy manner.

Elaine continued after a moment. "I, on the other hand, was raised in a home where my parents were very good people, they just didn't go to church nor did they see the purpose of it. They both believed they were good enough people and didn't need a God to tell them how to be better or to impose a bunch of rules on them. When I was twelve I was sexually abused and never told my parents. I was afraid I would ruin our 'good family' image and kept it to myself."

Elaine noticed Sophia's eyes mist over as she reached a hand to her mouth, fully engrossed in Elaine's story. "By the time I reached my

155

teen years, I believed I was nothing more than trash, used up, worthless."

Stan reached a hand over and squeezed his wife's hand.

"In my early high school years, I dated many boys and felt like all I was good for was for them to use me and then discard me at will. Eventually I became suicidal."

"Oh, Elaine. This breaks my heart for you. I have a teen-age daughter and I can't imagine her going through such pain." Sophia's soft heart was visible to all.

Ed watched the admiration for her mother cross Lindy's face. He could tell she had heard this story before but stopped to listen again. A sweet smile graced Lindy's face as she looked at Elaine.

"Thank you, Sophia. My story may be difficult to hear but I promise it has a happy ending. Anyway, I will never forget the day as long as I live. It was a Wednesday. I planned to take my life in a women's restroom at a local shopping center. I didn't want anything to stop me at home, nor did I want my parents to be the first ones to find me after I died. I had a bottle full of pills in my purse and had just purchased a soda to wash them down with. In the restroom, I found it was empty so I chose the last stall away from the door. Closing the lid on the toilet, I sat down and dug out the pill bottle and soda. I opened the pill bottle and set it on the toilet paper holder and reached for my soda. My heart rate was so fast I am surprised that I didn't have a heart attack and die just from the stress of what I was about to do, but I knew the pain inside me had to end *that day*. I drank half the soda before I worked up the nerve to down the pills. Then I reached for the pills and noticed a slip of paper, a pamphlet of some sort under my pills on top of the toilet paper holder."

A teary smile interrupted Elaine's words. She stopped for a second to compose herself.

Will reached for his handkerchief in his shirt pocket and dabbed at his eyes then handed it to his crying wife. She gladly accepted it.

"You may need to pass that around the table, Sergeant. She's got us all choked up!" Ed blew his nose unashamedly and loudly on his napkin. Everyone laughed and savored the needed chuckle.

Taking a deep breath, Elaine continued. "Here comes the good part. I don't know why, but I picked up that piece of paper and began reading. I only remember a few words but they were like a life line thrown to someone drowning. The cover showed a picture of a silhouette of a woman, arms raised above her head, light shining all around. The simple words under the picture said, 'Freedom can be yours! Freedom from pain, depression, sadness, and hurt.' I stared at it unbelieving for a minute. Then I flipped it over and saw a church's name and address on the back. Somewhere in my darkened mind, I wanted that light to shine around me, to make me free from those very things the cover listed that I could be free from. I looked at my watch and realized that the next service started in less that fifteen minutes. Without giving myself time to change my mind, I recapped the pills and stuffed them in my purse and promised myself that if that church didn't deliver on its promise then I would return right after the service and take my life once and for all."

Elaine stopped her story and looked around the rapt faces before her. "I'm sorry. I just realized I have monopolized this entire conversation. I am almost done with my story. Anyone want dessert?"

"No way! This *is* dessert!" Ed seemed to speak for the entire table so Elaine felt encouraged to continue.

"I don't remember a word the pastor said that night, only the feeling I had of someone watching out for me. I should have been dead right then, I wasn't. That startled me the longer I sat there. I *wasn't dead* and I should have been. How could a piece of paper influence me so much to change my plans? Sitting on the back row, I literally felt love wash over me like never before. It grew stronger and more intense the longer I sat there. My mind kept telling me to get up and leave before anyone walked up to me after the service, but my body couldn't respond. I remember praying, 'God if You're real, show me.' And within thirty seconds, this guy walks up to me and says, 'Hi, I'm Stan. Have you been here before?'"

Stan put his arm around Elaine's shoulders and smiled at the memory.

"My real name is Eleanor. For some reason, I told him my name was Elaine. I liked the sound of that better than Eleanor. As a child I would imagine myself as an Elaine because it sounded prettier. And part of me didn't want anyone to know Eleanor. Anyway, I thought Stan was hitting on me when he invited me to go for a milkshake after church. He said his father was the pastor and he would have about an hour to kill before they went home and he wanted to treat me to a shake. I searched his eyes for any sign of him wanting *more* than a milkshake with me. It wasn't there. I hesitated so he pressed me further and promised me that I could leave whenever I wanted to if I thought he was boring or I just didn't like him as I person. That struck me as odd, but I was intrigued. I also felt a pull to something I saw in him, a genuineness, a joy, a peace that I desperately wanted. That night I met Stan Hudson and Jesus Christ and I have never been the same since."

"Wow! What a wonderful testimony!" Sophia was still dabbing her eyes as she spoke.

Stan finished up where Elaine left off. "Elaine got connected with some really precious women in the church and received the help and healing she needed. We started dating and married within two years of meeting each other. I went to Bible school and became an associate pastor, then later a pastor. She worked with young women in the community that had experienced much of what Elaine had, then we got connected with a mission board and began doing local then short-term global outreaches. After we had Lindy, Elaine and I both felt the call to do more missions and found out about AMRA. We served under them for years and recently got sent to Datka. We actually feel like we are home now, strange as that may sound. I do know that wherever God calls you to go, *that* is home."

"Very well said." Ed piped up. He looked at his watch and told the group he had about fifteen more minutes to visit then had to go back to work. Turning to Lindy, Ed asked, "What do you think about coming with me? There's plenty to be done before Luka and Yuri's wedding and we can use all the hands available."

"Ummmm.....Mom?" Lindy was used to her mother giving her a way of escape from uncomfortable situations such as these, so the answer she got wasn't what she had expected.

"Sure, Ed. Lindy is free. That would be great for her to connect more with the people here."

Ed saw Lindy's eyes widen at her mother. *Maybe she doesn't want to go,* he mused.

Excusing herself from the table to go change into work clothes, Lindy heard the conversation return with the adults.

Ed's sincere look and request for her to join him flashed across her mind.

*There's no reason for me not to go. And Ed didn't have to ask me. I need to get over myself and get to know people, get out of this bubble I keep forcing myself to stay in! This is no fun at all hidden away all the time.*

Quickly changing shirts, she grabbed her hairbrush and ran it through her dark brown waves. Flipping her hair to one side, the scar stared her in the face in her mirror. Horror struck her as she realized that she had sat on Ed's right side with the ugly, scarred, left side of her face towards him. She hadn't thought to keep her face covered with her hair as he chatted up a storm with her through lunch. Then reality hit her full force.

Not only was he on the 'bad' side of her, but she had completely forgotten about her scars.

And they hadn't bothered her once in his presence.


Back at the lunch table, Will observed and enjoyed the comradery among them all. During Elaine's story, he kept seeing eleven faces flash before his eyes. Those of Rita and the girls in her home.

*God, is there a connection here? Is this one of the reasons You wanted me to come meet this family?* Will prayed silently during Elaine's story.

When she was finished and Lindy and Ed had left to go work on the church, Will felt as if he would burst if he stayed quiet any longer.

Within a matter of minutes he gave a quick summary without too many details about *Rita's Place* and Berta's kidnapping. Instantly he could see the interest on Pastor Stan and Elaine's face as they listened.

Plans quickly shaped up for the Hudsons to come to Seal Harbor and do what they could for the girls that were so desperately lost and hurting. Elaine knew these girls were experiencing much more pain than she ever endured at that age, but she also knew she had just the answer these girls needed.

# CHAPTER 15

Cursing silently under his breath, the man raked his hands back through his hair for the hundredth time. Like a caged, rabid dog, he paced and schemed, only to change his latest plans yet again.

"Where *is* he? Where did that Aleutian piece of trash go?" Propelled by a mixture of panic and anger, the man began storming through his house. The first thing to go flying was the bottle in his hand. Crashing into the wall across the room, glass shards scattered across the linoleum floor.

Next, he kicked a kitchen chair and sent it careening through the room. Hands in his hair again, he could almost hear his heart beat in his ears pounding out a rhythm that would rival that of an Indian war drum.

"Where did he take her? That's not how this was supposed to go!" Knowing he needed to calm down before the neighbors came to see what all the commotion was about, the man did his best to reign his anger in.

Fear vied for anger's place and momentarily won.

Pacing.

Panting.

Planning.

Talking under his breath, he worked out his next moves. "I need to get out of here. Get out of town before Peter or the girl talks. No, Peter's too scared, but the girl won't be. Uhhh!!! How did she get out and where is Peter?"

Moving quickly to his bedroom, the man snatched a large tattered suitcase from the upper shelf of his closet and began throwing everything into it he could fit making a mess of the rest of the house in his haste to pack.

Stuffing last month's rent money into an envelope, the man ran a few houses down and knocked on his landlord's door. Impatience burned in his gut like a smoldering fire. "Come on, old man," he mused under his breath.

A dog inside the house began barking. "Shut up, mutt!" He heard someone inside shout at the yapping dog.

His landlord opened the front door and appeared to have been awakened from a nap. Dressed in a t-shirt riddled with holes and stains, the landlord grumbled, "Yeah?"

The man thrust the envelope towards the landlord. "Here's your rent money. The house is all yours again. I've got a family emergency and have to leave. Don't know when I will be back....." He backed down the steps and headed up the street to his car.

Finally aware of what the retreating man was muttering, the landlord hollered, "Hey! What do you mean you won't be back! You didn't give me any notice...." He watched as the man quickly got in his car and drove off, tires screeching in his haste.

*******************

Surprised yet pleased that she said yes, Ed led Lindy to the work site. Adjusting his old coach's cap on his head he asked her, "What type of work do you like to do, Lindy? I can hand you a paint brush or a hammer or a pair of gloves. What do you think?"

Unsure of what to do, Lindy let her hair lower over the scars on her face and neck and looked at the ground. "I can work where ever

I'm needed. Not afraid of hammers, paintbrushes, or gloves. So you tell me."

"Great! Then I will get you to work with me unpacking these crates of new supplies. We truly are almost done with this project of finishing the church's repairs. Less than a week before it's needed for the big wedding!" Ed grabbed two pairs of work gloves and a couple of crow bars and handed one of each to Lindy.

She followed him over to six wooden crates that contained new Bibles, cushions for the church's benches, chairs, and various other assorted items that the church would need. AMRA had outfitted the new little church with what they would need to start weekly services along with sending the surprise of dark red cushions for the newly-constructed benches to go in the small sanctuary. Lindy loved the feel of the soft cushions. She unpacked them from the crates and took them into the small sanctuary and lovingly placed them on each bench.

Joy arose in her heart as she worked side by side with Ed setting up the interior of the little chapel. Excitement consumed her as she saw the value of the little things that would bring such comfort and beauty to the place. God's house on Datka Island would be beautiful indeed. And seeing the faces of the young and old gathered within would only add to its beauty.

Time quickly passed as the two finished with the last of the crates. "Want to help me haul these boards off from the crates and get them stacked for firewood later?"

"Sure, Ed. So tell me, where are you from? You have a strong accent and I can tell its somewhere in the south."

Ed's drawl was very distinctive and was his trademark, so to speak. "Thanks for noticing, Lindy. I am Texas born and bred."

"So, that explains it. A cowboy that oozes charm. I have been trying to figure out a good description of you all day. A charming cowboy! Perfect!" Laughter flooded from Lindy as she saw Ed's momentary discomfort. Surprised at how much she felt completely at ease with him, she realized the shyness and self-consciousness she normally felt had vanished as quickly as the full crates. Brushing her hair from her eyes for the hundredth time that day, Lindy picked up another load of wood from the opened, empty crates.

"Charming cowboy, huh? Well....I've never been called that before." Ed removed his ball cap and placed it on Lindy's head. "Here you could use this to tame your mane. Maybe it will keep you hair out of your eyes while we finish up. You know how girls twist their hair up in a ponytail and shove it through the back of the cap? That should help some."

"Thanks, Charming, but it's okay down." Lindy took the cap off her head and held it out to Ed.

"No, go ahead. I don't mind. You need it more than I do."

"But I never wear my hair up and no charming cowboy will ever talk me into it. It stays down, whether it's in my way or not." Insistence colored Lindy's words.

In his innocent way, Ed pressed further, "But why if it bothers you?"

"Because of my scars, okay?"

"I'm sorry. I forgot about your scars, Lindy."

She whirled around and stared him in the face. "What? How can you forget something that stares you in the face all the time?"

Holding up both hands in self-defense, Ed just shook his head. "Look, Lindy, I didn't mean to rile you up. I am just being honest."

Watching her take a deep, shaky breath, Ed knew he had touched on a tender subject with Lindy without meaning to. "Here." He took his cap out of her hands and turned her around so she had her back to him. "Now pull your hair up into a ponytail and I will cram it in the back of the cap and that will get you to where you can see again, Little L---" Stopping himself mid-sentence, Ed knew he had almost called her "Little Lady," the name he reserved for Jade. Thankfully Lindy had never heard him use the name before so he quickly recovered his mistake. "Little Lindy." Stuffing her ponytail through the cap's hole she grabbed the bill and pulled it over her eyes. Quickly she adjusted the neck of her shirt as she saw Ed glance at the very visible scar that traced itself down her cheek and neck into her shirt.

Unfazed by her scars, Ed reached for the bill of the cap and tweaked it until it was no longer crooked. He watched Lindy take another shaky breath and glance away. Placing both hands on her shoulders, he gave them a gentle pat. "Now, let's get back to this project, Lindy. Aren't you glad you can see now?" He gave her a little nudge.

She muttered a quick thanks and grabbed up her work gloves.

Ed was something else on the Island she was just going to have to get used to.

And she realized instantly that she wanted to get used to this charming cowboy.


As the two finished with the remainder of the crates, Ed watched the activity all around him. By the end of the day, the little church would be completed, all except for the steeple being put in place. That would happen on the church's dedication night that the ladies of Datka had planned. There would be a big meal to celebrate the new church, the new pastor and his family, and a few days later, the little church would hold its very first wedding.

Edward Hamilton felt the old familiar ache deep in his chest at the thought of a wedding. Oh how he wanted to meet the right girl, get married, and live life with her! Not alone anymore, but someone to share all of life's experiences with. That much he knew he wanted more than anything.

The only question was *who* that woman would be.

Jade Miller and her spunky personality and athletic beauty flashed in his mind. Was there still something for the two of them? Their relationship had been filled with such fun times and equally such argumentative times. Could they ever reconcile their differences? Differences that were due to his past and what he believed his calling entailed? Would she ever see that God could use him to help the hurting? Time would tell.

Maybe when he went to Fairbanks soon, he would see if he and Jade had matured enough or changed to make things work out between the two of them.

*God, You know my desires and dreams. You know what I want and what I need. Help me to keep it all submitted to You.*

Ed had prayed these words so many times it was almost laughable. But deep inside he knew that God did have his best interests at heart. That God would lead him to that special someone. Some day.

For now, he would continue to do the one thing he knew to do. Trust.

# CHAPTER 16

As soon as he arrived at the AST office, Sergeant Walker headed straight for the coffee percolator and started it up. The smell of freshly brewing coffee began to awaken him as he pondered the trip to Datka, the lunch with the Hudsons, and his talk, or lack thereof, with Andrew.

Unwilling to spill any other information or details, Andrew had once again frustrated Will to no end as he remained tight-lipped about Berta's disappearance. Will just knew the man was withholding information from him about the case. But why? It would reason that Andrew would tell Will anything to help find her kidnapper, but the opposite was happening. Knowing Andrew was clearly upset about Berta's disappearance only added to the mystery of his silence.

Frustrations mounted in Will as he downed his sugary coffee and poured a second cup. Glancing at the clock, he realized that his patrolman was late that morning. *Where is Dorne? Usually he's here before me.*

Will began the day and answered all the usual calls that came into the office, made his morning rounds, and filled out the customary paperwork that came with the job. In one more attempt to find a piece of missing evidence, the Sergeant took the file out with the missing girl's information. He read back over the interview notes, looked at the photos and notes on the evidence he and Hughes had found, and finally gave up with a resigned sigh.

He hadn't missed anything.

Glancing back at the clock, he noticed that Dorne had neither shown up nor called with an explanation.

Reaching for his AST cap, Will grabbed the keys for his patrol car. Something wasn't right and he was about to find out what was going on.

Will headed straight for his patrolman's house. He pulled up to the street's edge and noticed Dorne's car was gone. Walking to the front door, he pounded and yelled, "Dorne! You there?"

No answer.

Will jiggled the doorknob and found it to be locked. Walking around to the back of the house, he tried the back door and found it locked too. The backyard was empty as well.

No Dorne anywhere.

*Maybe he had car trouble on the way to work. I'll retrace his route and see if I spot him broken down somewhere. That's just not like Dorne. He's not home, doors are locked, car's gone. Just where is he?*

Will headed back down the route Dorne would have taken to work that morning.

There was no sign of his car anywhere.

That deep gnawing in Will's gut started up again.

*******************

Rinsing the last of the lunch dishes, Berta rolled her shoulders to ease the tension. So far that day she had baked a loaf of bread, worked in the garden, cooked breakfast, cleaned those dishes up, changed the bedsheets, swept the floors, and now she was contemplating her next chore. She spent her days as busy as she could so when she fell into the bed at night, she was so exhausted that sleep instantly claimed her body and mind.

170

If she stayed physically exhausted, she slept at night.

If she worked hard during the day, she could keep her mind occupied and not think about her sister and her friends at *Rita's Place*.

If she occupied her time taking care of the sweet elderly lady who hired her to cook and clean, then Berta didn't have time to grieve her losses.

If her days were filled with gardening and laundry and shopping, she wouldn't ache for Andrew.

Barkersville was now her home, if she could just ever see it as so. Markus had given her instructions to come here with the money Peter had given her in the bag the day of her escape. He said there would be a widow looking to hire someone for room and board and a little bit of money. The job was hers if she went to Barkersville. It was the only way to stay alive and to keep Ana and possibly the others from further danger.

But could she really believe that or was it a lie?

She had to believe it or go crazy with worry. After nearly a month of living here and no one had shown up to give her any trouble, Berta was beginning to believe.

Believe that maybe after all she could live here and never return to prostitution again.

Believe that she could be safe again.

Believe that God was truly watching out for her.

All she had to do was believe. And daily she chose to do just that.

Gratitude welled up in her chest as she paused for the millionth time to thank God for this blessing of a house, food, and safety. And for the millionth time she asked once again for His help so she could endure the pain of separation from those she loved. She wanted more than anything to return to Seal Harbor, but she felt deep in her bones she needed to stay put for a while longer.

The widow, Mrs. Tucker, had proven to be a treasure for Berta. The elderly woman possessed a deep knowledge of the Word of God and eagerly shared it with young Berta who soaked it up like a sponge. She had been honest with the widow upon her arrival and told Mrs. Tucker all about her past life, leaving out the kidnapping, Peter's role in it, and Andrew. She spoke freely of *Rita's Place* and her life prior to Barkersville when she was living with Miss Rita and the girls.

Mrs. Tucker hadn't been deterred one bit by Berta's past. It only pushed her to love the girl more and to show her God's love each day she lived there. Daily, during their morning coffee and toast, Mrs. Tucker would read passages from the Bible to Berta as she relished in the lilt of the old woman's voice and her love for the Word of God. It brought a deep peace to Berta's troubled soul.

But today's passage seemed to do more than bring peace. It brought instruction. She had asked Mrs. Tucker to read it again twice as she tried to memorize the few words from Isaiah 30:21.

In a clear, strong voice, Mrs. Tucker read the sacred words to Berta once more. *"Your ears will hear a word behind you, 'This is the way, walk in it,' whenever you turn to the right or to the left."*

Berta knew she definitely needed to hear someone tell her when to turn to the right or the left especially when she felt so unsure about her next move. Each day she thought about going back to Ana, but again, she would feel an overwhelming sense that she needed to *stay where she was.*

So she did just that. She stayed put.

Turning from the sink to gather Mrs. Tucker's tea cup, the lady reached for her hand just as Berta was about to pick up the dish. Gently she squeezed Berta's hand and pulled her to the chair beside her. "Sit, dear Berta."

Berta looked into the aged eyes of Mrs. Tucker. "Yes, ma'am?"

"I want to ask you a question. And I want you to think about it before answering me......Do you know Jesus? I mean *really* know Him?"

Berta hesitated a minute.

"Have you asked Him to come be the Lord of your life? Have you invited Him into your heart's home just as I asked you to come into my home?" Mrs. Tucker sat silent a moment.

"Not in so many words, I guess." Berta fumbled with the hem of her apron.

"I didn't think so. If someone has invited Jesus to live in their heart and take over their life, there usually is a peace, a contentment, an inner joy. I look at you, Berta, and see unrest and fear and sorrow. Jesus can remove that for you and help you through your troubles. You only need to ask." The widow's light blue eyes captivated Berta's.

Berta wanted what she saw in Mrs. Tucker's eyes. That rest, and peace, and joy.

"What do I do to get that?" Berta's simple, child-like question brought a smile to the older lady's lips.

"Oh, it is so very simple. Just like when you believed there would be a job here and you came to my door and asked me because someone told you there was one available. I am telling you there is peace and love available if you only ask. Jesus died for our sins, our troubles, our sorrows, our hurts. He is God's Son and God sent Him

173

just for me and you and the whole world. We only have to believe and ask Him to come live in our heart's home. And He does, without hesitation!" A huge grin lifted the corners of her mouth.

Berta's eyes shone with desire to know more.

"There's one condition though. When we ask Jesus to move in, then we have to ask some other things to move out."

"Like what things?" Berta asked.

"Well for starters, God doesn't want you to ever live with doubt, worry, fear, troubles. In this life we will have troubles and trials, but we don't have to be controlled by them or go through them alone. We exchange our worries and fears and doubts and troubles with God's love and protection and help. Does that make sense, Berta?"

"Yes, I think so. This is all so new to me. I do believe in God. I have started praying and I do believe He has been leading me and watching over me lately. I never asked Him to until a few weeks ago and now I see how God has helped me time and again. But I want to know more. I want you to teach me about the Bible and Jesus. I want you to help me understand, Mrs. Tucker." Berta's eyes pled with the woman before her.

"You have my word, Berta. I will do my best to show you and teach you. Shall we begin?"

Berta rose and poured another round of tea for the two of them, her afternoon chores quickly forgotten. She had something new to occupy her time with, something greater.

She *had* to, *wanted* to learn more about God and His Son, Jesus.

# CHAPTER 17

Their last day to finish the church for the dedication dinner and Luka and Yuri's upcoming wedding, Ed looked around the little group of Aleut men he had grown to love. Hard work, a shared project, laughter, and friendship were forging this group into a strong unit.

Looking around at the men, Ed watched Andrew closely. He seemed more withdrawn and distracted these past few days which had Ed concerned. Knowing Andrew couldn't just shut Berta completely out of his mind, Ed felt a deep sympathy for him. Just yesterday, Ed had tried to encourage Andrew to talk to him about what was troubling him, but Andrew remained silent for the most part and blamed his demeanor on the hard work and readjusting to the Island.

But Ed knew better. He had seen how Andrew's mother and sister had welcomed him back home with open arms. Natalia and Rose were treating him like the prodigal son in the Bible and were spoiling the man whenever the chance arose. Their forgiveness and love for Andrew was evident to all.

The other men had done their best to make Andrew feel part of the community again too. Yuri, who Andrew had stolen from, was even going overboard in an attempt to include Andrew in what was going on at the moment. After the way Andrew had treated Yuri, he could have remained aloof and detached from Andrew.

Something was brewing in the young man's troubled mind and spirit.

"Penny for your thoughts, Charming." Ed couldn't control the big grin that covered his face.

"Well, hello, Lindy. You definitely caught me deep in thought."
Ed removed a handkerchief from his back pocket and mopped his face
off. The unusually warm sun and hard work had made him sweat.
Evading her comment, Ed replied, "Looks like you brought lunch."

He saw a shadow of disappointment pass briefly over Lindy's
face when he didn't share any of his thoughts with her. Ed would like
nothing more than to take a long walk and have an equally long talk
with the girl standing before him. He had found her company to be
very enjoyable and he looked forward to any moment they shared
together.

Lindy was becoming a true friend.

"Sure did. You guys look hungry and thirsty." Looking around
the church grounds, Lindy surveyed all they had done. "It looks
wonderful! You and the men have accomplished a lot."

Lindy set the baskets of food on the make-shift table and the
guys immediately came for lunch. Lindy laughed easily at the men as
they unashamedly began removing food and water from the baskets.
While they ate, she entered the small chapel and began looking around
and enjoying the peace and solitude for a while.

Ed suggested they pray first and then he would lead them in
his customary short Bible study while they ate lunch. It was a time for
laying down their hammers and work gloves and enjoying a meal
together and the Word of God. At first when Ed suggested it, they were
silent through the reading and no one would comment or answer any
question he would ask other than with one or two word answers. But
slowly, Ed had watched the men open up just this very week and find
their voices. He had proven to them that this was a safe place to talk
and ask questions without fear of judgment or ridicule. Surprisingly,

one of the men even asked that they begin to pray for Markus' return to the Island. He too had been part of the cause of the fire. With Joshua and Andrew back with them, the others wanted to see their friend, Markus, back where he belonged and restored to his friends and family. Ed's prayers were being answered as the men began to participate a bit more each time they were together.

Each time Ed spoke, he tried to reinforce what he shared with an object lesson. Today Ed's lesson was on how God loves to take the trash and rubbish of our lives and make something beautiful out of the mess. With the last few days consisting of clean-up duty, it was easy to use that as a lesson. They had all grumbled and complained occasionally about the mess and the hard, back-breaking work it required to get the job done. But they also were able to rejoice at the beauty that came from the clean-up. Ed hammered home how they needed to allow God to show them what needed cleaning up in their lives and hearts and to do the hard work of removing the trash and rubbish, like unforgiveness, sin, worry, and doubt. The beauty left remaining would be a great reward. Ed pointed out that it was so very easy to overlook the rubble in our lives and become accustomed to its daily presence. Then before long the piles only grew bigger and our lives messier and more miserable. Clean-up was a necessary part of the Christian life and couldn't be overlooked. Today's discussion was the liveliest Ed had ever seen with the guys. They talked about how difficult it was at times to take on such projects in their lives and how to manage their messes. But doing these things with someone else, with a fellow believer, made the load more bearable.

Ed desired to see the men grow closer to each other and not live such independent lives and today he was seeing that maybe they were headed in that direction. Lord knows, he had needed and still did need men in his life to make it through each day.

Winding down his talk, Ed looked around the group, pride filling his chest. These men had worked so hard for each other, for their Island, and its months of recovery from the fires and damage. Not only damage to structures, but to relationships had occurred. But things were definitely changing.

Ed stuffed his hands in his back pockets and smiled appreciatively at the men seated before him. "This is redemption, men. God has redeemed so much over the last few months. Just look around you. It is evident. Do you see it?"

Ed noticed Joshua's frown deepening as he spoke. "Joshua, what is it?"

"Will you explain *redemption*? What do you mean?" the man asked.

Forgetting the breakdown in communication at times, Ed was happy that Joshua asked. He wanted them all to understand. Ed walked over to the stack of old boards and retrieved one from the junk pile that was splintered, slightly burnt, and had crooked nails sticking out in all directions. Next he chose a brand new piece of lumber from what was left in the construction process. "Someone paid the cost to get us these new boards so we could exchange them for the old ones. That person who funded this repair job wanted to see the burnt structures on Datka redeemed, restored to an even better condition than before. It's exchanging the old for new and better." He paused and weighed his next words. "Andrew, when you stole Yuri's traps, he offered you forgiveness which in turn redeemed your relationship with him, making it better and stronger, not eaten up with unforgiveness and anger and distance. Does that make sense?"

Heads all around the group nodded in agreement.

Ed stood to signal the meeting was over and they needed to get back to work. Turning from the table he saw Lindy standing in the doorway of the church watching him and the others. She had listened in on part of their talking. Ed was somewhat embarrassed at her presence.

Approaching Lindy, he said, "I didn't know you were listening."

"You have a way with those men, Ed. They respect you and hang on every word. It's obvious you were sent here by God to influence their lives. I like that about you. Not afraid to leave what was familiar and come to a far-away island to help the people." Lindy looked him in the eyes as she spoke.

A slight chuckle escaped his lips. "Thank you, Lindy. I appreciate that. Not everyone would agree with your opinion of me though."

"Do their opinions matter?" Lindy queried.

Ed looked up at the sky before answering her. "I used to think they did, but now I am not so sure anymore."

"We are called to be God pleasers, not man pleasers, right?"

"Or woman pleasers! Thanks for that reminder." Ed breathed deeply of the truth before him. He noticed the questioning look on Lindy's face at his response. "Oh, before I forget. I won't be around for a few days."

"Oh really? So where is the charming cowboy headed to now?" Lindy enjoyed teasing with Ed. They definitely had an easy relationship, one she had never experienced before with another man.

"I have to leave tomorrow for Fairbanks and meet with the AMRA board."

"Fairbanks, wow, that's not very close is it? Where will you stay?"

"With some friends, the Millers. I worked this past summer with them here on Datka after the fires."

"Ahhh." Lindy could almost hear the jealousy in her voice and she hated the sound of it. *The infamous Jade Miller.*

Ed began helping her gather the lunch things and put them back into the basket. When it was all tidied up, he said to Lindy, "Don't miss me too much when I am gone."

Trying to inject some humor in her tone, Lindy responded quietly as she picked up the baskets and left him to work. "Don't worry. I won't."

Deep in her heart she knew this was far from the truth.


The next day, Ed was enjoying the change in scenery as he disembarked from the small plane in Fairbanks. Having to leave Andrew behind was more of a challenge that he realized. Ed had to face one important fact.

He was not the one in charge of Andrew.

God was.

Yuri had promised to keep the young man busy for the two days Ed was gone. There was always plenty to be done on the Island. Ed finally accepted he wasn't responsible for Andrew's outcome. He could only offer help and assistance and pray for the man. The cloud of depression that had settled over Andrew had influenced Ed as well. This break would be good for him.

Ed was also anxious to hear what his best friend, Gabriel Parker, had decided about the job with AMRA. Communication with him was completely shut down since the Parkers return to Washington so he was curious how Gabe's life would play out. Ed knew without a doubt that Gabe and Rose were in love with each other and would hopefully marry. But a lot had to be worked out for that to happen for his best bud.

*We all need you, God. There are so many decisions and twists and turns in life that we can't face without You.*

Bringing Ed out of his reverie, he heard his named called from across the little airport.

"Ed! Over here!" Jade Miller was furiously waving in his direction, her bouncy waves spilling around her shoulders.

*She's a sight for sore eyes.* Unable to contain the smile on his face, Ed walked in the direction of the Millers.

Without thinking, Jade ran towards Ed and flung herself at him. Easily a head taller than the petite brunette, Ed hugged her and lifted Jade off her feet leaving her squealing with delight.

Quickly remembering the Millers, Ed sat Jade down and gave Jill a quick hug and peck on the cheek then shook John's hand. He had missed these three so much. It was good to be back in their company.

Ed grabbed his suitcase off the ground and followed the Millers to their car. John unlocked the trunk for Ed. Flinging his suitcase in the trunk, Ed looked inside the car and noticed another occupant in the front passenger seat. Before he knew what was happening, he saw the passenger door fling open and was immediately engulfed in a huge bear hug by his best friend Gabe.

Caught completely by surprise, the others couldn't contain their laughter any longer at the sight of Ed's shocked expression.

"What.....where......how....." Finally Ed burst into a round of laughter and hugged Gabe all over again.

Gabe decided he better explain himself. "I wanted to surprise you, Ed. I had to meet with AMRA with my decision and John clued me in that you were coming today so I planned my trip to Fairbanks around you....of course, without you knowing."

Ed couldn't contain the huge grin on his face. "You sneaky rascal! This is a great surprise!"

After the excitement settled down, they drove Ed to the Millers' house and let him freshen up and drop of his suitcase before they had to meet AMRA's director for a dinner meeting. The entire drive to their house, Ed could feel Jade quietly watching him to the point he was uncomfortable. He caught her eye and she blushed furiously more times than he was comfortable with. This was unlike the Jade he knew, always self-assured and never shy or quiet around him. Pushing that aside, Ed focused on the discussion around him.

John had just asked Gabe to update Ed on his situation.

Gabe couldn't contain his joy. "I finally reached a decision and accepted the job with AMRA before my week was even up after returning home. I talked it over with Pastor Greg and I guess you could say he helped me see clearly what I wanted to do. So these past few weeks I have spent time with Mom and Dad, packed up my things, spent countless hours on the phone with AMRA trying to settle everything we possibly could before I arrived.....and here I am! I start immediately as the Missions Director. We have needs on other islands in the Aleutian Chain so I am excited to begin the work."

Ed clapped Gabe on the shoulder. "You don't know how hard I have prayed for you, man. I know this was a big decision. How are Rand and Becca with this?"

A cloud quickly passed over Gabe's face before he answered. "They are accepting of it. Mom and Dad both know it is the right decision and I will be doing what I am passionate about. But it won't be easy being so far away from them." The cloud lifted before he continued. "But, AMRA has promised me I can return every 3 months to Washington for several days at a time. So that was some consolation for them....and me."

Unable to contain the question any longer, Ed questioned, "Does Rose know?"

The unmistakable look of a man in love crossed Gabe's countenance. "Not yet, but I can't wait to tell her!"


The dinner meeting was held in one of Fairbank's nicest restaurants. Ed enjoyed the food immensely. Though he loved the simple island fare, this was a wonderful treat to eat steak, baked potatoes, bread with extra butter, and salad again. With Jade on his left and Gabe on his right, it felt like old times.

But surprisingly, Ed found himself longing to see another face beside him.

Another pretty, petite, brunette, with a slight red scar on her face and neck that only made her the more beautiful to him.

Bringing his thoughts back to the table, Ed focused on the rest of the conversation. Brent Jackson, AMRA's director was hammering him with important questions about his work on both the construction projects and the young men he was leading. After Ed had answered all the questions, Brent laid his cloth napkin on the table by his plate.

The waitress took their coffee and dessert orders, then Brent continued. "Ed, I like what you have done over the summer with the initial fire and what you are doing now. I want you to consider staying on at Datka and Seal Harbor for a six months trial. You are filling a great need there. I want you to have time to think about this, but tell me now if it interests you at all."

Completely taken aback at the offer, Ed wiped his mouth on his napkin. Grateful for the interruption of the coffee and dessert being delivered, Ed threw a quick prayer heavenward. *God, please let me know if this is You leading me.*

The familiar feeling of an active beehive in his chest reminded Ed of the stirring he had a month ago that maybe coaching wasn't what he was supposed to do. He felt instantly drawn to this proposition on the Island. Reaching for the creamer for his coffee, Ed noticed his hand shake slightly giving his nervousness away.

Everyone was momentarily preoccupied with their food so he hoped no one noticed, until he felt a small hand give his knee a gentle squeeze. Glancing to his left, Jade quietly said, "Follow your heart, Tex."

Had he heard her right? The girl who was always giving him such a hard time about the type of work he was doing on Datka? Maybe she had changed her mind about him after all. A tiny spark of hope ignited within his chest.

"Sir, my first instinct is to want to say 'yes' to this six months trial. It's very appealing to me, especially since I have been questioning my life's direction lately. But, I would like time to pray about it first. Can I have a day or two to decide?" Ed looked Brent straight in the eye as he spoke.

"Of course, Son. Take all the time you need. Let me ask a few more questions that you may want to consider before accepting a position like this. I am hoping the six months trial will turn into something permanent."

"Okay. I'm all ears, Sir." Placing his fork down, Ed placed both elbows on the table and gave Brent his full attention.

"Where do you see yourself in the future, Ed? Do you have plans to marry, have children, make missions work your vocation? These are all important factors you need to consider when making this type of decision. It *will* affect your future." Brent leaned back and looked him squarely in the face, not expecting an answer but giving him much to ponder.

Ed cleared his throat before answering. "If you had asked me that eight months ago, Sir, my answer would have been different. But in light of the last eight months, I need to think that through."

Thankfully no one around the table noticed, but Jade could feel a pink blush settle on her pretty face. Sipping her coffee, she couldn't help but think to herself, *Maybe, just maybe we do stand a chance after all.*

The meeting had wound to a close with Gabe returning to his hotel and Ed to the Millers' home. Jill had insisted that he stay in their guest room for the one night he would be in town so Ed had accepted her invitation since money was tight for the moment.

Before they retired for the night, Ed remembered to invite the Millers to Yuri and Luka's wedding. "We are having the church dedication dinner next week on Wednesday and the wedding will be

Saturday. Yuri and Luka wanted me to ask you to come. All of Datka would be glad to see you."

"Oh, that would be wonderful, Ed! What do you think John?" Jill couldn't keep the excitement from her face. She loved a good wedding and this one was something entirely new to her.

"If we can pull off a trip to the Island in less than a week, then I am game."

Jill hugged John and she and Jade began making plans while the two men discussed Ed's proposition.

As their conversations ended, John and Jill excused themselves to retire for the night. "Ed, there's plenty in the refrigerator if you get hungry later. Make yourself at home, Son."

"Thanks, Miss Jill. You know my stomach will find food if it gets desperate."

After saying good-night, Jade invited Ed to sit with her on their glassed-in back porch. "The Northern Lights are gorgeous here! Maybe we can catch a glimpse. Want to join me?"

Ed hesitated a moment but finally decided he would enjoy their visit. "Sure, Jade."

"Need something to drink? We have some soda if you want one."

"Do you have orange?" Ed wiggled his eyebrows up and down and Jade couldn't help but laugh at his expression. Yes, things were feeling like old times.

After grabbing two orange sodas from the kitchen, Jade led Ed to the back porch. Taking side by side chairs, the two settled into a peaceful quiet.

Suddenly the greens, blues, and pinks of the Northern Lights appeared before their eyes. Gasping, Ed reached for Jade's arm in his excitement at the breath-taking sight. "Wow! You were right, Little Lady! What a view!"

Ed quickly removed his hand from her arm and wondered at the quick way his mouth formed the nickname he used to call Jade so easily.

Jade looked up at him in the darkness. "It is beautiful, isn't it?"

Momentarily mesmerized by her equally green eyes, Ed had to force himself to look away from her. "Yes....yes, it is, Jade." Taking a long swig of his soda, Ed told himself to settle down. He didn't need to get worked up again by this girl.

Jade broke the awkward moment. "You're different, Tex. I'm starting to like this new you." Reaching out her elbow, Jade nudged Ed playfully.

"New, huh?" Ed pushed her back with his arm.

"Yeah. I'm not quite sure what the difference is, but I like it. I was listening to you during dinner when you were talking about the future. You seem.....I don't know.....more resolved."

Ed's half-grin appeared. "Well, maybe I am. These past few weeks have made me question my future plans and now there are some new cards on the table."

"Yes, there are, Tex." Jade stood and stretched. She walked closer to the glassed-in wall and looked up at the sky. "I'll be right back. I have something for you."

Jade left the room and with her exit, Ed looked back up at the gorgeous night sky before him. So many changes and questions danced before his mind's eye. As swiftly as the Northern Light's

187

display changed from green to blue to reddish-orange, Ed's thoughts swirled in and out of focus. One minute he was enjoying his time with Jade, the next minute he was thinking about the new trial job offer, and then Lindy's face would appear.

He needed to pray. *God, You created me and my passions and desires just like You created this beautiful sky. You know everything about my past, present, and future. I just need You to clue me in on it all. What do I do? Which road should I take? I don't want to miss what You have for me. Help me see and know what's best.*

Instantly a verse from the book of John that Ed had read that week flitted through his mind.

*My sheep hear My voice, and I know them, and they follow Me.*

Taking a deep breath, Ed smiled at the new sense of peace that surrounded him at that very moment. God would show him what to do, where to go. And for now that was enough.

Jade approached Ed without him hearing her and she startled him as she placed her hand on his arm causing him to jump. Giggling lightly, Jade took the seat beside him.

Ed watched her finger a pink envelope in her hands a moment. Curiosity was getting the best of him.

"I wrote this for you and was going to mail it, but never did. I think I should give it to you now, but I want you to promise me you will read it after you leave Fairbanks, okay?" She looked at him in the growing darkness and waited for his answer before releasing her grasp on the letter.

"I, Edward Hamilton, do solemnly swear, to read the previously mentioned letter upon my departure from Fairbanks, Alaska....."

Simultaneously Jade and Ed erupted into laughter, something they did so often when together, at least when they weren't arguing. Recovering from her bout of Ed-induced giggles, Jade was grateful for the lighter air that floated around them. "Seriously, Ed. You can't have the letter without agreeing that you wait to read it."

"Hey, I was serious. I promise, Jade. Now hand it over." He reached for the mysterious letter and took it from her hand then folded it and placed it in his shirt pocket. "Now, it's getting late and I have an early morning meeting then an afternoon flight back to Seal Harbor, so I better get some shut eye."

"Understood, Tex. If you need anything let me know. There's towels in the cabinet in the bathroom for you to use and extra blankets in the chest at the end of the bed."

"Thanks, Jade." Ed stood to leave and paused at the doorway. "I've really enjoyed spending time with you again."

Jade's eyes lit up brighter than the moon. "Me, too, Tex. It has been good."

With that Ed headed to shower and go to bed. He had much to think about after tonight's meeting. And his evening with Jade.

Finally resting his weary head on the pillow in the guest room of Jade Miller's home, Ed closed his tired eyes and visions of a brunette danced before his mind. Only, it wasn't the girl who he had just spent half a day and night with.

It was another dark-haired beauty on Datka Island.

His mind held thoughts of Lindy Hudson.

# CHAPTER 18

Glancing in the rearview mirror of his patrol car, Will noticed the deep crease right between his eyes on his forehead. Forcing himself to relax, he rolled down the window for some fresh air and rolled his shoulders backwards to ease some of the tension.

He dreaded what he was now forced to do.

Pulling up to the curb beside Dorne's house, Will eased his tall frame out of the car's seat. Still no sign of Dorne's car in the driveway. Looking up and down the street, Will saw a couple of children playing ball in their front yard. One house down from that, a man sat in a rocking chair on his front porch smoking a pipe. The man stood and looked Will's way when he saw him. Will stayed by the car and watched as the man approached him as he continued to puff on his pipe.

Around billows of smoke, the man asked Will, "What can I do for you.....Sergeant?" Glancing at Will's badge and car the man waited for Will to answer.

"Do you know the man who lives here?" Will questioned.

"Sure do. Can't tell you where he is though. He done packed up and moved out on me. Broke his lease. I'm his landlord. You don't happen to know where he is, do you? I'd like to get my hands....." The landlord didn't finish his sentence. Instead he stuck his pipe back in place.

"How do you know he left?" Will's gut churned even more with this new bit of information.

"Cause he told me so. Paid last month's rent yesterday and said he had a family emergency or some such nonsense. No warning or nothing, just broke his lease agreement, left me with an unrented house, and I need the money."

"Do you have a key to the house? This man is one of AST's patrolmen and it would be helpful if I could get inside his place. There are keys that were in his possession for the office and I need to get them back." Will watched the man fumble in his pockets and withdraw a wad of keys. This was turning out much easier than Will had thought.

"You can only go in there if I am with you. That's rightfully my house."

"Fine by me." Will followed the man to the porch and entered behind him. There on the kitchen table, Will spotted the extra patrol car keys and Dorne's office keys. He pocketed those and walked around each room looking for something, anything that would lead him to Dorne or his whereabouts. Spotting an ashtray on an end table in the living room, the green striped cigarette butts stared Will in the face. His heart started pounding as he looked around for something to put the butts in. Finding a paper sack on the kitchen counter, Will placed the entire ashtray and its contents in the sack.

Moving to Dorne's bedroom, Will looked in the closet and dresser drawers. Empty. So was the bathroom. No trace of Dorne's personal items were left.

The kitchen sink still held a stack of dirty dishes. Within the cupboards and refrigerator, Will found food items still in place. The trash can was still full. Dorne was obviously in a hurry when he left.

Stepping out onto the back porch, Will surveyed the tiny backyard. He walked a few feet in each direction and returned to the porch. Sitting by the back door was a pair of boots with dried mud caked on the soles. Will picked up the boots and found the landlord. He had seen enough.

Dorne was clearly gone.

Thanking the landlord for letting him look for the keys, the landlord locked the place back up and said, "If you see Dorne again, tell him I'm looking for him. He owes me one more month's rent and an explanation."

Under his breath, Will replied, "You're not the only one looking for Dorne."

With that, Will got back in his car and headed for the office.


By the time Will reached the AST headquarters, Hughes had arrived for his weekend shift. Thankful to see him, Will greeted Hughes warmly. "I am so glad you are here, Hughes. I could really use your help about now."

Eyeing the sack and boots Will brought in, Hughes asked, "What's in the sack, Sergeant? That your lunch?"

"I wish it were so. I just got back from Dorne's place. He didn't show up for his shift yesterday morning so I went by his house so see if he was there. No car, nothing. I retraced his route to work hoping to find him broken down somewhere. Nope." Will headed for the coffee pot and sugar bowl before continuing.

"Is he alright? Did you find him?" Hughes asked, concern marking his features.

"I'm sure he's fine. I didn't find Dorne, but I did meet his landlord. Said Dorne left yesterday on a family emergency and won't be back. Paid some of his rent but still owes him more. The man was a bit upset. He let me in Dorne's house to look for his set of office keys. I found a few items of interest there." Will pointed to the sack and boots.

Hughes looked in the sack and left the contents inside. "Hmmm....these look familiar." Picking up the boots Hughes looked at the mud-covered treads. "I think we need to look at the photos I took of the boot prints and cigarette butts by the shed where the girl was held." Hughes began rummaging through the file drawer. He couldn't find the files of photos or any of the investigation notes. "Sergeant, did you move the file to another place? I don't see it here. You don't think....."

Will emitted a deep sigh that nearly rattled his bones. "Yes, I do think. Dorne took the file before he left. I was afraid he would if he became worried we were on to him. But don't worry, I had double copies of every note and photo made and even added some false notes to the file last weekend that would make Dorne think we were onto someone else."

Reaching into a locked drawer in his personal files, Will brought out the real file folder. "Honestly, I have been very suspicious of Dorne, even before you and I talked and you raised your concerns. I am disappointed in him. A man in our own department....." Will let his sentence trail off.

The next thirty minutes were spent comparing notes and photos and thoughts. Sure enough, the boots' treads matched the ones around the shed in Hughes' photos. The cigarette butts were the same as well, even down to the amount left on each butt. Will went so far as to gather the few butts by the front door that Dorne had never thrown away and compare them to the ones from Dorne's house. They all looked identical.

Walking back to his desk, Will sat down heavily. He reached for the telephone on his desk but didn't lift the receiver.

Hughes saw his hesitation. "Want me to do it, Sergeant?"

"No, Hughes, but thank you all the same."

With a heavy heart, Will dialed the number to call the State Headquarters. Waiting for the call to be answered, Will's heart beat double-time.

Hughes detected the weight in his Sergeant and friend's voice as he spoke on the phone. "This is Sergeant William Walker located at the Seal Harbor AST headquarters. I need a report to be issued at all AST locations to be on the look-out for a suspect on the run. His name is Patrolman..... Thom---Thomas Dorne, who also worked at this AST location. Suspect is five-foot-five, two hundred pounds....."

Hughes could see Will age before his eyes as he finished the phone call. Head in his hands, Will ached from head to toe with these new discoveries and confirmations of what he had hoped wasn't true.

Now there was no doubt. The truth had just hit him square in the gut and he would be reeling from its punch for days to come.

*******************

Anxious to escape his tormenting thoughts, Andrew stood on the Datka shoreline awaiting the small boat that would take him to Seal Harbor to meet up with Ed. Yesterday he had been very busy helping Yuri and Luka finish up some preparations on the church for their wedding. Grateful for the distraction of work, Andrew threw his whole being into the job.

Then night fell, and along with it, the circling thoughts returned that nearly drove him to madness. Thoughts like circling vultures swooped in closer and closer. Nights were the worst for Andrew.

*Where is Berta? Is she still alive and well, or is she being tortured or dead where I can never find her? Should I risk everything and tell Sergeant Walker what I know?*

On and on, his thoughts went. Reliving, rehashing, remembering.

*How could I be such a coward and keep my mouth shut while I have information that might help find Berta's kidnappers? What can I do?*

Now with the chance to get his mind on something new, Andrew looked forward to the trip to Seal Harbor and being alone for the first time in ages. Ed had left him a list of what to purchase in town and when to meet him after his arrival back in town. It would be simple enough, but it felt good to be trusted again, to be in charge of even a small task.

The choppy boat ride came to an end and Andrew disembarked. Stepping on the wooden dock, a flood of memories assaulted him full force. Here on this very dock was the first time he had ever laid eyes on Berta. She had gotten his attention and made him feel special, singled out. And now, where was she?

The familiar burning in his gut was starting up. The anxiety and stress was about to kill him if this didn't come to an end soon. Heading to the center of town, Andrew saw the AST office ahead on his left. *Should I go talk to Sergeant Walker? No! You can't risk causing more harm to Berta if she's still alive!*

196

Andrew knew without a shadow of a doubt that if word got out that he had blown the kidnappers' cover, there would be bloodshed. Berta's and his. Silence was the only way to keep them both alive. But after a month, was Berta really still living?

Andrew's heart rate increased steadily. Within seconds, sweat beaded up on his forehead and upper lip, the cool air doing nothing to bring his body's temperature down. Andrew reached a shaky hand up to wipe his forehead, his vision beginning to blur. His breathing picked up pace as well and tiny black dots began to form before his eyes. Catching a glimpse of an alley to his left, Andrew ducked into the shadows and staggered to the end of the narrow alley. Bending over his knees, he knew the routine. Shutting his eyes, Andrew forced himself to take slow, deep, cleansing breaths. He willed his mind to focus on something different.

*The list.....I have a list in my pocket....what is on it?* Andrew made his mind tick through the list of items that Ed wanted him to purchase. With each item, he breathed even deeper, feeling his heart start to slow to normal. After ten minutes of this, Andrew leaned his head on the cool brick wall behind him. Slowly, he opened his eyes and looked around. The drumming in his ears was now gone. Andrew thought he could make it now.

A bit disoriented, he looked up and realized he was near the backs of a row of buildings. Looking around, Andrew started to turn back the way he had come until something familiar caught his attention. A brown bottle lay on its side at his feet. Empty.

Nearly able to taste the amber liquid that would have been found inside the bottle, Andrew kicked it aside in disgust. He knew what those brown bottles held.

197

Heart rate picking up speed again, he walked in a tight circle trying to get his mind back to the list, but the bottle kept taunting him. He also knew where to get one.

Just one bottle, then he could get what was on the list for Ed.

Just one drink from the bottle would calm his nerves and help him survive these torturous thoughts.

*I am with you, Andrew. Look to Me.*

Ignoring the persistent voice, he looked behind him once, checked his pocket for enough cash and headed in the direction of his old source.

*Just one bottle and I will never go back. I need it now. It's too much,* Andrew thought.

Again the voice. *But I am enough. When life is too much, I am enough.*

Andrew refused to listen.


Ed impatiently patted his foot against the sidewalk. He paced a few steps in one direction and then back the other way. *Where is that boy? Maybe he's just running late.*

Deciding to see if Andrew was still at the last stop on the list Ed had given him, he headed to the hardware store a couple of blocks down. Opening the door to the front entrance, Ed was greeted with a friendly hello.

"Hey, Mack. Have you seen my sidekick? The Aleut man who is usually with me when I am in town?" Ed waited for Mack's answer.

Mack scratched his balding head. "Hmmm.....no, Ed I haven't seen your friend today."

"Are you sure? He hasn't been in at all? I sent him for some things and we were supposed to meet up twenty minutes ago." Exasperation colored Ed's tone of voice while worry crept up his spine.

"I don't know, Buddy. Hadn't seen him around, but if I do I will tell him you are looking for him."

"Thanks, Mack." Making a hasty exit, Ed headed in the direction of Andrew's first stop.

Ten minutes later, Ed had received the same frustrating report. No Andrew.

Now panic was easing its way into Ed's mind. *Ugh! I shouldn't have left him. I shouldn't have trusted him this soon!*

Turning in the direction of the AST office, Ed quickly entered under the clang of the brass bell.

"Oh, thank the Lord, you are here!" Ed said as soon as he saw Will at his desk.

"Now that's some greeting." Will's broad grin quickly vanished when he saw the look on Ed's face. "What's wrong, man?"

Ed quickly launched into his story and ended with Andrew being gone. Understanding Ed's fears, Will formulated a plan for the two to hopefully find the missing man. With instructions on which locations to hit for any sign of Andrew and the plan to meet back in the AST office in thirty minutes, Ed was grateful for something to do to help locate Andrew.

Within the half hour mark, both Will and Ed came up empty handed. Anger tinted his cheeks as he told Will of one store owner who had seen an Aleut man in the alley when he had taken out the trash. He showed Ed the direction the man had taken but that was the only clue they had to go on.

"So now what, Will?" Ed was trying his hardest to control his anger with Andrew.

"There's not much else we can do right now but pray. I do know for sure that his boat arrived and that he was seen headed into town around the time he should have been. And there haven't been any more boats hired to return to Datka. He's here. I just hope he didn't take matters into his own hands with his missing girlfriend." Will shook his head, at a loss as what to think.

Ed pounded his fist on the nearby desk. "Uhhhh, I shouldn't have given him this responsibility on his own. It was too much too soon. I could kick myself."

"Bottom line, Ed, is this. Andrew's a grown man. He alone is responsible for his own choices. Not you."

"But I am responsible for keeping an eye on him so this kind of thing doesn't happen."

Will placed a hand on Ed's shoulder. "You can't control the universe, Ed."

"I know, but this shouldn't be happening."

"Well, it is. God's not surprised by any of this. Now, let's head to the house for dinner and get some new perspective. Hughes will be here all night and will ring the house if he hears anything. We have told everyone in town that we have spoken with to call the office if they think of or see the slightest thing." Will guided Ed to the patrol car.

When they reached the Walker's home, Ed went to his tiny hunting cabin on the property to get a few more things he needed. He opened the door and immediately the smell of booze hit him full force. There sitting at the small dining table was Andrew, empty brown bottle tipped over on the table, his head resting on his arms, and snoring like a sleeping baby.

"What the-----," Ed was overcome with a mixture of relief and fury at the sight of the passed out Andrew. Without thinking, Ed kicked the legs of Andrew's chair startling the man out of his stupor.

"Hey!" Andrew stood on shaky legs and blinked a few times in Ed's direction.

"Don't you 'hey' me!" Ed had Andrew by the shirt collar and was giving him a good shake. "What do you think you are doing? What is this?" Ed grabbed the bottle off the table and shook it in Andrew's face.

"I can explain......I—"

Without giving him a chance to explain, Ed literally drug Andrew back to Will and Sophia's house. Before he reached the front door, Ed began shouting, "Sergeant Will, you won't believe who I just found!"

Recovering from his initial shock, Will looked Andrew in the eyes. He instantly got a whiff of the alcohol the man had consumed. "Boy, what do you have to say for yourself? You had us chasing all over town looking for you and all along you were off getting drunk....." Will paused when he watched Andrew's look go from humility and embarrassment to anger then outright fury.

Andrew's eyes darkened and his nostrils flared in anger. "How dare you call me that! So you are no different than your patrolman." Alcohol affecting his better judgment, Andrew made a move towards Will and stopped short when Ed jerked him back.

"Hey now, Andrew! You better watch yourself and remember who you are speaking to!" Ed tightened his grip on Andrew.

Cocking his head to one side, Will eyed Andrew. "How dare I call you what?"

Through gritted teeth, Andrew ground out his next words. "You call me *boy* just like your patrolman. You don't see me any different that he did. To you and him, I am nothing but a filthy Aleutian, a boy!"

"Whoa, Andrew. I meant no offense by the term. My concern is that you don't go backwards and that you stay the course you are headed down. I have *never* seen you as a 'filthy Aleutian' nor a child. I didn't mean anything by calling you 'boy.' Now what has you so angry at me all of a sudden and you thinking I am no different than my patrolman? What's that supposed to mean, Andrew?" Will placed his hands on his hips, looked him squarely in the face, and spoke slowly, but firmly. "The least you owe me is an explanation about my own patrolman."

"Sit, Andrew. I'll make some coffee. You could use a pot or two." Ed shoved him down in the kitchen chair.

Will took the seat next to Andrew and waited for an explanation. "You're better than this, Andrew. You've come a long way. Don't go back down the path you once took. Why the booze today?"

Self-remorse hung heavy on Andrew's shoulders. He shook his head slowly and looked at his clenched hands resting on the table. "I couldn't take it anymore. I just wanted one drink and then I was going to do what Ed asked me to. I failed."

"But why? What triggered such a decision?" Will wouldn't let up. He knew people opened up more when they were a bit inebriated, so he hoped he could get some information out of Andrew.

"What made you do it, man?" Ed took the seat across from them and tried to encourage Andrew to talk.

"Berta.....well, no, me. I chose to drink. I made the wrong decision, ---huh—" A humorless laugh escaped his lips. "And I even heard a voice tell me not to, to come to God. I didn't. I was afraid and worried and hurting. For Berta. For me." Andrew's words came slowly but at least he was talking.

"Andrew, what did you mean when you accused Sergeant Will of being like the patrolman? What made you so angry at him?" Gently Ed pressed further.

"The patrolman, Dorne. When I was in jail—he—" Andrew stopped.

"Go on, Andrew," Will coaxed. "What you say will not get you in trouble. I only want to know what you meant."

The two men watched Andrew's face darken again and his nostrils flare. "He called me a boy the day of my arrest. He called me a filthy Aleutian.—And he...."

Fear made Andrew's face pale noticeably. Both Will and Ed saw the change in the man sitting in from of them.

"He what, Andrew?" Will sat as patiently as he could not wanting to shut Andrew down.

"He threatened me when I was in jail and beat me up. Your patrolman enjoyed being rough with me when no one was there to see." Andrew hung his head in shame.

Will reached out and touched his shoulder. "Andrew, I believe you." Will went to the coffee pot and poured three cups and brought them to the table.

For a moment all three men were silent. Will finally spoke up. "Andrew, what do you need to tell me about Berta? If you are afraid of Dorne, my patrolman, you have nothing to fear right now. He has moved away and won't be working in my office again. Nor will he return to this area without being arrested. I have learned some things about him lately that hopefully you can help me figure out."

Ed's eyebrows rose as he looked at Will. Will simply nodded his head to affirm that he was on to Dorne.

Andrew quickly stood from the table and walked to the front window. Both Ed and Will stayed on his heels. They weren't about to let him escape.

Sighing deeply, Andrew turned to face them again. "Dorne threatened me. He said that if I ever told anyone about—about some things, then he would kill Berta. I found a note in my house the day Ed and I moved my things out. I *know* Dorne put it there. It was another threat to Berta. I couldn't tell you before because I feared for her safety. Now it has been a month since she has been gone and I am afraid she is dead. They want me to keep my mouth shut about—"

"Who is 'they?'" Will asked.

"An Aleut friend of mine, Peter and Dorne. They wanted me to stay quiet about the booze. I know where some of the stills are. Dorne and Peter were afraid I would give information to save myself from jail and they would be busted. There you have it, Sergeant. So now what do I do? Sit and wait for Dorne or Peter to kill me or drop Berta's dead body somewhere for me to find? Do you know how difficult this has been?" Tears sprung to his eyes. A mixture of relief and fear tumbled in his gut. He held no more secrets but getting them out in the open could be dangerous to the one he loved. Falling into the chair beside him, Andrew openly cried, a welcome release from the shame of this day, the shame of his past, and fear of the future.

Will spoke quietly but strongly. "Thank you, Andrew. That took courage to tell us. I promise you this. We will find Berta, hopefully alive, and her kidnappers will be punished."

A shuddering sigh shook Andrew's frame. Looking up at Ed, he said, "I am sorry I messed up. I failed today, Ed. I understand if you want to quit on me and leave me to myself. I deserve that. I will go get a boat and have someone take me back to the Island. You don't need to watch out for me anymore. I know you don't trust me and I can't blame you."

Ed's anger had long ago melted towards Andrew. Clapping him on the shoulder, Ed laughed heartily, "Buddy, if you think you are going to get out of this mess that easily, you are mistaken! I have invested too much in you to give up now. You are stuck with me a while longer. *We* will get the supplies we need and *we* will return to Datka together."

"But—" Andrew began.

"Redemption, Andrew. Remember that. We talked about it. Don't disregard the redemption you now have been given. And no 'buts!' Unless you do something like you did today, the only 'butt' you need to worry about is yours."

A slow smile spread across Andrew's face at Ed's silly remark. "You have a deal."

"Remember the one thing I have told you from the start."

Before Ed could finish, Andrew said the words for him. "God is the God of second chances."

"That's right. And if we need them, third and fourth chances."

Will uttered an agreement, "Amen."

# CHAPTER 19

Having seen Pastor Stan, Elaine, and Lindy Hudson off over an hour earlier on their excursion to Seal Harbor, Rose lingered a while longer on the shore. Hopefully they made it safely to town before the storm hit. The boatman felt they were well ahead of the storm but they needed to hurry before the rains came. This was the only foreseeable chance for the Hudsons to purchase the food and last minute wedding items for the two big celebrations a few days off.

Black thunderheads rolled across the Bering Sea to the North of little Datka Island. With each crash of thunder, Rose felt as if her heart was splitting. Oblivious to the coming rains, she ran her fingers through the thick, soft coat of her Malamute.

Rose wondered how much more she could take. The condition of her heart wasn't from the threatening weather and crashing thunder but from the longing to see one handsome face. The one that danced before her eyes during the day and invaded her dreams at night.

The face of Gabriel Parker.

What seemed to be decades ago was in reality a mere month or so. Gabe had promised, and she had only to believe. But with each rising and setting of the sun, Rose had to work harder not to doubt. With absolute certainty, Rose knew she loved Gabriel and that she wanted to be his wife more than anything.

The very day he boarded the small plane and left the Island for his home state of Washington, her mind began churning with the how-to's and what-if's of their strange relationship. She, an Aleut woman, he, an American man. How could they possibly make this work?

But love has a way of making the impossible seem very, very possible.

Now Rose no longer stewed over the how-to's and what-if's of their relationship. She worried more over *when* and *where*. When would Gabe return? When would she become his wife? When would they begin their life together? Where would they marry? Where would they live? Where would Gabriel choose to be employed?

A distant crash of thunder startled Rose back to the present. Having watched many gathering storms from this very shoreline, she knew she had a few more minutes left to linger in this rare moment of being alone. Allowing her thoughts to have free reign once again, Rose continued her musings.

*I wonder what more is out there left for me to see? I love Datka, but is there more calling my name? I want to* do *more, see* more, experience *more! With Gabriel!* A sweet smile touched her lips followed by a tiny tear of longing to see him again.

*Creator God, what do You have for me?*

Rose let her thoughts drift back to a recent conversation with Elaine Hudson. The pastor's wife had taken Rose and the other young women Rose's age under her wing and became to Rose the big sister she never had. Elaine had begun to spend as many hours with the girls as she could afford, setting up weekly times with each of them. Rose had instantly connected with the older woman.

After Elaine heard Rose's story of Gabe rescuing her from the icy waters, she began to share with Rose how God had indeed saved her for a purpose. Rose admitted to Elaine where she and Gabriel's relationship was headed and of their professed love for each other. Elaine was an excellent resource for Rose and peppered their talks with heart-searching questions for the young woman. During their last conversation, Elaine asked Rose a very poignant question when they were discussing Rose and Gabe's relationship.

*"Rose, what are you afraid of?"*

*With a slight shrug of her shoulders, Rose responded, "I do not know, Miss Elaine."*

*Giving her a friendly nudge, Elaine pressed further. "Yes, you do. Dig deep, Rose. Take your time. This is a very important question."*

*Taking a deep breath, Rose sat quietly for a moment. She toyed with the dark brown bread spread with jam on a plate in front of her. "Maybe I am afraid of failing....of messing up so badly it can't be undone."*

*"Hmmmmm.....I understand that fear. Rose, how many loaves of bread have you made in your lifetime?"*

*Scrunching up her nose at the silliness of the question, Rose emitted a light laugh. "I've made so many I have lost count."*

*"And who taught you to bake such wonderful bread? Did you take lessons from your brother? From a childhood friend?"*

*"No, from my mother and Aunt Aggie." Rose wasn't making the connection between bread-baking and relationships.*

*"Of course you did. And how many loaves did you mess up in the beginning?" Elaine asked.*

*Recalling her countless batches of failed bread, Rose replied, "Again too many to count."*

*"I bet you added too much of one ingredient or not enough of another, right? But you kept at it and worked with the best teachers until you got it right." Elaine let those words settle in around Rose.*

*"Yes, you are right. Aunt Aggie and Mother wouldn't let me quit until I had learned to make perfect bread."*

*"Rose, relationships are like bread-baking. We add too much of some things or not enough of another and end up with a mess at times. But that's when we go to the ones we know can get it right and have them help us, give us a refresher course, teach us a better way.....does that make sense? You don't have to do this alone. Surround yourself, you and Gabe, with people who will help you get it right and you won't fail! I promise you, there will be messes. But you don't have to stop there. Messes can always be cleaned up."*

Grateful for the words of truth, Rose smiled as peace settled around her. Yes, she and Gabe could do this, messes and all.

If they surrounded themselves with people who would help them get through the hard times.

Again, thunder crashed, then was followed by the first big plops of rain. Stormy whined at her side and began licking her hand signaling Rose it was time to turn back towards the community she loved dearly. To her family and friends. To life as she knew it.

For now at least.

On the trail back to the center of the Island, Rose's tears mixed with the growing rain drops and splattered her shirt front. The two combined, tears and rain, to momentarily bring a fresh cleansing of the longing woman's heart.

On the other side of the fence of Seal Harbor, "The Harbor" and *Rita's Place* were receiving the brunt of the storm. Within intervals of ten seconds, lightning split the skies repeatedly followed by deafening booms of thunder. Rain and hail pounded so loudly on the roof it sounded as if multiple machine guns were being shot at once.

The usual customers headed for home with the first crash of thunder, so Rita and her girls huddled in the kitchen with cups of tea and a steaming pot of stew and cornbread. Grateful for the warm food and dry house they did their best to keep each other's spirits up through the deafening noise.

Another round of lightning and thunder signaled heavier rain and even larger hailstones.

"Rita, this hail is as large as the pool balls! I have never seen it this size!" Felicity stood looking out the window into the back yard. "It is literally ripping branches off the trees!"

Felicity had no more uttered those words when a crash shattered through the house so loudly it sent all of the girls into screaming fits. The old Sitka spruce tree had been hit by lightning and crashed through the kitchen window close to the terrified group.

Rita gathered her wits about her first. "Is everyone alright?"

A chorus of yes's rung around the room. After the shock of the noise was over, Rita and the girls began to survey what had just happened. Their kitchen was getting drenched, hailstones covering the floor and counter under the window.

"Oh no!.....What will we do now?......Get the broom.....grab the trash cans and some buckets, anything to hold water.....Get the mop!"

Amidst the flurry of activity a loud knock sounded on the door. One of the neighbors stuck his head in and yelled over the commotion, "Miss Rita, you and the girls okay in here?"

"Oh, Frank, no! We aren't. I mean, yes, we are, but the house is not!"

Girls were scurrying to clean up the mess and gather the hailstones that had made it into the house. "Don't slip.....here's some more towels......watch the broken glass!"

"Miss Rita, I will get my son over here and we'll get the tree out of your kitchen and the window boarded up for you. Don't you worry!"

"Thank you, Frank!" Rita continued with the clean-up. She felt a drop hit her curly head. Looking up, Rita uttered a deep moan. "Oh, no! Not the roof, too!"

The dripping increased and buckets were placed under the leaking ceiling.

"With that amount of rain and the size of the hailstones, I'm not surprised," Liza commented. Hugging her mother, she did her best to comfort Rita.

Very soon, as quickly as it started, the storm abated. Rita heard the sound of saws as the neighbors began removing the tree from her kitchen window. After dragging it back outside, the men quickly boarded up the broken window and climbed a ladder to check on the condition of the roof. Soon Frank had a report on the roof's damage and it wasn't encouraging.

"Miss Rita, there's a good-sized hole in your roof and shingles are blown off on this side of it. We will do our best to patch it up for today until we can get someone to repair it for you. I can at least keep it from leaking anymore. Hopefully the storm is over and this is all the damage you will have."

Hugging her neighbor, Rita said, "Frank, thank you so much for seeing to us. What would we do without you?"

Frank left after sealing up the broken window and hole in the roof temporarily.

Rita sat down heavily in a nearby chair. Running her hands through her unruly hair, she said, "Oh, girls. This place is just too much for an old woman like me. I should just sell it."

"Miss Rita, don't talk like that....where would we go?.....we need *Rita's Place*.....You can't mean it!" All at once the noisy bunch worked to change her thinking before it took root.

Shaking her head slowly, Rita just looked at her soiled, patched up kitchen and felt the weight of the responsibility on her shoulders, not only of the business, but of these ten girls.

"Why don't you go lie down awhile, Momma? Get some rest and we will tackle the rest when the storm is over. The girls and I will get someone to fix the place up and it will be as good as new. This little storm won't stop us." Trying to sound cheerful, Liza ushered her mother to the stairs and up to her waiting room.

Rita didn't argue.

Heading straight for her room, she lifted the old cigar box from its hiding place. Removing a wad of bills from her skirt pocket, Rita added these to the box and returned it to the back corner of her closet where it was nestled under shoe and hat boxes. Knowing she had enough money for the repairs did nothing to change her train of thought from earlier. And seeing the box of money only did one thing.

It helped resolve in her what she knew she wanted to do next.

Something she had spent the last few weeks planning. Now she just needed to finish up her last few plans to make things fall into place.

213

Shaking her head slowly, Rita gathered up her papers and pen and began yet another letter. She muttered to herself before pen touched paper, "Change the past. Change the future."

Her hand writing as fast as her mind was going, Rita paused to push away the red tendrils that tickled her cheek. She knew what she had to do.

For Liza, for the girls, and for herself. The only problem, there was just one more missing piece to the puzzle of her plan. Hopefully it would turn up soon so she could proceed with what she wanted to do.


Placing the phone back in its cradle, Sergeant Walker looked across his desk at his friends. Stan, Elaine, and Lindy Hudson had stopped by to say a quick hello before returning to Datka.

"Well that was interesting. Are you guys interested in another project? This one could have a couple of implications."

Always ready to help out where they could, Stan asked, "What's going on?"

Will leaned back in his wooden desk chair and began explaining to the Hudsons about the differences between The Harbor and Seal Harbor. He told them about Rita, the girls, and the pool hall, leaving out the fact that he suspected there was more to the business than appeared. "I have wanted a way to get more involved and make more of an appearance on that side of town. With the AST office being short-staffed and under-funded, I do good to take care of issues here in town. There is sort of an unspoken "understanding" that The Harbor people take care of their own and don't appreciate anyone in their business, law or not. With the AST being only a year and a half old, we are still working on some issues like this all over the state. Almost all of the larger cities have this problem as well. When we get more money and troopers that will help tremendously. Sorry I didn't mean to get on my soapbox." Grinning sheepishly, Will continued. "Anyway, my point was, I now have a reason to get involved with some of the people in that area. *Rita's Place*, the pool hall I just spoke of, has hit by the storm last night and they have some extensive roof and structural damage. I can use some of the men here in town but......Pastor Stan, I know you will understand me when I say this. I *really* feel strongly that Elaine needs to meet Miss Rita and the girls that live there. Every time I think about them it's like I see Elaine connected in some way. Maybe to help them. I don't know. They definitely will need to hire some workers for the roof and kitchen. I didn't mean to spring this on you when you just get to town, but with the storm and what has happened, I see an open door."

Elaine's face glowed with the excitement of a new undertaking. Her desire to help and meet new people was undeniable. "If Stan agrees, I am more than willing to help out! I would love to meet them."

Stan spoke up next. "The only things that will be a hindrance are we have a dinner and church dedication tomorrow and a wedding two days later on the Island. Maybe Monday we could return and help out. I could arrange for a few of the men to help too. They will need another project to keep them occupied and maybe make a few extra dollars."

"That sounds great! This will give me a few days to arrange workers and supplies here and coordinate with Miss Rita. The neighbors helped patch things up until something else could be done permanently. Sophia and I will be at the wedding. Ed invited us before he left for Fairbanks so we can wrap up the plans after the wedding. Will that work?"

"Perfect. Our boat arrives soon so we better head out. See you in a few days!"

Handshakes and good-byes went around the room. Will returned to his phone and called to arrange the details for the upcoming week at *Rita's Place.*

*You even use the storms in our lives to set things in motion, don't you, God?* Will finished with a silent *thank you* sent heavenward.

# CHAPTER 20

It kept staring him in the face until finally Markus shoved the crumpled letter into his pocket for the hundredth time. A month had passed since his promise to deliver Berta's letter to her sister, Ana. Stalling was getting him nowhere. Markus knew the deed had to be done. Tired of thinking about it daily, he didn't give himself another chance to back down.

Rain drizzled from the gray overhead skies. The storm was over and now Seal Harbor was left with a dreary on-and-off mist of precipitation. Pulling his hood over his jet black hair, the Aleut man took the path to the other side of the fence and on to *Rita's Place.*

On the lengthy walk there, Markus began to analyze once again why he had delayed bringing the girl the letter. First, he wanted no part of his past life, from any ties with Peter or alcohol or the girls. Markus just wanted a new life, a better life. Nightly regret and shame kept him awake into the wee hours of the morning. Everything in him wanted to return to his family and community on Datka, but memories lit his mind like the fiery sky the night he set Datka's homes, boats, and school ablaze, reminding him of a real fire and booze and the craziness he had gotten himself into that kept him from considering returning to his Island. Markus just knew he *couldn't* return, not after all he had done. But, oh how he missed his sister Luka and his parents. He would give anything to turn back time and relive some of his past decisions and choices and make new and better ones. But that would never happen. Regret had become his constant shadow; shame was his friend.

Nearing *Rita's Place*, Markus noticed the damaged building and its patched up roof and walls. There were stumps and limbs lying around on the ground along with broken glass and splintered wood.

Datka flashed before his mind. What did the tiny Island look like now? It had been months since the fire and he wondered if its damage had been fixed. What sort of damage had he and his friends caused that one horrible night? They never stayed to find out.

Reaching the bright red building, Markus tentatively knocked on the door. He hadn't seen Ana or the other girls, except for Berta, in months and hoped someone he knew would answer the door.

Instead a strange face greeted him. "Can I help you? No one ever knocks here. The pool hall entrance is around the corner."

Starting to shut the door in his face, Markus stopped the girl. "Wait. I am looking for someone. For a girl named Ana."

The pretty face before him changed instantly. A look of sadness clouded her features. "Ana won't be seeing anyone right now." Again she tried to shut the door.

"No! I just want to talk to her. Please. It won't take long."

Pausing, the girl considered his request a moment. "Who can I say is asking for Ana?"

"Markus. She will know who I am."

"Okay....Markus. Wait here and I will go get her for you."

A girl he hardly recognized met him on the porch within a few minutes. Blonde hair hanging straight around her shoulders, frailer than he remembered, and dark circles that made her look even older, Ana's face showed she at least recognized him. "Yes?"

"Ana, remember me, Markus from Datka?"

"Yes, of course. I—I don't think you should have come....I am not—"

"That's not why I am here. I have something for you." Reaching into his pocket, Markus withdrew an envelope.

Tentatively she held out a hand and took the envelope. "What is it?'

"It's a letter. From your sister. From Berta."

Instantly the girl's hand flew to her mouth and she swayed on her feet. A pitiful sob escaped her lips. Markus grabbed her arm and led Ana to a nearby porch chair.

"Sit, Ana."

Obeying Markus, she sat heavily in the chair. "From—from Berta? How...."

Clearly he needed to quickly explain things for the distraught girl. "Ana, your sister came to me about a month ago. She wrote a letter to you and asked me to deliver it. I have delayed and for that I am sorry."

Turning to face Markus, Ana gripped the arms of the chair she sat in and tried to keep from scratching the man's eyes out. "You have had this for a month and are just now bringing it to me?" Her eyes flashed dangerously with red-hot anger.

Markus watched the color quickly return to her cheeks. Laying a calming hand on her arm, he said, "Ana, tell me what happened to Berta."

"She was kidnapped! Several months ago! Did you see her? Tell me everything, Markus!" Forgetting the letter for the moment, Ana focused on his unbelievable words.

"First, Peter came to me and gave me little information. He left money for me, maybe to shut me up or make me do what he wanted. Peter said I was to expect Berta to come to my house, that he had been forced by someone to kidnap her and she would die if he didn't help her escape. He also said that Berta figured out it was him and he was disappearing for good. That's all I know. Then Berta sought me out. She had escaped from her kidnappers with Peter's help. I don't know the other man, but Peter gave her money and instructions for her to leave in the night and come to me. So she did. She could only stay the night and had to leave immediately so the other man wouldn't hunt her down. She would have been killed if she had stayed. The next morning before sun up, Berta left. I don't know where. She wrote you a letter and asked me to deliver it."

Grabbing the forgotten letter from her lap, Ana ripped it open with shaking hands. Devouring each word, she let tears course down her cheeks as she read.

*My dear sister,*

*I am writing this letter to assure you that I am fine. Well, I wasn't for a while but now I am. Markus has helped me escape from the man who kidnapped me. I am not even sure how long ago that was. All I know is that my heart is breaking because I have to leave you. Again. This time is so much more difficult than the first. I have to leave now for my own safety and for yours and the girls at Rita's.*

*I know the man who kidnapped me would do unspeakable things to you and the girls if he could. I don't want you in harm's way.*

*I promise to come to you when I think it is safe. For now, I will stay away and somehow I will get to you again one day.*

*I love you.*
*Berta*

Turning the paper over in her hands, Ana looked for more words, more clues to where and how Berta was. A quiet laugh and cry burst from Ana.

"She's alive. She's alive!! Markus, my sister isn't dead!" Ana clutched the letter to her heaving chest and breathed for the first time in weeks. Truly breathed.

"How did she look, Markus? Was she hurt? Do you know where she was kept? Please tell me all you know."

Fear welled up inside Markus as he listened to her questions, knowing that if he divulged all he knew concerning Peter and Berta's kidnapping, he could face serious trouble himself. Markus looked down at the frantic girl's tiny hand on his arm. "I am sorry, Ana. I don't know any more than that. She was well, not harmed. Just dirty, hungry, and thirsty. I could tell she had been through more than anyone should have endured. But I assure you, she was unharmed. And that is a miracle, especially since Peter was involved."

Tears sprung to Ana's eyes again as she pictured her sister in such conditions. "Thank you for bringing this to me. I know you didn't have to, but you did. Thank you."

Looking sheepishly at his feet, Markus stood to leave.

Ana grabbed his arm again and pulled him down. "Markus, I have to call the AST office. They have been looking for Berta and need to know about this."

Fear clouded Markus' face. "Don't mention me, Ana. I am trying to stay away from trouble. All I did was let her eat and sleep at my house for one night."

"Wait, you are here in Seal Harbor and not on Datka?"

"Yes, I moved here a few months ago."

"What about your family and friends? Do you ever go back?"

A deep sadness enveloped the man. "No. I haven't. I....made some mistakes and don't think I should go back. Not now. Maybe not ever."

"But you can't do that to your family, Markus! Berta is all I have left in this world and I can't imagine not being near her if I could. You have to go back. For your family's sake. Surely they miss you."

Longing surged through Markus. Standing again, Markus looked at Ana. "I hope you see Berta again soon. She is brave and strong and will be fine until she can return to you. I know she will be back." With that Markus left Ana sitting on the porch watching him leave.

Before she could notice, he wiped a tear that escaped from his own eyes. Maybe he should take the girl's advice and go back to Datka.

Maybe.

*******************

The mid-week activities were under way. So much had to be accomplished before tonight's church dedication and steeple raising.

222

Pastor Stan placed his arm over his wife's shoulder and kissed the top of her head.

"Elaine, did you think we would be bored on this little Island without much to do except lead church services?"

Laughing at his question, Elaine looked at her husband. "Honestly, yes, I did wonder about that. But since we have arrived, there has been so much to do. I love it! After the wedding, we will be needed in Seal Harbor at *Rita's Place*. We are gaining more construction skills than I had hoped for, though."

Laughing at her humor, Stan replied. "Doesn't look like there will be a dull moment for quite a while. Now, let's get Lindy to lend you a hand with decorating these tables for the dinner." Stan reached for a box containing the new Bibles that he had brought back from their last trip to Seal Harbor.

Elaine went back to their tiny Island home she had come to adore. It was perfect for the three of them. Loving simplicity in her life, the no frills, easy-to-maintain, house was right up her alley. Entering the house, Elaine called out for her daughter. "Lindy! I need some help at the church. Are you here?"

Hearing a noise from Lindy's room, Elaine headed in that direction. She saw Lindy sitting on her bed with her back facing the doorway, mirror in hand. Elaine could tell from Lindy's sniffling noises that she had been crying.

"Honey....." Elaine sat on the bed beside her, took the mirror from her daughter's hands, and instantly wrapped Lindy in her arms. "What happened? Why the tears? Did someone hurt your feelings?"

Sniffing loudly, Lindy tried her best to get ahold of her emotions. She had done so well these last few months and was surprised at the onslaught of insecurity this morning. Out of nowhere, she was getting ready for the day and there it was again. Staring her in the face like every morning, only today the angry red mark seemed to be longer, redder, uglier. Knowing it hadn't changed at all, Lindy felt shame for letting herself grieve that fateful day all over again.

"It's no one's fault but my own, Mom. Honestly, I am more frustrated with myself for getting upset and insecure today than I am over the scars. I don't understand this. Why today? I am getting too old for these outbursts!" Lindy tried to laugh at herself, but it wasn't helping any. Pulling away from her mother, Lindy tried to stand. "Anyway, we have *lots* to do, Mom, so we better get going."

Grabbing her daughter by the hand, Elaine pulled her back down beside her. "Wait a minute, Miss. You aren't going anywhere. Stuff to do or not, *you* are the most important thing on my to-do list right now. Talk to me. We can get through this, but not by ignoring it."

Fresh tears glistened in Lindy's sapphire blue eyes. "Oh, Mom. I'm sorry about this. I am as caught off guard by these crazy emotions as you were when you walked in here."

"So tell me, sweetie. What were you thinking about when it all started? At breakfast you seemed fine."

"I was.....until I got to thinking about the wedding.....and how I should dress and do my hair.....and then I tried a new style and there were my ugly scars staring me in the face. Again. You would think that since I have had these since I was three years old they wouldn't be as bothersome."

"Lindy, I am so sorry, honey. I still wish I could turn back time and erase that day. I never would have put the boiling water so close to the stove's edge. I would have left it out of reach of your little curious hands. I would never have walked out of the kitchen and left you there for those fateful two minutes....but I did." Tears gathered for the millionth time in Elaine's eyes as well.

"That's why I hate talking to you about this. I never want to make you relive what happened. It wasn't your fault. It was just a silly, innocent mistake I made as a little girl. I have never blamed you, Mom. I have always regretted it for you more than me, honestly."

"I know, Lindy. But I would change it if I could. Don't you find it interesting though that your dad and I chose the name Lindy for you? It is so true of who you are, scars or no scars. Remember, *Lindy* means *beautiful.* Your name should always remind you of that truth."

"Yes, it should. You remind me of it often." Reaching a hand to her face, Lindy continued. "Why do I let these scars dictate how I feel about myself? How my mood is? How I react to people? When I hear myself say that, it sounds so childish. And why now? I thought I had made such headway in not allowing my scars to define me."

Giving her shoulders another squeeze, Elaine hugged her tighter. "Well, here's my opinion. Since we have the wedding to think about, it is natural for you to plan your clothes and what you will do with your hair. All the girlie things we do to feel beautiful. And added to that is the possibility of a handsome young man who may or may not have caught your eye...."

Lindy reached for her pillow and gently smacked her mother on the head. Elaine didn't miss the unmistakable blush that covered her daughter's face. "Mom!! This has nothing to do with Ed!"

"I wouldn't be so hasty to ignore that fact. He *is* attractive, godly, hard-working, funny. All those things that I know you like in a man. There's nothing wrong with wanting to look your best, honey.

But don't hide behind the fear of what someone might think about you. Please God and the rest will take care of itself. We aren't supposed to be man-pleasers. Only God-pleasers. And the man who falls for you and your beautiful self will see *you*, not your scars."

Lindy's smile returned. "Thanks, Mom. I needed to hear that."

The two hugged and went to help finish the preparations for that evening's dedication dinner. There was so much to be thankful for and excited about in the upcoming days. Lindy decided that she would enjoy the day and not stay bogged down in the fears and insecurities that tried to hold her back.

No, she would charge ahead, confident in who she was, not distracted by what she thought others would think of her. Grabbing her green sweatshirt from the end of the bed, Lindy pulled it over her brown wavy hair. Next she tied her hair back away from her face and neck with a matching green ribbon. Then Lindy did something she hadn't done in a while.

Looking in her hand mirror, she smiled at her reflection and was pleased with what she saw looking back at her.

*******************

Their boat bumped onto the shore's rocky edge. Ed and Andrew disembarked and began unloading the last of the things for that night's dedication dinner and Yuri and Luka's wedding. He smiled just thinking about the contents in the boxes. Per Elaine's instructions, Ed had purchased the ingredients to make two luscious cakes, one chocolate and one vanilla with a berry filling for the wedding. They decided to stick to a more traditional meal for the dedication dinner

226

and splurge for the wedding festivities. He could almost taste the cakes just thinking about them. Grateful for the best of both worlds, Ed could see how living in Seal Harbor and on Datka would benefit him. He did enjoy the comforts and pleasures of the mainland, while at the same time, Ed soaked up the time on the tiny Island with his Aleut friends and their simple, charming customs and life.

Time was wasting away and there was much to accomplish before the evening's festivities. The two men hauled their load to Aggie's busy kitchen. Rose, her Aunt Aggie, Natalia, Luka, and a handful of other women worked so quickly Ed could barely follow their motions and instructions that swirled in the air around the smiling women. The room smelled of smoked meat, vegetables, berries, bread, and sweets that made his mouth water.

Laying down their burdens on an empty worktable, Ed snatched two berry tarts from a nearby tray and quickly secreted one to Andrew. The two men smiled as their mouths tasted the tart, sweet treat. Instantly both were smacked on the arm by Natalia and Aggie; their deed had not gone unnoticed by the older women. Shielding himself from further friendly assault, Ed laughed at the sweet ladies and their stern looks.

"My compliments to the chefs. These are wonderful! Do you need us to sample any more food for tonight? We wouldn't want you ladies to serve something that tasted bad to the group, so Andrew and I would be willing to sacrifice ourselves to taste-test this feast."

Receiving another smack on the arm, he drug Andrew out of the kitchen and onto their next project.

A rare smile lit Andrew's eyes. "That was close! You know how to make the women angry, don't you, Ed?"

"You could say that's been my track record, but one I am trying to change."

The two men headed towards the church so they could lend a hand. When the freshly painted building was in sight, Andrew stopped in his tracks. Confused, Ed turned and looked back at his friend. "What is it, Bud?"

Heaving a deep sigh, Andrew stayed quiet a moment before answering. "It is still very difficult to see the church."

Frown lines creased Ed's forehead. "I don't understand. Explain what you mean. Why would it be difficult to see this beautiful place?"

"You see beauty and I see destruction."

"How? What, Andrew?"

Andrew looked Ed in the eye before continuing, imploring his friend and mentor to understand. "I helped destroy this place, the homes, and school. It's my fault, my stupidity, my destruction that ruined what was once here. That's all I can see...." Andrew's voice broke off mid-sentence. He reached a hand up to rub his eyes as if he could clear his vision from the offending sights.

Understanding crossed Ed's face. Placing a hand on Andrew's shoulder, he guided him to a nearby boulder. The two sat a minute in silence. Ed stuffed his hands in his back pockets of his jeans and felt the crumple of paper, a reminder of the letter he hadn't yet read that Jade had given him. He had all intentions to read the letter on the plane, but forgot about it. A fleeting thought flashed across his mind. *Funny, I forgot to read that letter from Jade.*

Returning to the present, Ed turned to his friend. "I have told you my story many times, Andrew. You know how bad and broken and miserable I was. You know the ways I destroyed my own life over and over and over. You also know that when I met the Parkers, I met Jesus and His forgiveness. And His redemption. I know you don't see it right now, but I promise you.....one day soon, you will see redemption in your life instead of pain and destruction. And when your eyes are opened to look through the lenses of forgiveness, when you can even forgive yourself, you will see something redeemed. You will see yourself redeemed, new, bought, ransomed, important enough for Jesus to die for you. And all the pain and destruction that is still in front of your vision will clear away like the Aleutian Islands fog. Trust me on this. Okay?"

"Yes. I will trust you on this, Ed. So far, you have been honest and true. I believe you, though I can't see it yet." Tears weren't far from the surface. Andrew stood and squared his shoulders. "We have work to do."

Ed understood this was his cue to stop talking; Andrew had heard him. Smiling to himself, he said, "Yes, we do have work to do."

Reaching the church, Andrew joined a group of men working on setting up tables and benches. He jumped right into the activity, ready for a distraction from his troubling thoughts.

A flash of bright green caught Ed's attention. Looking in the direction of the color, he stood a moment and watched. Lindy. Her back was to him as she worked, but he knew it was her.

A tightness filled his chest as Ed realized how much he had missed her company while he had been away at Fairbanks and the AMRA meeting. He wanted nothing more than to take her hand and go for a long walk while filling her in on the meeting and upcoming prospects with AMRA.

Turning in Ed's direction, Lindy noticed him standing there. A huge smile lit her face as she walked towards him. Never had she looked so at ease and gorgeous to Ed. He couldn't contain his smile if he wanted to.

"Well, hey there! When did you get back?" Lindy gave Ed a quick, friendly, side-hug.

"Just today. Got here in time to help with the finishing touches for the dedication." Ed's eyes flashed his pleasure at seeing her.

Unconsciously reaching a hand to her scarred cheek, Lindy said, "So how was Fairbanks?"

"Great! I had a really good trip!" His mind raced with all the things he wanted to say, but time wouldn't allow for it now. Not able to interpret the look on Lindy's face, Ed continued as her smile fell away.

Brushing her bangs out of her eyes, Ed caught sight of a deep scratch on Lindy's hand. "You're bleeding....what happened?"

Reaching for her hand, Ed turned it over to look at the offending cut. Quickly he took out his handkerchief from his back pocket and began dabbing at the cut.

"Oh, I didn't even realize I was still bleeding. I knew I cut my hand earlier on a staple on a box I was unloading, but I thought it was better. Thanks for the handkerchief." A slight coloring touched her cheeks as Ed tenderly wrapped his handkerchief around her hand.

"You better go get a bandage on that, Lindy."

"Yeah, I guess so. Thanks again."

"I better go help these guys while you get that hand fixed up." Ed turned in the direction of the work that was beckoning him as Lindy watched him leave.

*Don't be so silly, Lindy. He would have done that for anyone. Remember, he is "Charming."*

Watching him walk away, Lindy stood a moment before going for her bandage. Something pink lying on the ground caught her eye. Picking it up, she turned over an envelope. It had one word scrawled in a pretty script across the front.

*Tex.*

Without allowing herself to think further on her actions, Lindy stuffed the pink envelope in her pocket and headed for a bandage, her gut tightening with each step she took away from Ed.

# CHAPTER 21

Glancing down the long table where she sat, Rose looked from one face to another. Yuri and Luka, Andrew and her mother, Michael and Lydia, her mother Ola, and sweet daughter Lillian, Pastor Stan and Elaine, then Lindy and Ed. All precious people Rose loved dearly.

Everyone at her table was smiling except for two of the faces. Lindy and Ed's. Their countenances emitted discomfort. She knew they were friends, suspected possibly more, so what would be troubling those two? Rose puzzled over this but soon returned to the wonderful plate of food before her. Her stomach growled as everyone began eating.

Pastor Stan had offered thanks for the feast they had before them, and each person surrounding the long tables dove in gratefully and enjoyed the food and companionship immensely. God had done such a work among her people. The tragedies that threatened to harm them had only worked in their favor. Rose knew this was simply God's miracle-working grace.

Her own face turned sad as she missed the one man she would have given most anything to have seated beside her. Thoughts turning to Gabriel, Rose yanked them back as she would have yanked on Stormy's collar when the dog would have tried to chase down a rabbit. It was pointless, especially tonight when it was supposed to be a night of celebration, to allow her thoughts to run away with her. No, she wouldn't allow it.

All she did know about Gabe was he had sent word that he was detained in Fairbanks getting accustomed to his new job with AMRA and couldn't leave for a while. Knee-deep in planning a trip for a mission team, he couldn't leave the job undone and escape even for a few days. This trip was critical and demanded Gabe's expertise.

So Rose accepted the fact that Gabe wouldn't be at the dedication service, though deep down she wanted nothing more. Turning back to those surrounding her, Rose determined to enjoy the feast. Anxious for the remainder of the evening, the young woman fought to keep her focus on each moment, treasuring them as they came. Life was too precious to waste a single second in longing for what she didn't have. It stole the joy from what she *did* have in her possession.

This night.

Her people.

Love, healing, redemption.

The ache in her chest eased a bit as she relished the moment.

After everyone had finished eating, Pastor Stan instructed them to lend a hand in clearing the dishes, food, tables, and benches and asked the group to go to the church when finished. Quickly the tasks were done, and the clean, sparkling church received its guests one by one, both Aleut and American faces filling up the rows of newly cushioned benches lining the gleaming wooden floors of the sanctuary.

Approaching the front of the seated group, Pastor Stan looked at the beaming faces before him. Pride for these people swelling in his chest, he silently thanked God for directing him to Datka Island. Clearing his throat he began, "You as a community have long awaited this night. You have worked hard for what you have. This wonderful building, these strong relationships, this close community. Suffering and tragedy haven't destroyed Datka or its people. Difficulties and challenges haven't hurt but helped each of you."

Andrew felt Pastor Stan's eyes catch his. Looking back at the Pastor, he only saw acceptance there. Ed was right. His vision was changing, little by little. He just needed to continue to believe.

The Pastor continued. "Each of us have made certain choices throughout our lives that weren't for the best. No one sitting in this room is faultless. No one. Therefore, no one can point a finger nor cast a single stone at another for their actions and choices. Instead, we choose to offer forgiveness and love because it's what we all need. You are sitting in a building built on that foundation, a lasting foundation. As the Pastor of this church, in this community, I am so....." Tears halted Pastor Stan's words. "So very proud to call this place home for as long as God allows it to be. So very proud to know each of you and your strengths and struggles. Thank you for accepting me and my family."

Elaine turned in her seat and glanced back at all of the smiling, tear-stained faces seated across the chapel. Gratitude filled her heart as well. She was so happy and fulfilled here, with these people she had grown to love. Turning back to her husband, Elaine listened as he finished.

"So, as a reminder of the challenges you have overcome and the one true reason this community has stayed undivided, tonight you will erect the very first steeple on this Island! May it remind us, as it points heavenward to God, that He is our strength, our hope, and our reason for living. Each time that you look at the steeple on this church, your church, may it call you to worship, privately and corporately as one body. God bless each of you. Now, Elder Dan and several other men will be ready in a few minutes for us to join them as they lift the steeple to its rightful place. Please join us outside."

Excitement rippled through the small group as everyone filed out to the surrounding church yard. As soon as each member had taken their place, Elder Dan, Michael, and James all worked to hoist the gleaming steeple upright. As it was set securely in its spot, they all watched as Yuri deftly anchored it to the church's roof.

The sun broke through the filter of late evening clouds and touched the steeple's highest point as if God had reached down and laid a finger on the gleaming spire. Cheers erupted from the group below and shouts of joy surrounded the small church.

Rose wiped tears from her cheeks as she recalled the day the steeple was brought to Datka. AMRA had given it to the community to inspire them to repair and rebuild and to continue to worship together as a community. And they had done just that. All repairs were finally completed. Relationally as well as physically. Some repairs were newer than others, but still they were there like the fresh coat of paint on the church's walls.

Fresh, bright, beautiful.

Pastor Stan turned to the aged elder. "I have asked your Elder to dedicate this church to God and to His worship."

The older man looked around the group through dimming black-brown eyes. Holding up one hand toward heaven, he spoke as loudly as his voice would allow. "Before my people of Datka Island, I stand and commit this church, this community, and this Island to the service of God and each other. Our commitment to God and His people is what will make this Island strong and great. I pledge my heart and life to God and to Datka and ask anyone willing to do the same to raise your voice in agreement with mine."

Not more than a second passed before the air was filled with joyous, heartfelt shouts of affirmation, each voice joining with that of their elder.

The very ground of Datka Island felt the reverberation of the people standing, shouting on its soil. Strength, unity, and hearts turned toward God is what would keep this community alive and well.

Ed sauntered up to Lindy's side hoping to gain some understanding on the awkwardness between them during the dedication dinner. He simply just didn't understand women at times. One minute they were friendly and chatty, the next they were giving you the cold shoulder and glaring looks. This was something he had expected from Jade Miller, but not Lindy Hudson.

"What did you think of the dedication service, Lindy?"

Turning her shoulder towards Ed she said coldly, "It was fine."

"*Fine*? Just *fine*? Surely you thought more of it than that."

Not responding, Lindy seemed to be distracted by her fingernails for a bit.

"Did I miss something, Lindy? I know I can be thick headed at times, but is something wrong?"

"No, Ed. Everything's fine. I'll see you later. I want to go talk to Rose." Leaving Ed standing in her wake, Lindy took off in Rose's direction.

"What the heck?" Ed scratched his head in confusion.

"Problems? You seem a little disturbed." Michael stood at Ed's elbow holding his daughter, Lillian, who always seemed to want to run off.

Ed huffed. "Women! I can't seem to figure them out, Michael."

Laughing at Ed's statement, Michael answered, "I have been married several years now and still don't have them figured out. Just when I think things are going well, Lydia gets mad at me for something I didn't even realize I did. But give them time and what has them mad or upset usually comes out soon enough."

"So you're saying they need space? To cool down and then they will come explain?" Ed was trying to understand Michael's words.

"I can't promise it always works that way, but yes, give them space if needed. Is Lindy the particular young woman giving your heart fits?" Michael gave Ed a friendly jab in the ribs.

"How could you tell?" Ed's reply was full of sarcasm.

"Oh, it is written all over both of your faces. You can't hide those emotions!" Laughing at Ed's discomfort, Michael patted him on the shoulder. "Don't give up yet, friend." Leaving Ed's side, Michael put little Lillian down and followed off after the toddler.

"Space," Ed muttered to himself. "That's just what I *don't* want to give her." Before he could decide his next move, Ed watched across the crowd as Lindy turned to the house she and her family shared. "So much for talking to her tonight."

Ed watched Yuri and Luka head for the empty chapel, hand in hand. He longed for the love and friendship he saw between the two. Life was uncomplicated and unencumbered for them. Days would stretch ahead of them, sweet and simple. Though life was often difficult on the Island, Ed knew Yuri and Luka would make life good and rich. It didn't take *things* or *careers* or *achievements* to make life good. It would take God, hard work, love, and remaining faithful to those in your life.

He could do that. He *wanted* to do that, *be* that for a special someone.

Just figuring out who that person was seemed to be the challenge.

And of course waiting on God's timing.


Yuri laughed at the shyness written all over Luka's face. He gently tugged on her hand as she gave in and entered the dimly lit church's sanctuary after him.

"I won't bite," Yuri said with a twinkle in his eye.

"You might." Luka teased back.

Wrapping his arms around her waist, Yuri pulled Luka to him. "I have waited so long for this day to finally arrive. Tomorrow you will be mine, my sweet Luka." Bending his head to reach her, Yuri placed a gentle, reverent kiss on her lips. "Very soon."

Luka wrapped her arms around Yuri's neck and leaned in for one more kiss. "Tomorrow cannot arrive soon enough."

Breathing deeply, Yuri looked into her eyes. "Can I ask you a question?"

"Yes."

"Do you regret not having a place of our own? Alone? You are marrying a man with an instant family. You not only get me, but Michael, Lydia, Lillian, and Ola. Do you think you will be able to stand such a change? Maybe I should have asked them to leave since I am getting married. I just don't want you to have any regrets, my future wife." Yuri stole another kiss from Luka.

"I have none. I would never ask you to lose one family just to gain me. You have suffered enough when your own family died and you were alone. You don't deserve that kind of hurt again, Yuri. I love you more than I love myself."

Tears clouded his vision momentarily. "Luka, I could search the whole world over and never find another woman as beautiful and sweet as you. Thank you so much." Hugging Luka again, Yuri's voice took on a husky tone as he whispered near her ear, "Even with a house full of people, I promise to guard our privacy with my life."

Giggling shyly, Luka whispered back, "And I will remind you often of the promise you just made me."


Flopping down miserably on her bed, Lindy buried her face in her pillow and let out a little groan. "Ughhhhhh."

Instantly she was filled with regret at her actions. She hated being snotty to Ed. He was so nice to her and she had returned it with a sour disposition and leaving him in confusion. Contrary to her emotions, Lindy's heart was teetering precariously close to falling for this man. And now she had read that stupid letter, but at least she knew where she stood with him.

But for her heart, it was too late to stop the fall. She was already plummeting over the edge. From the safety of the solid ground of friendship, her heart had leaped over the cliff's side and was falling hopelessly in love.

With a man she couldn't have.

Heat flushed her cheeks. Embarrassment colored her face as she remembered several conversations they had, even moments of innocent, sweet flirting. Edward Hamilton was the first man to make her forget the scars. He said he didn't even see them. And that was when her heart started its downward descent.

240

Flipping onto her back, Lindy reached over to the low table and lit the lamp. Then she grabbed her favorite book, *Little Women*, and opened it until the pink envelope stared her in the face again. Face flushed, Lindy still couldn't believe the audacity she had. How could she have read a letter, written by another woman, meant for another man? A man she now loved. She should have called to Ed and told him he dropped the pink offending thing and immediately handed it to him. But curiosity had gotten the best of her. And now she felt at her absolute worst. Snatches of the girlish script floated across her mind.

*Tex, I hope you will give me another chance.....*

*Yes, we have our differences, but I believe we can overcome those and find the love we both want. Together......*

*I believe our friendship has the foundation to hold up a deeper, more meaningful relationship.....*

*I know you feel the same about me. I have seen it in your eyes often when we were working on Datka together.*

A toxic cocktail of anger, jealously, and shame filled Lindy's stomach. The churning of these emotions threatened to make her physically ill. Stuffing the letter into its envelope, Lindy knew she couldn't lie here any longer and keep rehashing the contents. What was she going to do? There was no way she could act normally around Ed.

And to think she had hoped and wished and almost believed that he was interested in her! Again Lindy's face flamed with shame. Tears rolled silently down her cheeks as she turned out the light, and without removing her clothes she pulled the covers up over her head giving into the torrent of heartbreak and humiliation.

# CHAPTER 22

The four walls of the *Seal Harbor Inn and Restaurant* threatened to crush him to death. Anxiety like no other choked Gabriel Parker, forcing him to pack his meager belongings and leave the tiny room. At six a.m., he was among the first patrons in the dining room that adjoined the hotel he had spent the night in. His plan was to grab a quick breakfast and secure the first boat to Datka Island. He had a mission, a very important mission on his agenda.

To see the one face that had haunted his every waking moment and every sleepless night for the past few months.

His sweet Rose.

And he couldn't get his breakfast ordered soon enough.

The waitress finally took Gabe's order of coffee, pancakes, and bacon. Surely it wouldn't take long to prepare it. He was hungry enough to eat more but didn't want to waste a single second to see his Rose.

His food finally arriving, Gabe poured the slow, thick, maple syrup over his pancakes as his thoughts poured out just as heavy and thick. It would have been laughable to the other patrons if they could see inside his brain and try to make sense of the tumultuous thoughts that swirled therein.

*God, thank You for this wonderful food and this day. The day that You have made. Help me honor You in all I say and do. And please, let Rose say "yes."*

His prayer quickly turned to ponderings.

*So how and when should I talk to Rose? I hope we get a few moments alone with no one around. Maybe I will take her to the rock where we talked so many times before that overlooks the shoreline. That's a special place for her.*

*Will she be willing to leave what is real and comfortable and her family and friends and follow me on another path? Will she want to? Was I gone too long and someone else has stolen her heart? God, I feel so unsettled.*

*Okay....stop thinking that way! Breathe. Trust. Believe God.*

Knowing it would take one more cup of coffee until his thoughts were settled at least temporarily, Gabe forced himself to relax and drink the last cup before leaving for the Island. His body warred within itself; part of him didn't want to leave the safety of the hotel's dining room and face the unpredictable, and the other part of him wanted to jump up and grab the next boat out of town to see Rose.

*Breathe, Gabe. Calm yourself, man. You don't need to end up having a heart attack.*

Mind briefly returning to his home in Washington, Gabe breathed a sigh of relief that God had indeed answered that prayer. Having made amends with his parents over his lack of communication and the distance he had placed between the three of them while on the Island, Gabe needed and wanted their blessing to ask for Rose's hand in marriage.

Unbeknownst to him, Rose had written a letter to Becca and snuck it inside his mother's bag when they were last on Datka. That letter had actually helped him as it had prepared Rand and Becca both to accept Rose and Gabe's love before he had really spoken to them about it. Time and prayer had a way of paving the way, especially a path that was difficult for others to see someone taking. A path that his parents neither expected nor fully understood at first. But after multiple conversations between Rand, Becca, and Gabe, they came to see how much he really did love Rose and more importantly that Gabe knew God had put the two of them together. He knew it was difficult enough for his parents to come to peace with him moving to Fairbanks to work for AMRA and head up future missionary teams to go to other Aleutian Islands. But for him to choose an Aleut woman for his future bride was jarring to say the least. Thankfully, both of his parents shared a common love for the Aleut people and their land.

The week before Gabe left for Datka, his parents had prayed with him about he and Rose's future, that he would remain at peace when he went to propose to her, that their future would be made crystal clear to the two. Gabe was so very thankful to have them on his side.

And now, here he was in Seal Harbor, Alaska headed to Datka Island to propose to the woman he loved.

One more self-pep talk and he would be on his way. *Whew....deep breath, Gabe. You are not alone. God is with you every step of the way.*


The last hour and a half drug by for Gabe until he finally saw the small Island and soon heard the crunch of rock against the boat's bottom. Quickly paying the boatman and grabbing his gear, Gabe stepped onto the very familiar spot of land and inhaled deeply. He needed this moment alone to regroup once again. The trip to the Island was a constant mental battle. At half past nine in the morning, Gabe physically felt like it had to have been midnight. Fear wasn't something Gabriel Parker was accustomed to. He would be glad to face his fears and get some heart matters settled soon.

Taking the path to the village's center, Gabe rounded the corner to a flurry of activity. Wedding preparations were in full swing. Flowers and baskets and streamers fluttered all around the little church and people of all ages raced to some task or another. A smile crossed Gabe's lips as he looked at the people he knew well and loved greatly. Their dark, shining faces lit up with the excitement of an upcoming wedding only added to how beautiful and wonderful they were to him.

And then, he saw her.

Rose.

Gabe stood without anyone taking notice of him for a minute and took the scene in. Standing a head taller than the rest, Rose was carrying armloads of blue lupines and laughing at something her best friend, Luka has said. Rose deposited the flowers in a basket and turned in Gabe's direction. The look on her face when she saw him would stay with Gabe for a lifetime.

Rose's hands flew to her mouth and she froze in place. Tears poured down her cheeks and she stood still just staring, crying.

Gabe set down his bags and took off towards the woman he had missed and loved so very much.

Squealing with delight, Rose's feet instantly took over and she ran into his arms and threw herself at Gabe. Joy mixed with surprise overcame her tears and Rose began laughing, nearly hysterically. "You came, Gabriel! You are here!"

Without a hint of shyness, Rose kissed him squarely on the lips without a care of who saw. All fear and worry evaporated in Gabe with that sweet kiss. He had nothing to worry about with Rose. Nothing at all.

Afraid he would squeeze her to death, Gabe made himself set Rose down on her feet. "Let me look at you, Rose." Gabe took in her hazel eyes, her tall frame, her beautiful smile. "I told you I would come back." Laughter consumed Gabe from the sheer joy of seeing Rose again. This time he lifted her off her feet and twirled her in the air.

Setting her down again, the two noticed they had attracted the attention of the entire village and blushed at the smiles, giggles, and elbowing among the ones watching. Instantly Gabe was welcomed by his many friends. He knew he was where he belonged. At least for now.

Things suddenly felt right and good in Gabriel Parker's world.


So happy to see her friend Rose with a constant smile on her face, Lindy knew she was watching the result of true love. It was bittersweet and precious all at the same time. Watching a couple together was affecting her in new and disturbing ways. Maybe because she thought she just might be getting close to that season of life herself.

All the more reason she had to do what she knew she needed to do. Lindy needed to come clean. She needed to remove any possibility of her heart falling any further for the charming cowboy. Someone who was clearly interested in another girl in Fairbanks. A girl who wanted to be with the man she wanted. But couldn't have.

And all the more reason to return things, if possible, to friendship with Ed Hamilton. He may never speak to her again after what she had done. Which would only help shut down the emotions she wanted gone from her aching heart.

Lindy had gotten up the courage to ask Ed if they could talk later that day, before the wedding. He of course accepted. Lindy knew he was puzzled about the way she treated him at the dedication dinner. Shame seemed to hound her right now, like a dog tracking a scent. One minute Lindy was embarrassed, ashamed, angry, hurt, disappointed. The whole gamut of emotions one person could possibly feel at one time. It was getting the best of her.

Hearing a noise, Lindy looked up from the fallen tree she sat on just outside of the center of activity. Everyone was so distracted with the wedding preparations, she and Ed wouldn't be missed for a few minutes. And here he was, not thirty feet away. It took all Lindy had inside her not to bolt.

"Hey." Her muddled mind wouldn't allow for any other words to escape her parched lips. Licking her lips nervously, Lindy motioned for Ed to take a seat beside her.

"Well, this looks serious." Ed sat beside her and gave Lindy a playful nudge. "I must have really screwed up. Ok, let me have it, Lindy. I can't stand the suspense any longer." He tapped her tennis shoe with his cowboy boot.

A small smile escaped, but that was all. Lindy stared at the ground looking for the courage to say what she needed.

"Take your time. I'm in no rush." Concern etched itself onto Ed's face.

Heaving a shuddering sigh, a lone tear coursed its way down Lindy's scarred cheek. Ed reached a finger up to brush it away as Lindy leaned back just enough for him to miss.

"Ed....I am the one who screwed up. Not you."

Trying to relieve the tension of the moment, Ed returned, "Now that's the funniest thing I have heard all day, darling!"

"Ed, seriously....let me say what I need to."

Nodding at her, Ed remained silent.

"I did something I am ashamed of. It's—it's why I was such a jerk at the dinner. I was....I don't know, mad, embarrassed, jealous, any other bad emotion you can name." Lindy stood from where she was seated and took a few steps away, her back to Ed.

Worry replaced his concern, but Ed stayed silent. He wanted to take her in his arms and tell Lindy there was nothing she could ever do to—

She pulled a pink envelope from her back pocket. Still not turning to face him, she held it by her side.

Ed instantly recognized the pink envelope with *Tex* written on the outside. A rush of anger so powerful it scared him hit Ed full force. Standing to his feet, he walked to Lindy's turned back and grabbed her shaking shoulders. Forcefully Ed turned her to face him.

"I'm so sorry, Ed. So sorry. I hate myself for not giving it to you after I saw you drop the letter. When you gave me your handkerchief for my cut, I should have—"Stuffing the offending letter in his chest, Lindy was about to bolt. Ed knew it so he grabbed her again, stopping Lindy in her tracks.

"Oh, no you don't, Lindy! Don't you dare run away from this— this....So you read it? Really? Without returning it to me first?"

"Ed, I don't expect you to ever be my friend again. I just had to tell you what I did! I couldn't stand myself another day for what I have done. I am so terribly sorry. I was wrong."

Ed just stood there. He had no idea what was even in the letter. Now Lindy knew before him what it contained. He felt like his privacy had been violated. By a friend, no less. By someone he knew he cared for. A lot. That just made the pain all the worse. Brushing past her, Ed stuffed the letter in his pocket and left Lindy where she stood, eyes tear-filled, crying out his name.

"Ed, wait!"

But he didn't. He couldn't.

Ed headed straight for the shore. There was really no place to go. He had no private house here on the Island and he couldn't just go invade someone's house and kick them out so he could be alone. So the path to the Island's rocky edge was his safest haven for now.

Reaching the end of the trail, he paced back and forth trying to calm himself. Red hot fury consumed Ed's being, burning hotter and hotter until he felt like he would self-destruct.

Falling to his knees, Ed scooped up a hand of rocks and threw them with all his might. *Why? Why would Lindy do this to me? Why would she read Jade's letter and just not simply return it?*

Instantly he realized he had no idea of its contents and someone else did. Snatching the letter from his pocket, Ed opened it. Lindy would have been able to tell that he had never even read it because it had been sealed. She read his unopened letter. That thought infuriated him!

Removing the pink paper, Ed scanned the words. Once. Twice.

Reality hit him square in the gut. The author of the letter now decided she wanted to pursue a relationship that was more than friendship. Jade, the girl who snubbed him because he was so *different,* on a different *level* as him all those months. Ed had finally come to realize that Jade was not the one for him and was just a good friend.

And now, the girl he had fallen for had betrayed him. The one who had affirmed his work with Andrew and the others, the one who didn't judge him for his past, the one who had caught his eye. And now this!

It was too much. Standing to his feet, Ed tore the offending letter into the tiniest of pieces and let the coastal breeze fling the little pink shreds in a thousand directions.

*How could she??? How could Jade?? How could Lindy?*

Back down on his knees, Ed cried out to God, knowing that was the place to take his anger and pain.

*God, what are these two thinking? One's messing with my head and the other is messing with my heart! Help me know how to handle both of them. I am really confused and angry and hurt. And I have to eventually face them both. Show me what to do.*

Rolling the tension out of his neck, Ed looked skyward. Sitting back on his rear end on the ground, he purposed to not let the anger consume him. And the disappointment, which was even more dangerous.

A snapping twig startled him to a standing position. His friend, Gabe, was coming down the path in Ed's direction.

"Looks like we both have a favorite place on this little spot of dirt." Gabe instantly noticed the turmoil on Ed's face. "Oh, man. What happened?"

Ed just shook his head in disbelief. Placing his hands on his hips, he motioned to the nearby boulder. "You better sit for this one, buddy. We may be here a while."

251

Gabe sat. "I'm all ears. Spill it."

The next half hour, Ed told the whole story to his best friend. He told about Jade, his shift in feelings for her, the letter, Lindy and his new-found feelings, her hurtful actions, and even AMRA's job prospect. He spilled it all. And it felt good to let go knowing he could trust his best friend to listen and advise.

Finally, Ed ended with, "I just don't understand why Lindy did this. It just doesn't seem like something she's even capable of doing. I don't get it. The girl I am very, *very* interested in basically slaps me in the face and violates my trust."

Gabe sat a moment in silence before speaking. "Ed, sometimes we all do or say things that aren't normally how we would act. Fear, insecurity, past hurts. They all play a part in causing us to act in ways we know we shouldn't. It sounds like Lindy was acting out of her insecurity. Especially if she is interested in you and is picking up on the fact that you might be interested in her too."

"So you're defending her actions?" Ed groused.

"No. Not at all. Honestly, I'm pretty angry too at how she treated you. Don't like it one bit. But if she really means that much to you, and you seem to think that God has His hand in you two meeting, then you may need to dig a little deeper than the surface of Lindy's actions and find out what might be at the root of them. Don't give up on something so special, so easily." Gabe stood and placed a hand on Ed's shoulder giving it a firm squeeze. "Just for the record, I never thought Jade Miller was the one for you, buddy."

Surprise flitted over Ed's face. "Really? I thought you—oh, never mind. Insecurity and fear, huh? Well, I'm going to need to do some thinking on that a little longer. Mind if I keep this spot for a while?"

Gabe chuckled at his friend. "Be my guest. As long as you promise to work through this and not leave it as is."

"You have my word."


Gabe left Ed alone to work through what was on his mind. He *had* to find Rose. That was why he went to their boulder in the first place. Seems like he needed to talk to Ed first.

Nearing the fields of blue lupines dancing in the breeze, Rose was gathering more of the bright blue flowers along with baskets of fuchsia shooting stars. The brilliant pink and blue blossoms made for a perfect backdrop for the tall girl with the hazel eyes. Gabe's breath caught at the sight.

Looking up when he approached, a smile broke out over Rose's flushed face. "Gabriel! What are you doing here? Surely there is more manly work for you to do than picking extra flowers. If Luka had her way, the fields would be empty and they would all be gathered for her wedding!"

"Rose, you are so beautiful." Taking the basket from her hands, Gabe looked deep in her eyes. "You are right. There is other work for me to do, but I can't do a single thing until we talk."

Fear flashed across Rose's face. Gabe kissed the crease that formed between her eyes. "Don't be afraid, Rose. I am the one who is nervous and afraid to talk with you, but I need to. Now." Taking both of Rose's slender hands in his, Gabe said, "Rose, I have had so many hours since we have been apart for my mind to run away with itself. I need to say some things to you and hear what you have to say in return."

Rose noticed a slight shaking in his hands as she held onto his. "Gabriel, you're nervous! Please, tell me what's on your mind!"

Releasing her hands, Gabe rubbed them on the fronts of his pants. "Okay. Well, first, AMRA has offered me a position in Fairbanks. They want me to head up future missionary teams to go to other Aleutian Islands and various locations in Alaska.....There are two positive things about this job. Number one, I will be in Fairbanks, nearer to you than I was in Washington with more opportunities to be here on Datka, and number two, it's the job I am good at and what I love to do!"

Rose watched the excitement on his face. "You are taking the job, aren't you?"

"Yes, I am. But.....I have a very important question for *you.*" Clearing his throat, Gabe ran a hand through his hair and tried again. "I want to hear your answer, but at the same time, I am afraid to. I have been so afraid that another man would come, one that would give you a home here with your family and friends, and make you forget about me. I was gone so long I was afraid you wouldn't wait."

Touching his cheek with one hand, Rose placed the other in her pocket and withdrew a tiny object. Opening her hand, palm up, Rose produced the little, pink, heart-shaped rock Gabe had given her before leaving Datka.

"You still have it." Gabe grasped her hand and looked her in the eyes. "Rose, would you be willing to leave Datka Island, your home, and go with me where God leads.....to live in Fairbanks, to travel to other locations in Alaska and serve other people, to follow God and me.....wherever that leads? Will you, Rose?"

Joy and excitement and hope filled her chest to the point of overflowing. Rose couldn't contain it any longer. "Yes! Yes! A thousand times, yes!! Gabriel Parker, I would count it the joy of my life to follow God and you, wherever!"

Tears of joy and kisses of love mingled with each other as the blue and pink flowers in the Alaskan field nodded their heads in affirmation of the couple's future. One full of promise, hope, love, and adventure.

Releasing her, Gabe went down on one knee and asked the only question he really wanted an answer to. "Rose, will you marry me? Let me be your husband and you be my wife." And now, removing something from his pocket. Gabe placed a delicate pink heart-shaped jewel set in a silver band on her finger.

Unable to contain the tears, Rose laughed and cried as she looked at the ring. Her ring. From the man she loved. The one who kept his promise and returned to her.

*******************

"Is this seat taken, Beautiful?" Ed leaned down close to Lindy's ear and whispered the words.

Startled for more reasons than one, Lindy smiled broadly and looked into Ed's eyes. "As a matter of fact, Charming, it isn't."

With a good fifteen minutes before the ceremony began, Ed settled in by Lindy, his arm brushing hers. "You look amazing."

255

"Ed, what did you just call me?" Lindy looked down at her hands in her lap.

His half-smile escaped and red touched Ed's face. Clearing his throat, he said quietly, but assuredly, "*Beautiful.* I called you *Beautiful.*"

Now it was her turn to blush. "No one has ever called me that, except Mom and Dad. And they sort of have to since I am their daughter. So does this mean I am forgiven or is it too early to ask?"

"Yes, you are forgiven. Lindy, I don't understand the *why* of what you did. We can talk more later. But right now, I do understand that I value *us* more than my anger or being right."

No words had ever touched her as deeply. "Thank you, Ed," she whispered. "That means so much to me."

"Now, Beautiful, we have a wedding to focus on." Giving her a quick wink, Ed leaned back in his spot, determined to wait for the right timing and speak with Lindy when she was ready, resolute in giving them another chance though he didn't understand at the moment the reason for her actions. Peace settled back between the two as they watched another couple's love and commitment be professed among friends and family.

Ed felt the tension leave his shoulders. He *wouldn't* stay mad at Lindy; truthfully, he *couldn't.* Allowing himself to feel the remnants of anger and frustration roll off his back, Ed glanced around at the crowd gathered for the ceremony. His heart nearly stopped in his chest.

There were Jade and her parents sitting across the church.

Jade was watching him; that much was apparent.

And the tension eased itself up Ed's back and shoulders, finally settling along the base of his neck. *Now what, God? I didn't even think about the Millers making it to Datka for the wedding.*

A sad smile stretched across Jade's face as she took in the dark-haired beauty beside Ed. Jade noticed the scar on her face, but more than that, she noticed the look in Ed's eyes for the girl before he caught Jade watching him. Her gut churned with a mix of emotions knowing her eyes hadn't deceived her. Jade couldn't deny the looks that had passed between Ed and the other girl. Struck at how much she favored the unknown girl, Jade had to force herself to look away, but not before giving Ed a little wave of her fingers.

Nodding his head in her direction, Ed acknowledged Jade and turned as the Pastor called the group's attention to the ceremony's beginning. He would have to deal with Jade later.

The simple, yet sincere, ceremony lasted long enough to leave nearly every attendee in tears at Luka and Yuri's profession of faithfulness and love. Lindy was overwhelmed with the beauty in the Aleut wedding ceremony. Not the same beauty from traditional American weddings she had attended before, but from the candlelit chapel and fresh-cut field flowers brimming from handwoven baskets the Aleut women had crafted, to the fact that Luka's brother, Markus returning to the Island the day before his sister's wedding, the love and forgiveness, the deep conviction of family, hard work, and unity....all of it surrounded Lindy with an overwhelming sense of what she wanted in her life.

Later the ceremony continued with the two decadent cakes the women had made, singing, dancing, feasting, laughter, all lasting into the wee hours of the morning. The Island of Datka knew how to celebrate!

At one point, Lindy was amazed at the differences surrounding her. She watched as Sergeant Walker and his wife, Luka and her brother, Yuri and three year old Lillian, Gabe and Rose, even her parents swayed and danced to the music, everyone laughing, learning new dances, living life together. There were no divisions, no differences in cultures, all human beings enjoying each other and the moment they were celebrating to the fullest.

Life. The life Lindy wanted.

The one she prayed and hoped for.

The only disturbing moment was when she saw the girl named Jade. The one Ed made a beeline to talk to immediately after the ceremony. Uncertainty mixed with trust swirled in her heart along with the lively music. Ed had proven himself a trustworthy person. He had given her no reason to not trust him, as she had done to him. Time would tell what the quiet discussion between him and Jade entailed. Honestly Lindy realized she didn't need to know what was spoken between them. The body language from Jade and the sad look on her face combined with a few tears let Lindy know the conversation didn't go as Jade had planned. Not gone longer than ten minutes, Ed returned to Lindy's side and claimed her attention the remainder of the evening. Lindy knew who he had chosen.

She knew Ed had made a decision about the letter concerning Jade's request for them to begin a new, deeper relationship.

And as the evening progressed, Lindy was left without a doubt that Ed had chosen her.

# CHAPTER 23

The echo of hammer against nail, shouts from one to another, men giving and receiving instructions on the best way to repair the storm damage at *Rita's Place,* filled the crisp, early morning air. True to his word, Sergeant William Walker had arranged a work party of about a dozen men and women from Datka and Seal Harbor combined. The Hudsons, Walkers, Markus, Joshua, Andrew, Ed, and Gabe all worked diligently to get the place back in working order.

Outside buzzed with activity, while inside the kitchen, Elaine Hudson and Sophia Walker made themselves right at home in the midst of the wide-eyed girls of *Rita's Place.* Even Miss Rita was a bit taken aback at the two women's eagerness to help out on the inside. They slapped paint on the freshly repaired kitchen wall, shined the new window, and repainted the scuffed cabinets. What amazed Rita the most was that someone, who remained unnamed, had paid for all of the repair supplies, paint, brushes, roofing materials, and every single nail that went into the job. Walker remained secretive and wouldn't reveal the source, leaving Rita completely baffled. To top that off, the men working only requested meals and beverages during the day when they took their breaks.

This left Rita and her girls happily preparing food and keeping tea and coffee made for the workers. Every now and then Rita would hear one of her girls marvel to another about the nice men who were volunteering to help them without pay. They had never been shown such kindness and care. Their world had always been one of survival until they came to Rita's and here it was still everyone pulling their own weight. These men were of another breed entirely. Interestingly a few of the girls recognized a few of the Aleut men from their Island excursions that Peter used to arrange, but no one let on they knew each other. Still they couldn't understand the change in them. These men from their past were no longer drunken, raucous, gambling, grabbing, expecting animals. Now they held hammers and nails and cut boards and said "yes, sir" and "thank you."

Leaving the girls to cook, Elaine convinced Rita and Sophia to take a break and share a cup of tea at the gingham clad dining table. The table had been shoved in the corner to afford room for painting and repairs, so the three sat tucked away in the large kitchen and enjoyed conversation.

Rita was so baffled by the women's treatment of her, in her own home, that she didn't know how to behave. Never had another woman treated her in this manner, with kindness, almost equality. It was a very strange thing. Maybe this was her missing link, the one she had spent hours at night trying to come up with. These women were kind, thoughtful, caring. They were perfect for her plan. As Elaine and Sophia sat and talked with Rita, she saw a genuineness in their faces and attitudes that put her at ease. Yes, this was it. Just what she needed. She could rest easy in the days to come.

Bringing her out of her reverie, Elaine was speaking to Rita so she focused on her words. "Where do you see these girls' future headed? I was once their age, in a desperate situation of my own and couldn't see any future for myself. What do you see for them, Miss Rita?"

A frown creased her brow. Rita shook her head, confused. "What do you mean, Elaine? I guess they will all live here and work here until—well......I hate to say this but I really don't see much of a future, as you call it, except life as they know it. And that's sad."

Reaching across the table for Rita's hand, Elaine felt the woman almost draw back at her touch, but Elaine held on. "Miss Rita, it doesn't have to be that way. We are all promised a hope and a future if we want it. God promises that to us.....Do you know God, Miss Rita? He sure seems to know you. Look at all of these people He sent to help you in your time of need, people who hardly know you, and yet they want to give their time and resources to you and the girls."

Rita hadn't thought of that. "Elaine, I know there is a God. I do believe, but I have made my own choices and life dealt me a nasty hand of cards that I could never get rid of. So yes, I know He is there, but I am too stubborn, too hard-hearted and hard-headed for Him to take notice of me. But these girls.....if there was something better for them than—than this....." Rita broke off her sentence and stared into her empty cup.

Sophia quickly reached for the tea pot and poured another round for all three of them. She didn't want this time to end here. This woman was desperate and Elaine was giving her truth. She would silently pray and keep the cups filled if that's what it took. Elaine sent Sophia a grateful glance.

Staring off into a faraway world, Rita twirled a red lock of hair on her finger then replied, "My mother used to say a quote about the future that never made any sense to me until lately. It goes like this, 'Change the past. Change the future.'"

Elaine repeated the six short words. "Interesting. I have never heard that. I don't think I understand it. What does it mean to you, Rita?"

"I know we can't go back and undo the past, but I do think we can do something to redirect its course so that the future will be changed. On a different path, so to speak." Astonished that she felt this comfortable talking to these two women, Rita was slightly embarrassed at her openness.

"Rita, that's so true!" Elaine burst out. "Yes. We can redirect the path of the past so the future can go in a different direction. I like that thought!"

"Me too," Sophia joined in. "I would venture to guess that some of your girls need their paths redirected," she gently stated.

"Maybe so," was all Rita would volunteer.


The clock in the hallway struck two a.m. Rita laid down her pen and folded the last letter placing it in its envelope. She scrawled a name on the outside, *Liza*.

Her third and last letter now finished, Rita stood from her bed and stretched. Donning her winter coat and scarf, Rita hefted the small suitcase in one hand and checked her bosom for the money's hiding place with the other. Yes, it was all there. She refrained from looking under her bed for the hundredth time for the locked metal box shoved in the far corner behind shoes and old hat boxes. It would be discovered soon enough.

Walking as quietly down the stairs as she could, Rita reached the kitchen she loved dearly. A tear trickled down her face. Angrily she swiped at it, resolving to not give into a bunch of sappy emotions. Now was the time for action, not tears and grieving.

Rita placed three letters on the gingham checked table cloth. Without looking back, she was overcome with a sense that she could only describe with two words.

Heartbreaking relief.

With broken heart, but relieved mind, Rita shut the white painted door and clicked the lock in place with the key as silently as possible. Saying good-bye to the lipstick red house was harder than she thought. But she had to do what was best. Sneaking away into the night, Rita met up with her ride, one she had secured to take her to the train station.

So she could board the noisy train that would forever take her away from her girls.

Without allowing any further emotion to engulf her, Rita turned to her driver, "What's the hold up? Let's go and be done with this. I'm not paying you to sit in a car and drive me nowhere."

*******************

A tired and dirty crew of men had returned from The Harbor after working on Rita's repairs. Lindy felt sorry for the bedraggled men as they strode into the village looking hungry and exhausted. She had spent the day alone for the most part, praying and planning. There was much she needed to say and Lindy didn't want to mess this up.

After a heart to heart talk with her mother the night before, Elaine encouraged her daughter to do what was right. She told Lindy to seek God, seek her heart's intentions about how she handled Ed and the letter from Jade, and really pray about how to apologize and get her friendship back on track with Ed. The best advice Lindy received was still ringing in her ears.

*Depending on the amount you value your relationship with another person will usually dictate how much you are willing to be humble and make things right no matter how difficult it is to do so.*

*Yes,* Lindy thought, *this will be difficult. I have never bared my heart with another man. But I do value Ed as a person and as someone I have grown to care about deeply. Very deeply. Okay, even love. I can't just ignore this and leave things as they are.*

Her cheeks flushed at her own admission. But down deep she knew it was true. She did love Edward Hamilton aka the Charming Cowboy. An unexpected, light giggle escaped from her lips over the silly nickname she had given him. Lindy continued to watch him finish putting away tools and say his good-nights to his friends.

Catching his eye, Lindy gave Ed a little wave. A hesitant, then huge smile broke out over his face. Ed sauntered up to Lindy and greeted her, "Hey, Lindy. Have a good day?"

"Yes, I guess so. What about you? You all look exhausted."

"Well, I won't argue with you on that. I am. What did you do today?"

"First, I have a question. Did you eat dinner yet?" Lindy watched Ed's half-grin escape.

"No, I haven't. And if what you did today has anything to do with cooking, count me in!"

"Perfect."

Ed looked down at this appearance. "I need fifteen minutes to get cleaned up and changed. Where are we dining tonight?'

Lindy waved a hand in front of her nose. "You can have twenty if you need it."

Ed playfully shoved her in response.

"How about we meet at the table and bench on the edge of the community bonfire. I think it will be warm enough tonight to eat under the stars. Does that sound good to you?"

"Wonderful. Meet you in a few."

"Bye, Charming."

Now it was Ed's turn to blush. That name she had for him seemed to affect him in the worst way.

Lindy ran back to her house and placed the last of the food items, plates, napkins, and utensils in a large basket then covered it all with a heavy blanket. Her parents entered the house just as she was finishing gathering the rest of their dinner things.

Stan looked at his daughter with a puzzled expression. "The wonderful aroma I smell better not be leaving *this* house in *that* basket, girl."

Lindy laughed at her father's words. "Hate to disappoint you, but it is. Oh, I did leave you and Mom a plate on the counter by the sink. And there's candles on the table. Sooo...while I am gone, I thought you two could enjoy a candlelit dinner alone. Be back in a couple hours. Love you!"

With that Lindy disappeared out the door. "Now where do you think she is headed this late, with food for more than just herself?"

"Don't worry, Husband. She has that look in her eye. Lindy has a plan and I just think she might succeed." Elaine winked at Stan. "Now how about cleaning up and I will get our candle-light dinner set out."

Kissing Elaine on the forehead, Stan responded, "You don't have to tell me twice."

Knowing she had little time according to how hungry Ed appeared, Lindy quickly took the blanket off the top of the food and spread it out on the table set at the edge of the tall, spicy-scented, spruce trees. This was one of Lindy's favorite spots on the quaint Island. Oftentimes she would rise early and bundle up with a cup of coffee in tow and her favorite book or Bible and spend the first few hours of her day here at this very spot. Or the chilly evenings would find Lindy staring up at the star-lit sky hoping to catch sight of the stunning aurora borealis.

But tonight she had a different agenda in mind.

Making amends with the Charming Cowboy.

Taking out the container of a tasty salmon dish she had prepared herself and the still warm bread, Lindy laid out the plates and utensils all the while trying to calm the nervousness swirling in her stomach.

"Hey, Lindy! That smells great! So that's what you have been doing all day." Ed smelled of soap and clean flannel which did nothing to calm the young woman at the table.

"Yeah, I guess you could say I have been busy today. Hope you like the way I prepared the salmon. And of course, what's a meal without bread and jam?" Lindy could hear the nervousness in her voice. Taking a deep breath to steady herself, she knew an explanation of the impromptu picnic was necessary. "I guess you are wondering why you were asked to stay up late after such a hard day of work and eat fish and bread under the stars with a girl who has been a jerk to you. Well.....I have an explanation for that. But can we eat while it's still hot? And from the way your stomach keeps growling, I don't think we can have much of a conversation over the noise."

"Sounds like a plan to me." Ed sat and began filling a plate then handed it to Lindy.

"You didn't have to do that. You can have that plate."

"Lady's first. Plus if I dish your plate with lady-like portions then I get the rest. Wouldn't want you to feel bad if I don't eat it all." Ed began putting a generous portion of fish and bread on his plate. "Mind if I pray?"

Lindy looked up quickly, pleasure in her eyes. "That would be nice."

Reaching for her hand, Ed bowed and offered thanks. "Father God, how can I express in words how thankful I am for this food, this beautiful evening, and this wonderful company? You are so good to me. Bless Lindy for making this meal. In Your Son's name, Amen." Giving her hand a gentle squeeze, Ed grabbed his fork and unashamedly enjoyed each bite.

Around a mouthful of fish, Ed asked, "Do I detect lemon and pepper on the salmon? It's amazing!"

"You detected correctly, Ed. Glad you like it." Barely touching her food, Lindy nibbled at her fish and bread and finally gave up trying. She did agree it was tasty and was glad Ed was happy with the simple meal.

The Alaskan sky sparkled overhead with tiny diamond-like stars. Uttering a silent prayer, Lindy looked up. *God, give me the words and the courage to speak them.*

Laying down her fork, Lindy began, "Ed, you know I didn't invite you here just to sample my cooking, even though I had fun cooking today all by myself. With Mom and Dad gone, it gave me time to experiment in the kitchen again. I've missed that....anyway, I am rambling, well....because I am nervous." Lindy cleared her throat and began again. "We need to talk about what I did. The letter from Jade."

An emotion Lindy couldn't decipher flitted across Ed's face. He laid his fork down and gave her his full attention, remaining quiet and giving her the space to gather her thoughts.

"I want to say again how sorry I am for reading Jade's letter to you. I shouldn't have invaded your privacy. I should have given it to you as soon as I saw you drop it and not let my curiosity get the best of me. Most importantly I regret doing anything to harm our friendship and cause you to distrust me. That is what hurts the most." Lindy watched Ed's eyes soften as she continued. "I hope you can find it in your heart to forgive me and to one day trust me again." Tears pooled in her sapphire eyes.

Ed reached across the table and laid a hand on her arm. "Lindy—"

Slowly Lindy pulled away from Ed and held up a hand to interrupt him. "Please let me finish, Ed. This is important."

Drawing his hand back to himself, Ed said, "Sure. I'm listening."

"Ed, I feel like a fool. My actions are unexplainable and unacceptable and shameful." Giving a mirthless laugh, Lindy continued. "What I have to say next is the hardest for me but probably the most necessary.....After reading Jade's letter to you, I want you to know that I will back away and let you pursue the relationship that will make you happy. Clearly Jade wants this. I know you were very close to her, but things didn't work out before. Maybe now they can. So, Charming. Here's your chance—" Lindy swiped at the annoying tear that leaked out before she could catch it. "Give it a try once more. I truly believe you two can—can make it and find a strong, good, wonderful relationship, the one that—you both....."

Ed had heard enough. Gently he interrupted her speech. "Stop. Lindy, listen. First of all, I forgive you. I told you the other night that I forgave you but I didn't understand. Well, time and sleepless nights have a way of making you see things differently than before. And I've had both." Reaching again for her hands, Ed continued. "I read Jade's letter. And, to put it simply, I don't want what she wants. Maybe a few months ago I did, or at least thought so. But now, there's something more important, more precious, more beautiful, more special that has my attention and I don't intend to let it slip through my fingers. That *something* is me and you, Beautiful."

Tears flowed freely now down Lindy's face. Ed reached a gentle hand up and wiped them off. "Hey, I didn't mean to make you cry. Why the tears?"

"You keep calling me that. Beautiful. It is honestly the very least way I see myself." She laughed softly. "Do you know what my name means, Ed?"

"Stubborn, hard-headed, wonderful....am I close?"

Slapping his arm, she replied, "No silly. Lindy means 'beautiful.' Ironic, huh? What man would want a woman with these scars to show the world?"

A flash of anger crossed Ed's face. "Do you really think me so shallow, Lindy? Do you think I am out for a woman with a perfect face, perfect body, and flawless in every way?  Listen to me now 'cause I will only say this once.  When I look at a person, I look at more than their outward appearance.  I look at what I want them to see in me.  My heart.  I am not after a perfectly modeled mannequin.  I want what's real and true.  And I find that in you, Lindy.  And I see beauty when I look at you, so much you take my breath away--" Ed's voice caught in his throat and he stopped to clear it.

"That is the sweetest thing anyone has ever said to me, Edward Hamilton."

"And you can count it the most sincere as well.  I mean that with all my heart.  I love what I see when I look at you, Lindy!  Everything about you is precious.  Everything."

# CHAPTER 24

Sergeant Will Walker received two phone calls, one right after the other, as soon as he opened the front door of the AST headquarters. Tossing his keys on his desk, a mixture of relief and disappointment pierced his senses.

Thankful he had hired Officer Brandon Hughes full-time, Will needed him today if this morning's calls were any indication of how things were headed. True to his usual punctuality, Hughes set the brass bell to jangling as he entered the office.

"Morning, Sergeant." Hughes sniffed the air. "Uh-oh. Something's wrong. I don't smell your usual witch's brew simmering. Are you sick?" Hughes chuckled to himself.

"No, Smarty. If you are referring to my morning coffee, I haven't had a chance to start the pot. I got two phone calls before my rear end could hit the desk chair. Let me just say that I am so glad that you decided to work for this headquarters." Will paused, shaking his head.

"Want to tell me about the calls? You seem disturbed." Hughes propped his hip on the desk's edge and gave Will his attention.

Getting the coffee grounds and percolator, Will began his story. "Well, the first call was from a panicked Liza. You remember, Rita's daughter? Sounds like Rita took off during the night and left a bunch of letters on the dining table including one for Liza. She wants me to come get the others and deliver them and give me the details of her mother's disappearance. It is definitely Rita's own doing; she wasn't abducted like Berta. Liza said she needed to talk to me in person, so I am headed there in a bit. Strange. I could never have guessed the woman would have ever taken off like that.....anyway, the other phone call was about Dorne. Long story short, he was spotted and arrested in Oregon. A patrolman on the run and a guardian and mother to ten girls has flown the coop. Strange world, Hughes, strange."

"Agreed. I'll stay here at the office while you go see what's happened with Rita."

Pouring his first cup of coffee and adding heaps of sugar to the black liquid, Will slurped it down and left to meet the hysterical girl who had phoned earlier.


Liza paced like a caged animal, auburn hair standing out in all directions. Looking out the window every few seconds, the other girls were afraid she would wear the curtains out. Finally, the AST patrol car appeared signaling tears to gather afresh in Liza's eyes.

Running to the door, the frantic girl flung it open before Sergeant Will Walker had a chance to place his boot on the bottom step of the porch. It took everything in Liza not to grab him and haul him the rest of the way in the door.

Will entered the kitchen and took in the solemn faces in the room. The scenario was oddly familiar from several months ago when he had first entered *Rita's Place* to investigate Berta's disappearance.

*God, help these girls,* Will breathed.

"Good morning, ladies. I understand you wanted to see me." Will touched the brim of his sergeant's hat.

Liza jumped right in. "Sergeant, thanks for coming so quickly. I don't really know what is going on. All I know is Momma left....she just left us." Her voice cracked with emotion. Liza motioned for the

Sergeant to take a seat at the dining table while the girls stood in groups about the kitchen so they could listen in.

"Can I get you some coffee?"

"No, I just had some. But thanks. Tell me what happened."

"Something woke me earlier than usual this morning, a wolf howling? I don't know....anyway, I couldn't go back to sleep so I came to the kitchen around 5 a.m. and put the kettle on for tea. The girls were still asleep so I was alone.....I fixed my tea and sat down at the table and noticed these." Liza shoved the stack of letters at Will.

Looking at the top much bulkier one, he saw it was addressed to *Liza Ann Holbrook* and she had already opened it. Written on the outside of the flatter sealed envelope of the second letter were the words *Pastor Stan and Elaine Hudson.* And on the last sealed one, Will blinked twice before registering the name on the third.

*Sergeant Walker.*

Will looked up at Liza and around the room of faces. He was stunned at the three envelopes.

"Liza, I don't understand. Why would your mother run off and leave these three letters? One to the Hudsons and one to me?" Will shifted again in his seat and rifled through the envelopes again.

"That's why I called you, Sergeant."

Laughing at how ridiculous his comment must have sounded, Will said, "Of course. I am just surprised. Can you tell me what was in your letter, Liza?"

Without speaking, the girl handed her letter to Will.

He took the envelope from her shaking hands, removed the folded paper and its contents, then read aloud.

"My Dear Girl,

I know this will all seem so confusing to you, but before I write anything, let me say this. What I am doing is what I believe will be for the best. For you and the girls and for me.

Liza, I have spent my life regretting my choices. The only one I have never regretted was keeping you when you were born. My own mother suggested I let another couple adopt and raise you because she knew it would be very difficult to raise a baby and live the life I was in. She had done the same with me. Raised a baby in a harlot's house. Not the best place, but still I couldn't bring myself to give you up. I thank the stars above that I kept you, my ray of sunshine in this dark world.

With that said, you know the rest of the story. Our story. So I won't rehash the past. You lived it with me. Every second of every day the last twenty years. I do have one regret. I never pushed you to leave the life your mother and grandmother before you lived. I was selfish and wanted you with me, no matter what. And it cost you dearly.

Years ago, I ran away once and now I am doing it again only the first time I ran away from the past. This time I am running to the future. For me, you, and the girls.

The day I ran away the first time, my mother gave me a little green book the moment before I left. She said she could see in my eyes for days that I was going to leave her. I am leaving the same book with you. Inside you will find a few pictures and quotes my mother liked. There is also a key and some money. Mother left me a $20 bill the day I left so I guess I couldn't help myself. I taped a twenty to the very same page she attached my bill. But in reality I leave you with so much more. On the page after the bill you will find a key taped to it. This key opens a metal box that is under my bed in the far corner. I have saved as much money as I could over the years from my work for you and the girls. It has always been my hope to better the place, to make it nicer. I am leaving a large amount and expect you to talk to Sergeant Will and Pastor Hudson after they have read their letters. There are specific instructions in each letter that I hope everyone will honor. This is probably the biggest risk of my life, but a necessary one.

Liza, I know you don't understand right now, but I hope one day you will, when your life and the girls' lives are different. This is your chance. Their chance to be better, do better. Please take it. If I didn't leave, I am certain, as well as I know that my hair is red, that you and the girls wouldn't have listened to me. I had to leave to make things better.

So I leave you with this quote from the little green book.

"Change the past. Change the future."

That's what I am doing, Liza. I am changing and redirecting the past so you all will have a better, different future. Know that I am in a safe place. I found a dear old aunt in Canada and I am going to her. I've always wanted to go to Canada. Please let me go for now. For your sake. For all my girls.

Love,

Momma"


Fighting tears of his own, Will sniffed loudly as he folded the letter and returned it to the envelope. Picking up the velvety green worn book, he looked at Liza, "May I?"

"Of course." She wiped at the tears on her face.

Thumbing through the aged pages, Will got the answers to some of his questions and suspicions from the yellowed photographs and the faces that stared back at him. A sense of awareness dawned afresh in him. How could he have judged someone so quickly when he didn't have all the facts and details of their past? How could he have jumped to conclusions so easily? Yes, Rita was a prostitute, and yes, Liza was too. And most likely, the majority if not all of the girls at *Rita's Place* were the same. But life had led Rita and then Liza to this place, this choice. What if someone, anyone willing, had stepped into their shattered worlds and offered them hope, a job, another choice? What if.....Arresting his thoughts, Will reached for the other two envelopes.

"Sergeant Will, what do you make of this? I just don't understand." Liza could hear some of the girls whispering behind her as they were taking in the contents of Rita's letter that had just spilled off the Sergeant's lips.

Sitting a moment in silence, Will finally spoke, "Sounds like your Momma wants something better for you, Liza. And for the girls." He cast a glance around the room and saw some of them fighting tears and others dealing with deep emotions, from fear to anger to confusion. He couldn't blame them. Sadly their world just fell apart right at their feet.

But he was determined to be that someone. The one who offered hope and help instead of judgment and lack of concern. He could do that for these scattered women. He and a group of others he knew that were willing. That was all it took. A willingness.

"Liza, I know right now it is difficult to see Rita's heart in her actions. You see abandonment; she sees support. You see loss; she sees gain. You see pain; she sees love. Make sense? The decision she made to leave you and the girls is, in her eyes, the very thing that will make your lives better…..and I personally think she needed to start over herself."

Liza wiped at the fresh tears on her face. "Thank you, Sergeant Will. I hope I can see what you mean one day. I do know that Momma wouldn't have hurt me or any of us for anything in this world. She had to have done this for our good." Pausing to blow her nose, Liza continued, "Now will you read your letter and see if it holds any further clues? Maybe help us understand more?"

"Yes. I will do that." Will slid his finger under the flap of the envelope and removed the short letter. Quickly he scanned the few paragraphs and then reread it aloud.

*"Dear Sergeant Walker,*

*I know this must come as a complete surprise to you. A letter from me. Please hear me out and think about what I am about to say as it will affect the girls I love dearly. I know it will also surprise you to hear me ask for help. But I need it.*

*I want my girls safe. I want them living different lives. I want them to have something I never had, hope. You can play a part in this for me. You must do all you can to keep them safe while things change and future decisions are made. I am not there to do this anymore. And I know that my ways weren't always the best or the safest. But when the girls were with me I knew they had food, a warm house, clothes, and each other. I could do that for them. But all of it was not done under the best of circumstances. And that's what I want for them now. For things to change while they still can.*

*So please, help me by keeping them safe. You have done so much for me and the girls already. And I still have hopes that you will find Berta so there can be closure and peace.*

*Thank you again for taking care of repairing a house for a woman so undeserving, yet so grateful. I can never repay you. And here I am asking for a bigger favor.*

*Please give the Hudsons their letter for me. It is very important! Please do this as soon as possible. I know they will understand what I am asking and will honor my requests. With you watching over the girls and the Hudsons helping with their future, I know they will be on the right road to better days.*

*Rita"*


They all sat silently and absorbed the few words. Not bringing much clarity except that he needed to deliver the letter to Pastor Stan, Will looked around the room full of frowns and sadness. "I will get this letter delivered straight to Datka today and to the Pastor. Girls, I promise to get back with you tomorrow. In the meantime, take a day off, rest, and call the office if you need anything. Officer Hughes and I will be there today and will come right over if you need us. Understand?"

Solemn nods went around the room.

A small voice spoke from across the room. The owner of it had constrained herself as long as she had been able to. With the news of Rita gone, another shockwave had rippled through the girls' home and made her momentarily forget what was constantly in her pocket. Plunging a shaking hand in her skirt's pocket, Ana moved towards the Sergeant. "Sergeant Walker."

278

Looking in her direction, Will knew the girl was Berta's sister. Sadness swallowed him because he had no answer for her.

Holding out something in his direction, Will stepped towards the girl. "What do you have, Ana?"

Laughing mirthlessly at the irony, she said, "Another letter. Except this one is from—from Berta, my sister."

Hope swelled in his chest. "What? From Berta? When did you get this?"

All the girls began talking at once. "We tried to get her to call you….she was too afraid….Ana just got it…..had it for a week!"

Holding up his hands, Will looked at Ana.

"It was delivered to me a week ago. It's from my sister. She's alive—" Ana's voice broke.

Will removed and read the letter from the missing girl. "This is good news! We know she's alive. Can I take this with me? Who delivered this to you?"

Hesitating, Ana finally answered. "Yes, you can only if I can get it back. It's very special to me."

"Of course, but maybe it will yield some clue."

Gathering her courage, Ana said, "An Aleut man, his name is Markus. I know him. He was a….a friend. Berta gave it to him after she escaped from a shed she was held in and he brought it to me last week. Markus said he had the letter for almost a month before bringing it."

Liza followed the Sergeant to the door. "Thank you, Sergeant Walker, for coming. I appreciate you delivering this other letter. I just don't know what she's thinking. Running away? How will that help us? It makes no sense."

"Liza, I promise you will have answers very soon."

Stepping off the porch, Will was struck by the fact that this was something he never thought he would encounter as an AST sergeant. Protecting and doing his part to insure the safety and well-being of a rag-tag group of girls loved dearly by one red-headed prostitute.

He now had to hire a boat and deliveryman to get the letter to the Hudsons on Datka. Today couldn't possibly hold any more interesting turns of events.

*******************

Like the waters swirling around the boatman's oars, thoughts swirled through Pastor Stan Hudson's mind. The last four hours brought many discussions and prompted this quick little trip to Seal Harbor. He needed a telephone and he needed one fast. Feeling an urgency, Stan left immediately after receiving the delivered letter from Rita and reading and discussing it with Elaine. At the last second, Stan asked Ed to go with him. Maybe this would give Stan the time on the boat he needed to have a chat with the young man who had caught more than his daughter's eye.

Ed was caught off guard by the Pastor's invitation to join him on the trip to Seal Harbor. His mind was running away with him as he tried to figure out the *why* of the impromptu request. Before Ed could ponder on it another minute, Stan was speaking.

"Ed, I am not good at beating around the bush....Elaine will vouch for that. So here it is. I need to know what your intentions are with my daughter."

Butterflies began somersaulting their way around Ed's stomach. He opened his mouth to speak but no words formed quickly.

Stan continued. "You know how much Elaine and I love our Lindy. And of course it would make sense that we care about her future and the man who might be interested in her as more than a friend. But mostly, Ed.....she's strong, yet very delicate. Lindy is fearless, yet timid. She's brave, yet needs protecting." Stan reached a hand to wipe the moisture that gathered near the edges of his eyes.

"Sir, the things you just stated about Lindy, those are the very reasons I am drawn to her, other than the fact that she loves God with all her heart. But I understand. I do see her as delicate and timid and in need of protection. So to answer your question, my intentions are hopefully, with your permission, to be that man, the one, to love her and look after her and be the godly husband she needs. I don't beat around the bush well either. So here it is. I love Lindy. I really do. And I think she might love me too. Whew! That was a mouthful! Sorry if I caught you off guard. I didn't ease into that very well, did I?" Now that Ed had admitted the truth in his heart, aloud, to Lindy's father, he felt the world lift off of his broad shoulders, but the butterflies were still tumbling on the inside.

A huge smile slowly spread across Pastor Stan's face. The man remained silent too long for Ed's comfort.

"Okay, Sir, say something. You're making me nervous. I just bared my heart in this tiny boat in the middle of the ocean and you are sitting there in silence." Ed raked a hand through his hair, waiting.

A deep laugh began in Stan's throat and spilled out loud and strong.

Ed emitted a nervous laugh of his own. *What is going on in his head?*

"Ed, I'm sorry, but I am just relieved, happy, astonished.....God is so good—" Stan paused as he choked up. Regaining his composure, he began again. "Elaine and I have prayed for a man like you to love our girl. And here you are, an answer to our prayers. I really didn't expect you to be so quick about confessing your heart like that. But now, neither of us have to worry. We both know where the other stands with Lindy. And that's a good thing. A very good thing."

Now it was Ed's turn to laugh, a sound of joy and relief blended together. "Yes. Yes it is, Sir."

"One thing, Ed. Stop calling me *Sir.*"

Holding his hands up in surrender, Ed replied, "Yes, Sir. Sorry, Sir. I can't help it....it's my Texas upbringing. But I will work on it, S— Stan."

"Another question. How do you see your future playing out? What about work or where will you live? What are your expectations over the next six months?"

"That's easy. AMRA offered me a job when I went to Fairbanks not long ago. They want me to live in Seal Harbor as my headquarters, so to speak, and continue my work on Datka. There will be future opportunities for mission work. I accepted the job on a six month trial basis and then AMRA and I will reevaluate the position and go from there. If it doesn't work out, which I truly believe it will, then I still have a position in Washington at the school I worked at before coming here. My hope is to stay in Alaska and do God's work. So Seal Harbor will be home for a while and mission work will be my vocation."

"Does Lindy know all of this?"

"No, she doesn't. We haven't really talked about my Fairbanks trip, haven't had the chance. I do know that both of us love mission work and both of us want to serve God in whatever capacity that involves. The only variable is that we haven't discussed putting our two dreams together. Not that I haven't prayed and thought and prayed some more about it."

"That's good to know. I like a man who prays."

"So.....I have your permission to pursue your daughter, Sir?" Not realizing he just called Pastor Stan the forbidden name again, Ed waited and held his breath for the answer.

"If and only if you remove *sir* from your vocabulary when you address me." Slapping Ed on the shoulder, Stan laughed at Ed's face. "Yes, Ed, I would consider it an honor for you to pursue my Lindy. You are a man worthy of that endeavor."

Ducking his head at the great compliment, Ed could only smile to himself at God's goodness, no, His *greatness*, in his life. It was almost too much to take in.

# CHAPTER 25

Reaching Seal Harbor, Stan set up a meeting time with Ed for when they would be taken back by boat to the Island. Heading straight for the AST office, Stan's hands were itching to make a phone call. After talking with Elaine, they both decided that it was urgent that he act now on the letter from Rita. Snatches of the letter buzzed in his mind as he took the ten minute walk to the AST office.

*I know Elaine will understand what I mean when I say it is time I change the past so the future can change. For me. For my girls.*

*My leaving will force them onto a better path, but only if you help. I fear for their future if you choose not to do as I request. My asking is very brazen or brave, whichever way you look at it.*

Stan chuckled to himself at that statement. A woman of her reputation worried about being brazen? In his mind, she was brave, so very brave. Leaving those you love for their betterment was the biggest sacrifice he could think of, other than giving your life for them. This had to be costing Rita's heart dearly.

Determination to help however God revealed quickened his steps. Stan continued to go over the letter mentally. Elaine explained to him what some of Rita's references in the letter meant based on her time with Rita the day of the work on *Rita's Place.* It all made sense to him. A desperate woman in desperate times wanted more and better for those she loved, and he had the power and means to help.

*When Elaine asked me what I saw in the girls' future, I guess you could say I had a wake-up call. Their future looked just as desolate and hopeless as mine had been. So if what Elaine said, that a hope and a future does exist for them, then please give it to my girls......*

*.....My hope is that you will find someone to look after them and turn things around for the girls. Lead them down a different path than I have led them. They need you. They need someone good and true in their lives. You can help me by helping them. Please.*

As the end of the letter went through Stan's mind, he placed a hand on the door knob of the office and burst through the door. Without much of a hello, he rushed to the Sergeant's desk. "Can I use your phone? It's important, Sergeant....Sorry, how are you doing? I didn't mean to be rude. My mind is spinning its wheels so fast I can't keep up."

Will Walker laughed at his new friend's urgency. "I take it you read the letter from Rita?"

"Yes, and I need your phone. If that's okay."

"Be my guest. I'll leave you to your phone call. Think I'll make a run to the diner. Want anything?" Will watched Stan as he stuck his finger in the number holes to dial someone. The man was obviously on a mission and didn't respond to Will's question. "Make sure the office doesn't burn down while I'm gone."

Stan listened intently as the other line rang. Finally he heard someone answer.

"AMRA, this is John Miller."

"John! Just the one I wanted. This is Stan. Got a minute?"

"Hey, man! How's Datka? I'm surprised to hear from you." John settled into his desk chair.

"Datka's great! I am so grateful for this job and the people. But that's not why I called. I have a problem."

As Pastor Stan launched into the story involving Rita and the girls, the other end of the line remained silent with an occasional question or comment from John. The head of the mission board gave his full attention to the problem at hand and prayed for a resolution as he listened.

Finally when Stan came up for air, John said, "You won't believe this but just last week I received a call from some long time missionaries. You have never met them but they are Gabriel Parker's parents, Randall and Rebecca. Rand called to say that he had decided to retire this past school year. He and his wife are both teachers and Rand said he had an overwhelming sense that his time was up. Becca learned that the school district voted to close down the elementary school she teaches in but she still had a job only it was across town. She wasn't happy about the drive and was toying with what to do. Rand said the two of them wanted to remain active as missionaries especially since their son was tied to AMRA. They just didn't know in what capacity, but Randall felt like he needed to call AMRA and tell me they would like to be considered for any opportunities. While you were talking, I kept thinking about my conversation with Rand and that they might be just the right fit for *Rita's Place*." John proceeded to give Stan some background information on the older couple.

After talking another twenty minutes, Stan hung up the phone with a satisfied sigh. Will entered the office just as he was ending the call.

"You look much less stressed than when you got here, Stan."

Heaving a relieved laugh, Stan replied, "Yes. I am! Have a seat and I will fill you in."

While Pastor Stan and Sergeant Walker put their heads together over Rita and the girls, another young man was working on his own schemes. Ed Hamilton entered Seal Harbor's finest restaurant, *Aurora's*.

So far the front door answered Ed's first question. He needed to know the hours of this place, especially for Sunday. *Yes! They're closed on Sundays*, Ed inwardly rejoiced. Several hours before the Friday dinner crowd, Ed found the place mostly empty except for a few workers.

"Can I help you?" A middle-aged lady dressed in a beautiful, simple knee-length gown approached Ed.

"Yes, ma'am," Ed drawled. "I have a little plan in mind and I hope you can lead me to the person who will help me make it happen."

"Well, sir, what does this little plan involve?"

A broad smile spread over Ed's handsome face. "Me, a girl, and love."

"I'm all ears. Follow me." The beaming, pretty lady led Ed to a quiet table so the two could talk and scheme.

*******************

Liza stared open-mouthed at Pastor Stan and Sergeant Will. She was having a difficult time wrapping her mind around the turn of events in the past few days. Blinking her eyes at them both, she just shook her head, no words forming in her mouth. The rest of the girls stood around the kitchen with nothing to say either.

Pastor Stan spoke again. "Liza, I know this is a lot to digest, but I don't think your mother has made a bad decision. I do understand why you and the others are upset and disturbed by it. It would shake up anyone's world if their mother or guardian left unexpectedly. Rita

288

has done this with the intent that you all would have a life she never had. A chance at something better. Do you understand?"

Finally she found the words. "Yes, I understand the *why* behind her actions. I am just surprised that she would leave. She loved this place and me and the girls. At least I thought so. Momma always gave everything she could for us but we had to work hard and help out too. She always said nothing in life is ever free." Liza jumped up from her chair. "I have to show you something."

A moment later she returned with a metal box in hand and a green book. Sitting at the table, Liza turned to a page in the book and removed a key. Placing the key in the lock on the metal box, Liza turned it until they all heard the tiny click. Before opening the box, she said, "Momma left instructions in the letter for me that there would be a box and that I was to talk to you about the money she left. Honestly every fiber of my being wanted to take all of the money and run and go look for her, but I can't. I won't go against her wishes and I can't leave my friends with nothing. This money is all of ours, not just mine. It is for *our* future, not mine alone. I am just so confused."

Easing the lid open on the box, the men gasped as they took in its contents. The girls sucked in deep breaths of exclamation as they peered over Liza's shoulder. "Can you believe all of this money? Momma must have saved every dollar she earned and then some of our money too." Her voice broke as the realization hit her afresh.

Jocelyn spoke first among the girls. "Liza, it's going to be okay. We will figure this out. I promise you we will."

Next Felicity was at Liza's side handing her a handkerchief for her tears. "Don't cry. We still have each other. And it's time we all got our heads together and made something of this place. Something better. Since Berta's disappearance, you know as well as I do things have been different. Our patrons have even dwindled down. There are too many stories and too much gossip. I think everyone in town is afraid to get within a hundred feet of the place. Afraid they will be considered a suspect or afraid the law will see them here. No offense, Sergeant Walker."

"None taken. Rita asked me to look after you girls until things get situated and you know what the future holds. See, that's just it. Rita's point to all of this is your future. Now it's up to you all to decide what that will look like. You can carry on with things as usual or you can listen to Pastor Stan's plan." Sergeant Walker looked around the small room of girls. Some fidgeted with their collars or cuffs while others looked at him with expectation in their frightened eyes.

Milly spoke next. "My plan is to take the next bus out of this town and start over somewhere else. I've had my share of Seal Harbor's disappointments and hard work and heartache. Anyone with me?"

Ever the peacemaker, Emily implored, "Milly, you just can't leave us. We are all family."

"I'm sorry girls, but I have to think about myself too. Count me out of your little plans. So nobody's willing to go with me?" Milly asked.

No one responded to Milly's request. It looked to Sergeant Will that Milly would be on her own. "Milly, you don't have to leave. We have a plan."

"Just not my kind of plan, Sergeant."

Will knew there was nothing more to say to the girl. He watched as she quietly left the group and headed upstairs. He and

Stan had to work to convince the rest to join the scheme, to do what Rita would want.

"Ladies, I want you to consider that the decision you make, to stay or go, is yours to make. No one will force you to do anything. Just know that what you decide will have an impact on everyone in this room."

Stan picked up where Will left off. "I have a friend that I called about this situation. He has asked an older couple if they would be willing to come to Seal Harbor and help us help you open a restaurant. It would support you all, it would give you employment, it would pay the bills, and most importantly, it will give you all a future and honor Miss Rita's wish. With so many of you living here, you won't have to hire anyone else and the work load will be easy with this number of people. We can also offer housing and jobs for young girls off the streets who have stories much like your own that *need* a family, need a home. Like Miss Rita did for you all."

Pastor Stan could see he had reached the girls with his words. A few had tears on their cheeks while some had a hopeful faraway look in their eyes. Hope. That was what they needed instilled in their lives.

"What do you say, girls? I am willing to try it if you are." Liza looked around the room at her friends and family.

A chorus of *yes*'s and *okay*'s went around the room, some spoken timidly, some with a hint of gusto. Hope always did that to a person, it gave you a reason to live, a reason to carry on. Stan prayed the girls would feel this purpose and reason to live and move toward a promising future.

Now he needed to make one more phone call.

He needed to hear Randall Parker add his final *yes* to this group of lonely, desperate girls.

********************

"Okay, Rand. Fill me in. This sounds good." Becca beamed after her husband had hung up the phone, anticipation written all over her face.

Placing both hands on Becca's shoulders, Rand kissed her squarely on the lips. "Seems like not too long ago we were both wondering what God had up His sleeve for us two fifty-somethings." Rand took her by the hand and led Becca out to their patio that overlooked the mountains. Opening the door for both of them, they sat in two matching lounge chairs and took in the scene.

Playfully Becca shoved Rand's shoulder. "I'm waiting."

"I'm sorry, honey. I'm still trying to take it all in. I think you heard most of the conversation with John Miller. Basically in the matter of a few hours we have been chosen to move to Seal Harbor and take over a group of misfit girls and help them open a restaurant. The details are very interesting, though." Rand continued telling Becca about the background of Rita, her girls and *Rita's Place.*

Becca sat silently after he finished talking. Finally, she turned to Rand and said, "Well, we wanted to be near our son and his future bride, but whoever thought a prostitute and a group of hopeless girls would ever have made that happen?"

Laughter full of purpose and joy poured from both of them. Becca and Rand took a moment to join hands and thank God for giving Rand the urgency to retire and for making her unsettled in her job.

292

God's leading was always an adventure and they were both ready for a new one.

# CHAPTER 26

Lindy held tightly to the sides of the small watercraft that was taking her on a mysterious date with the man beside her. All Ed would tell her was she needed to 'dress up' and 'trust him.' So that's exactly what Lindy was doing and enjoying every moment of it.

Ed wore an uncontainable goofy smirk on his face, which made him all the more adorable to her. "So when will you give me another clue?"

"Beautiful, don't you worry your pretty self at all about today's plans. I have it all figured out. Remember, trust me."

"I find that easier and easier to do every day I am around you, Ed."

The remainder of the boat ride, Ed watched the woman of his dreams seated across from him. Gratitude overwhelmed him the closer they reached Seal Harbor. He knew this was the right decision.

Feeling the rough bump of boat against deck, the boatman tied them off as Ed helped Lindy out of the craft. Looking down at her feet, he started laughing. "Um....since we are in town, you may want to head over to this bench and take your boots off and put on your dressier shoes."

Lifting her chin, Lindy spoke in a teasing manner, "So you don't like Aleut boots with a dress? You just don't understand fashion, Sir." Looking down at her pretty dress she had worn to the wedding, Lindy laughed at the oversized boots peeking out from beneath. "I think I will take your advice." Stepping over to a nearby bench, Lindy withdrew a dainty pair of shoes from her bag. Holding up a booted foot, she looked at Ed, "Excuse me, Charming, but Cinderella needs help with her slippers."

Dramatically kneeling down in front of Lindy, Ed pulled her boots off and placed the dress shoes on her feet. "Better?" he asked and stood giving Lindy a deep bow from the waist. Ed picked up her boots and shoved them in a large canvas bag that he brought.

"I really like my boots, but it's nice to wear normal shoes again." Taking his arm, Lindy said, "Okay, now on to our adventure."

Leading her down the nearly empty streets of Seal Harbor, Lindy remarked, "The town looks deserted. What did you do, run everyone off?"

"It is a Sunday afternoon, so everything's closed today, remember?"

She followed Ed down another block and they turned the corner onto Main Street. Nearing *Aurora's,* Lindy looked up, startled to see candles gleaming in the restaurant's windows and lights on inside. "I guess they stay open on Sundays."

Taking her arm, Ed replied, "Well, let's go inside and see."

"Ed, that's *Aurora's.* You know how pricey that place is. We can't go there. Anyway, they are probably closed too."

"Let's go see." Taking Lindy by the hand, Ed pulled her into the door. Before Lindy could speak, much less look around the room, a woman wearing a midnight blue, knee-length gown approached them.

Holding out her hands, she reached for Ed. "Edward.....so good to see you. This must be Lindy. Welcome, young lady. I hope you enjoy your time at *Aurora's.* I have a table prepared for you two. "

"Thank you, Mrs. Aurora. This is perfect." Ed glanced back at his speechless Lindy. Pulling out the chair for her, he guided Lindy into the seat.

As Mrs. Aurora left them alone for a moment, Lindy finally spoke, "Ed.....what on earth? No one else is here! What have you done?" A beautiful mixture of confusion and delight crossed her pretty face. Lindy reached an unconscious hand to the scar on her face and covered it discreetly.

Reaching for both her hands, Ed said, "Well, Beautiful, I guess the secret's out of the bag. You and I have the whole place to ourselves. Let's just say I used some of my charm and convinced Mrs. Aurora to open up for a couple who hardly get any time alone together. Surprised?"

"I'm glad I chose this dress and shoes! Oh, Ed....I am still speechless. This is incredible! Candlelight, dinner, me and you...."

"Speechless? Sounds like you have plenty of words to me. Lindy, have I told you lately how beautiful you are? You look so pretty today. You make the room light up."

"Silly, it's the candles everywhere." Looking around the room, Lindy noticed the soft music playing and the delicious scents coming from the restaurant's kitchen. It was perfect, something she never would have dreamed up nor expected Ed to be able to pull off.

Mrs. Aurora reappeared and brought them glasses of water. From somewhere, she produced a vase of deep red roses. "Shall we proceed as planned, Edward?"

"Yes, ma'am. We are ready when you are." Ed gave the woman a quick wink, pleased that all was going according to his wishes.

"You planned all this for me? Ed, you are wonderful! I have never been treated so special before." Ed reached for the card tucked in the beautiful roses and handed it to Lindy.

Opening the card, she read his manly scrawl. *"May today be only the beginning of further adventures with you."* It was signed *"Charming."*

Tears sprang to Lindy's eyes, "Oh, Ed." The meaning of those words settled in around Lindy bringing a sense of security and an overwhelming rush of joy.

Two plates of salad and a loaf of crusty, hot bread appeared at their elbows. Aurora simply said, "Enjoy. Lasagna will be served shortly."

"What? Lasagna? How did you know that is my favorite meal?" Shock was written all over her face as Lindy wondered what other surprises the day held.

"Okay, I confess. I asked your Mom."

Dawning crossed Lindy's expression. "Mom and Dad know about today?"

"Only some of it. I left a few details out." Clearly Ed was enjoying every minute of the surprise he had planned for her. "Now eat your salad and bread."

Soft laughter escaped her throat before she began her salad. "This is so far the best day of my life. Thank you, Ed." Reaching a hand for his, Lindy gave it a gentle squeeze.

The two ate in contented silence, enjoying the beginnings of their meal and the soft music. After the salad plates were cleared, Mrs. Aurora asked if they were ready for the lasagna.

"Give us a bit. I hear some music calling our names."

298

"Whatever you wish, Edward." Aurora left the two alone again.

Ed rose from his seat and took Lindy's hand. "Will you do me the honor and dance with me?"

The faint blush that Ed had grown to love tinted Lindy's cheeks, making her all the more beautiful to him. "I'd love to."

For the next thirty minutes, Ed and Lindy swayed to love songs, ballads, and violin-laced instrumentals completely forgetting the world outside the two doors they had entered earlier. No one else was even on the planet as far as they were concerned. Dancing tentatively at first, Ed and Lindy quickly matched their steps and bodies to each other. The two were soon moving across the quiet carpet like they had danced together for years.

Looking deeply in Lindy's eyes, Ed whispered, "I have wanted to do this for a while now, Beautiful."

"What? Dance with me?" Lindy whispered back.

"No. This." Ed lowered his lips to Lindy's and placed a gentle, sweet kiss on her lips. "Is that okay with you?"

Without an answer, Lindy lifted her face to Ed's, inviting him to kiss her again.

And he did without hesitation.

"Wow! Our lasagna is going to get cold if we keep this up."

"What lasagna?" Lindy playfully kissed him once more. She took Ed's hand and they both returned to the candlelit table.

Quickly, Aurora brought out plates of steaming food and refilled their glasses. Smiling contentedly, she replied, "You two love birds let me know if you need anything."

Blushing furiously both Ed and Lindy looked at each other and smiled sheepishly.

Lindy tasted her food. "Finest lasagna in the world! This is now officially the best day of my life, Ed!"

"What? Is the lasagna that good?" he teased.

"I'm not talking about the food." Lindy shyly ducked her head before continuing. "I'm talking about you. Us. I am so blessed." Overcome with thankfulness, she could hardly continue.

"So am I. I never in my wildest dreams imagined a girl like you in my life."

Somehow the couple finished their lasagna as the candles continued to melt around them. Time seemed to stand still for them. Eventually, Mrs. Aurora cleared their plates and asked if they were ready for dessert.

"Would it be okay if we took a short walk first?" Ed waited for Lindy's response.

"Sounds great."

"Take your time, you two. I will keep dessert waiting."

Ed and Lindy rose from the table and went out into the gathering dark. With the streets deserted, the couple felt as if they had the town all to themselves. A gathering of trees with a bench nestled underneath caught their attention. Ed could hardly contain himself as a deep reality seeped into his bones. He loved Lindy and Lindy loved him.

Without a doubt.

Turning sideways to face Ed, Lindy settled herself on the bench and tucked her feet under her dress. She didn't even try to stop smiling. It would be impossible even if she wanted to.

"What are you thinking?" Ed asked as he intertwined his fingers with Lindy's.

"I guess I need someone to pinch me to let me know I am not dreaming."

Quickly giving her cheek a gentle pinch before she could slap him away, Ed asked, "Did that work? It's real, Lindy. Neither one of us are dreaming." Unable to wait another second, Ed stood from the bench, turned and faced the woman he loved, and got down on one knee in front of Lindy.

Inhaling deeply, Lindy's hand flew to her mouth.

"Lindy Jane Hudson, I have looked high and low, from Texas to Alaska, for the woman to spend my life with. And I finally found her. It's you. Like my card said in the roses, I want future adventures with you. Not just as my friend, but as my wife. Lindy, you're it! You're the one I choose. Will you choose me in return?" Ed reached into his pocket and withdrew a tiny velvet box.

Tears ran in rivers down Lindy's face. Her hands flew to wipe them away. Before Ed could even show her a ring, Lindy nearly knocked him over with her excitement. "Ed! I can't believe this is happening! Yes! Yes! Yes! I want to have adventures with you, as your wife!"

Ed stood to his feet and stuffed the little box back in his pocket. Picking Lindy up off her feet, he twirled her until they both were laughing. Setting her back down, Ed said, "I wasn't sure, but was that a 'yes' or do you need to think about it some more?"

"Oh, Ed! I love your humor and I love you! Absolutely without a doubt, yes! Now can I see what's in the little box?"

"What box? Oh, this one!" Ed teased her mercilessly. "I was hoping I could get my money back since you didn't seem interested."

"Stop it!"

"Okay, sit back down and let's try this again." Lindy sat and Ed kneeled a second time. "I am probably the only man on earth who had to propose twice in one day."

"Go on." Lindy could tease him just as easily as he teased with her.

Love shined so deeply in Ed's eyes that Lindy thought she would drown in their depths. "Lindy, will you be my wife? Ready to go where God leads, do what He says do? With me, forever?'

Fresh tears appeared in her eyes, but she remained quiet.

Ed retrieved the velvet box a second time. Slowly he opened it and turned it to Lindy. Inside was a white gold band, delicate like his woman. A square-cut diamond winked back at her surrounded by three tiny stones on each side. Unable to catch her breath, Lindy looked back at Ed. "This is exquisite! I don't deserve something so beautiful."

"Don't ever let me hear you say that again. Lindy, you deserve everything beautiful and good and true in this world.....do you like it or should I return it?"

Her senses returning, Lindy reached for the beautiful ring. Ed took her hand and placed it on her finger then kissed the ring. "Never forget that you are more beautiful to me than these precious stones. I love you, Lindy.

"And I love you, Ed. Yes, this is *definitely* the best day of my life!"

For another few minutes, the lovebirds lingered. Finally, Ed said, "Dessert's waiting and I know for a fact that Mrs. Aurora is too. She can't wait to see the ring on your finger."

Lindy stood and grabbed Ed's left hand with her right so she could admire her ring as they walked back to the restaurant. "I hope this is all you have planned after dessert because I may die from sheer joy if there's more."

"After dessert, that's it. We have to head back to the Island soon before it gets dark."

"I can't wait to show Mom and Dad! And Rose and Luka....."

Nudging her playfully, Ed said, "So what do you think about a double wedding? Me and you, Gabe and Rose?"

Stopping in her tracks, Ed turned as Lindy threw her arms around his neck. "That would be wonderful!"

He planted one more kiss on her lips as the two entered the restaurant where their day's adventure had begun, hand in hand, head over heels in love.

# CHAPTER 27

As soon as the newly engaged couple returned to the Island they sought out their friends, Gabe and Rose. Since Gabe's return to Datka, the two were nearly inseparable so it was easy to find them both in their usual spot. After getting off the boat, Ed and Lindy took the path to the village and found Gabe and Rose on their special boulder, hands linked and talking quietly, heads bent low.

Startled out of their moment, Ed thundered, "She said *yes!*"

Lindy erupted into a fit of laughter as she held up her hand and showed them her engagement ring. Both couples hugged and congratulated each other with shared, heart-felt joy.

"So when have you two planned to marry? I haven't heard a day yet."

Rose looked at the ground shyly then back at Lindy.

"Well…..we were just talking about that before you two arrived. We really want to marry soon. Gabe's job is awaiting him and we have been apart so long, we both have agreed the sooner the better."

Gabe placed an arm around Rose's shoulder and looked at her intently, "I have been away from her for too long, I don't plan on waiting much longer for a wedding. We are ready to start our lives together."

Ed looked at Lindy and beamed. "Sounds like we all have had the same conversation. Lindy and I know we met such a short time ago, but I have already spoken with Pastor Stan about my feelings for his daughter. We want to marry immediately, mainly because neither of us see any reason to wait and things are different here on the Island. Our belief that God wants the two of us together serving Him and the fact that my job is also waiting for me is helping the two of us make a decision on when to marry. So.....we have a suggestion. How about we talk Pastor Stan into marrying the four of us at the same time?"

Lindy couldn't contain her joy another second. She began bouncing up and down and squealing like a schoolgirl. "What do you think, Rose? A double wedding ceremony? Nothing at all fancy, just the men we love and our families present? That's all I need and want!"

Rose looked at Gabe. "Gabriel?"

Scooping her up in his arms, Gabe hooted and laughed as he twirled her around. "Sounds like a plan to me! What more do we need but the girls, Ed?"

"Then I guess we should go have a chat with the preacher," Ed said as he led the way to Stan and Elaine's house.

Gabe set Rose down and the two girls linked arms and brought up the rear. Excitedly they discussed the simple ceremony and made plans like the best of friends. Before they knew it, Elaine walked out the front door when she heard the commotion.

"What a crew! You all are excited about something!" Elaine saw the sheer joy on her daughter's face and knew. It was done. Ed had followed through with his plan to propose to her little girl. Elaine's eyes were shining with joyful tears. So much had happened for Lindy in the past few months. Her mother's heart couldn't ache for long when she saw that Lindy was happy, at peace, and loved by a wonderful man. Reaching out her arms, Elaine embraced Ed and Lindy at the same time.

"Mom, we all want to talk to Dad if he is available."

"Okay......" Elaine asked the four to come inside. They all gathered around the table waiting on Stan.

Stan entered the room and took in the scene. Both couples were sitting hand in hand, beaming from ear to ear. Wearing a mock stern expression, Stan said, "This looks suspiciously like love."

"Oh, Daddy. Look!" Lindy extended her hand to her parents as they admired her beautiful engagement ring. "It's beautiful, isn't it, Mom?"

Stan kissed Lindy's hand and whispered, "Your eyes are sparkling more than your ring. I am so happy for you, Lindy-girl."

Wiping tears from their cheeks, the family embraced again and returned to Gabe and Rose.

"Sir, I mean, Pastor Stan, we have something to ask you." Ed spoke for the group. "Would you consider doing a double ceremony for the four of us......in two weeks?"

Coughing in his hand, Stan was clearly caught off guard.

"Two weeks!" Elaine exclaimed for the both of them.

"Well.....yes—"

Gabe took over from there. "Pastor Stan, I know this all seems so sudden. It *is* sudden. But life on the Island is different than life in the States. There's an urgency to begin our futures. We don't want or need a traditional ceremony. Ed and I have come to the conclusion that we only need our women, God's blessing, and someone to marry us. We want that to be you. And with my parents moving here in a week and a half, that will be perfect timing. Mine and Ed's jobs are awaiting us and honestly neither of us want to wait to marry. Why should we?"

Ed continued. "Both of us have found the woman we want to be with forever and why can't that start sooner than later?"

Stan reached for Elaine's hand. "I have no valid argument except I don't want my girl leaving home yet, nor growing up, nor marrying this soon. All of which are selfish reasons. I see your point, I know without a doubt that you all love each other and God and are committed to His plan for your lives. Yes, I would be honored to perform a double ceremony for you all. If you aren't wanting anything traditional and are simply exchanging vows then I don't see any reason to wait."

The next two weeks flew by in a flurry of activity. Another wedding was on the horizon but the two couples decided to keep the ceremony simple and sweet, no decorating or anything extra. All just wanted their family and friends there to witness the vows. Then Ed and Lindy would be off to Seal Harbor and moving into the small hunting cabin on the Walker's property where Ed had lived while in town. It was a temporary arrangement but one that made the couple extremely happy to be near the Walkers, yet on their own.

As quickly as the ceremony was over, Rose and Gabe were moving to Fairbanks so he could resume his position with AMRA. Already a trip to a nearby Aleutian Island was scheduled, something Rose was looking forward to as new beginnings shimmered like the sun at noon.

Randall and Rebecca were expected to arrive in a week and begin their work at *Rita's Place*. Pleased that his parents would be closer than Washington, Gabe was proud of them for taking on such a daunting task. Knowing his parents had a heart for others, Gabe never doubted they would be successful in this venture.

The only one on the entire Island that wasn't thrilled with the upcoming excitement was Andrew. Now two more couples were marrying, one of them taking away the person he had come to depend upon for strength and help and friendship. Andrew would definitely miss Ed's nearly constant presence. Yuri had taken Andrew under his wing as well, forming a bond that was a blessing to Andrew, something he never deserved from the man he had stolen from but who had offered him forgiveness and friendship.

But there again was the struggle for Andrew. When he saw Yuri and Luka, it was difficult to watch. It caused his heart and stomach to burn with jealousy and longing, creating a nauseating combination. Yes, he was happy for the couples, but it hurt him all the more to see them together; it stirred up longing for Berta and fear for her well-being. Andrew paused once more to offer thanks to God for Markus' return and the news about him seeing Berta alive and of her escape. Markus explained about the letter Berta had written to Ana that he delivered. After Markus left him, Andrew ran to the security and privacy of the trees and let out the months of pent up emotion from worrying about the woman he loved and longed for. Both Yuri and Ed had continually encouraged him to hold onto hope. He was trying, but some days it was impossible.

Like today.

Andrew stood outside the small chapel on Datka Island, his home. He wanted desperately to be the one walking down the polished aisle with Berta on his arm ready to begin a new life with her, ready to uphold his promise to her that he made so very long ago. Knowing Berta could never believe him that one day he would whisk her away from Rita and her job there, now it had happened, only not at all like Andrew had planned.

*He* wanted to be the one to get Berta away from the life she lived, not an abductor. Not someone who brought harm to her. Andrew still dreamed of the day they would be reunited, especially since he heard of her letter to Ana. All he could do was hope. Hope that it would happen. Hope that she was still longing for him as much as he longed for her.

It was time to enter the chapel and watch two more couples be united in marriage. He could do this. Taking a deep breath, Andrew entered the door with the remaining group of people coming to see the weddings. Though Andrew was very proud of Ed for finding the woman he loved, he also struggled with jealousy. Choosing to push any negative emotions aside, Andrew focused on the ceremony.

To the left of Pastor Stan stood Gabe and Rose, and to his right were Ed and Lindy. All four were beaming, full of joy and passion for their loved ones. Surrounding them were all of Datka Island, Rand and Becca right behind their son and his girl. Becca and Lindy's mother, Elaine were simultaneously dabbing at their eyes as tears of joy flowed. Pastor Stan cleared his throat and began.

"Thank you all for coming today as we witness the joining of these two couples in love and life. Their deepest desire is to be with the one they love and begin God's journey for them as couples. So today in the sight of God and each of you, their family and friends, I will proudly join them as man and wife."

This day couldn't have arrived soon enough for the Aleut and American couple. Gabe and Rose both felt as if they had waited a lifetime to finally be together as husband and wife, living, loving, and serving. Overwhelmed with joy, they both fought to pay attention to Pastor Stan's words and not lose themselves in each other's eyes.

"Gabriel and Rose, Ed and Lindy, I implore each of you to listen to and take to heart these words from I Corinthians chapter 13. If you *live* them, your relationships will never fail.

"'Love is patient, love is kind and is not jealous; love does not brag and is not arrogant, does not act unbecomingly; it does not seek its own, is not provoked, does not take into account a wrong suffered, does not rejoice in unrighteousness, but rejoices with the truth; love bears all things, believes all things, hopes all things, endures all things. Love never fails.'*

"As you two couples begin your life's adventures together, remember that two are better than one, and even better than that is the three-fold cord that cannot be broken, you, your spouse, and God."

Ed reached for Lindy's hand and gave it a gentle squeeze signaling her he was ready to embark on their God-adventure. Lindy's eyes turned an even brighter shade of blue as she looked into the man's face she adored. Excitement for their future pulsed through the chapel.

"Now, if you will please take the hands of your future spouse." Unencumbered by the traditional bouquet of flowers and rings, the couples grabbed hands with the ones they loved and turned to face their soon-to-be spouses.

Quietly, so only Lindy could hear, Ed whispered, "I love you, Beautiful."

Nearly unable to keep from kissing Ed before the Pastor said they could, Lindy whispered back, "And I love you, Charming."

"Will each of you repeat after me?" Stan led the men in what words to repeat while the two spoke their vows. "Gentlemen, 'With God and these people as my witness,'...."

"'I promise to love you and protect you'....."

"'To honor and consider you in all areas of our life'....."

"'To do you good and not evil, and to put no one but God before you'....."

"'As long as I live.'"

The two grooms' voices rippled through the church like far away rolling thunder. Truth and commitment resounded from each man.

Turning to the women, Pastor Stan asked for them to repeat their vows. "Please repeat these words after me, Ladies. "'With God and these people as my witness,'...."

"'I promise to be a wife to you'....."

"'Honoring, loving, and respecting you in all areas of our life'....."

"I will put no one but God before you and devote my love to you only'....."

"'As long as I live.'"

The brides' sweet clear voices rang like birdsong and touched the hearts of their men.

"And now for the moment you have all been waiting for....You are now husbands and wives. Grooms, you may kiss your Brides."

"Woo-hoo!" Ed let out a whoop and lifted Lindy off her feet planting a resounding kiss on her lips. Gabe and Rose forgot anyone was in the room with them as the two embraced and placed a sweet, lingering kiss on each other's waiting lips.

The room erupted with laughter, clapping, and sounds of celebration. The crowd ushered the couples to the waiting outdoors where food and dancing and celebrating ensued.

Looking around the group, Rose spotted her brother taking in the scene. She headed in Andrew's direction watching as one emotion after another crossed his face. Wrapping him in her arms, Rose spoke for Andrew's ears only. "Brother, do not give up. Your day will come. Have faith. Love will find you soon."

Andrew looked at his sister, the person he admired most on the planet. "Do you really believe that, Rose?"

"Yes. I really do. Now you just have to believe it." Kissing his cheek, Rose left Andrew to sort through the feelings vying for attention. Hope wrestled with discouragement and won, at least for the moment.

Choosing to celebrate the wonderful day, Andrew felt a small smile tug at the corners of his mouth. He grabbed Natalia by the arm and swept his mother into the center of the dancing. It was good to laugh and feel joy.

Andrew embraced the hope like a drowning man would a lifeline. He could and would hang on until his day came.

# CHAPTER 28

*4 months later*

Dipping the end of her paintbrush into the can of bright crimson paint, Rose dabbed the final touch on the wooden sign that would hang in front of the newly opening restaurant and home for girls in need of shelter and help.  Placing her hands on her hips, Rose stepped back to survey the sign.  There were two she had just touched up. One for the restaurant side of the oversized building and the other for the house side for Rita's girls and any others who might be seeking a helping hand.

Becca crossed the busy yard to her and Rand's new "home." Placing an arm around Rose's shoulders, Becca said, "Honey, it looks beautiful!  I can't wait to see both the signs hanging in their places."

Looking at her mother-in-law, Rose replied. "Thank you.  We have less than an hour before the newspaper reporter shows for pictures and interviews with you and Rand and the girls.  This is so exciting!  Becca, God is so good.  These girls needed help and someone to love them and care for them.  But poor Rand! Surrounded by all these women!  I bet he will spend more time in town than here just to escape all of the female influence."

"Actually he is looking forward to helping in the restaurant and being with the men patrons.  There will be a huge mission field just inside these restaurant walls for Randall."

"Very true."

Becca hugged Rose and went in search of her husband.

Twirling the ring with the heart-shaped stone on her left finger, Rose couldn't contain the smile that lifted her lips.  Reflecting over the past four months, she looked around at the newly painted building. No longer bright red, *Rita's Place* shone brightly in the afternoon sun. Its white coat of paint with gray trim and red front door looked beautiful. Amazed at the help from the townspeople and local churches, this little project had caused many from The Harbor on the 'other side of the fence' and many from Seal Harbor to come together for the sake of a group of lonely girls in need of help once again. Money was no problem, since Rita had left plenty of that. Workers were never scarce either. Both Aleut and American, men and women helped refurbish, repaint, and rebuild the large pool hall into a gleaming restaurant complete with new appliances, tables and chairs, counters and stools. Rose was truly proud of what had happened here, not only the work on the project, but the lives that were being touched.

Sneaking up behind his beautiful wife, Gabe wrapped his arms around Rose's waist and kissed her cheek. "Hey, you! What has you so deep in thought?"

Still overcome with the idea that they were finally married, Rose turned to face her husband. "I am just reflecting on what all has happened since we married. New job, new people, new mission trips, adjusting to life in the city, so much....and I love it all. God heard my prayer on the shore the week before you came back to Datka, that I wanted more in life, believed there was more and now, here we are. I am so happy, Gabriel."

"And so am I, Rose!" Gabe placed a lingering kiss on her lips. "We better stop this or we will miss the rest of the day."

"And what would be wrong with that?" Rose teased her husband.

"Okay, you two. Break it up!" Ed took every opportunity presented to him to tease his friends since they had arrived from Fairbanks for this special day.

"Why would we want to do that?" Gabe teased back.

"Because there's things to do right now besides kiss. Save it for later, Buddy!" Elbowing his friend, Ed laughed at their blushing faces.

The crowd that had assembled around *Rita's Place* parted as the flash from the cameraman's bulb went off. A newspaper reporter was interviewing different ones there. First Liza, then Pastor Stan, Sergeant Walker, and finally Rand and Becca. Taking in the scene, Gabe felt a rush of intense pride and gratitude for his parents. He was so glad God had orchestrated things so that he would still be somewhat near his parents and able to visit them when AMRA allowed. Grateful for their complete acceptance of his and Rose's marriage. Proud of them for committing to such a huge undertaking.

Finally Pastor Stan mounted the steps to the porch of *Rita's Place.* Much thought and prayer had gone into his little speech he was about to deliver. Raising his hands in the air, he quieted the crowd and got their attention. "If I could have your attention for a moment please. Many of you know there have been some changes made to *Rita's Place.* Before she moved, Rita left with one wish, one hope. She wanted a better, different life for her girls and their future. She enlisted the help of Sergeant Walker and myself to find the right couple to oversee what would happen here. After talking to her daughter and some of the girls living and working here, we decided to convert the pool hall to a restaurant....."

Stan paused when a few laughs and snorts went around the group of men standing off to the left of the crowd. Sergeant Walker shot a look of warning in their direction as one of his new officers moved to stand close-by the men.

Finally the AST had approved the hiring of three more officers after Dorne's fiasco. Now he had the man power to help do more about ridding Seal Harbor and The Harbor of illegal booze and prostitution. He had already assigned Brandon Hughes and another new officer to this side of town, mainly to uphold his promise to protect Rita's girls, especially during the transition from *what was* to *what would be*. Will knew they would have their hands full for a while but he believed with the new hires, all would fall into place.

Stan continued his speech. "With the support of this community we have been able to turn this place into what will hopefully be a successful business. I would like to introduce the new managers of this establishment, Randall and Rebecca Parker." Stan shot an arm towards their direction and the couple waved an acknowledgment to the crowd. "With that said, can we have the new sign lifted into place?"

Men moved to hang one sign above the restaurant's entry and another over the entry to the house side. Blazoned across the restaurant's sign in red letters were the words *Rita's Plate*. The crowd erupted in shouts and cheers as the sign was attached to its hangers. One little change to one little letter suggested a new establishment. From pool hall to restaurant.

Next the sign for the home's entry was hung. In equally red letters it said *Rita's Hope* across the white surface and in smaller letters underneath *Change the past. Change the future.*

Silence instead of cheers swallowed the crowd now. Pastor Stan continued. "Rita's *hope* was to do just what this sign says. To bring change for the future.  Thus the name change from *Rita's Place* to *Rita's Hope.*  Here, under the guidance of the Parkers, homeless or wayward girls can live and flourish and be a part of family while working at a stable job.  So in honor of Miss Rita's wishes, we present to you today, these two establishments with pride and joy!"

Now the crowd erupted along with the cameraman's flashing photography.  Cheers and welcomes and back slaps surrounded the Parkers and the girls.

Rand and Becca grabbed hands and thanked God for the support from the AST, the area churches, and from the community.  Changes were upon them and both were ready to run head-long into what God had in store for Seal Harbor.

*******************

The thump of the morning's newspaper sounded against the door of the Widow Tucker's house.  A kettle of tea simmered on the back of the stove as two heads bent over an open Bible.

"I'll get the paper for you, Mrs. Tucker."  Berta stood from her usual spot at the small round table and stretched.  "Looks like today's a good day for baking and housework.  These growing clouds will likely send rain our way."

Berta opened the creaking door and reached for the newspaper.  She cast another glance at the sky and went inside for another cup of tea.  Lying the *Barkersville Gazette* on the table, Berta went for the tea kettle to refill their cups.  Resettling herself at the table with her mentor and friend, Berta stirred sugar into her cup as she looked over the headlines on the front page.

"Yes, girl, I think you're right. Looks like a day of baking to me, too. What do you say about trying your hand at an apple pie?" Mrs. Tucker had done her best to teach Berta how to bake any number of things. Today would be pie day.

A sudden inhale of breathe drew the widow's attention to her companion. "Whatever's wrong, Berta?"

A hand flew to Berta's mouth and tears sprang to her eyes as she read the front page of the paper. "I don't believe it....."

"What is it, child? Don't leave an old woman in suspense!"

"It's my old home.....*Rita's Place.* Only now the name's changed. And look....." Berta couldn't continue. In the photo, she saw Ana's tiny face among the crowd gathered on the porch of what was now *Rita's Hope.* "There's Ana, my sister."

Mrs. Tucker pulled her chair closer to Berta's and placed her glasses on her nose. "Looks like I will just have to read it myself."

After a moment of silent reading, Mrs. Tucker said, "Well, girl, you best be packing your bags. You have a trip to make."

"What!?!? No, I can't go back. I won't leave—"

Holding up a wrinkled hand to interrupt Berta's protest, Mrs. Tucker said, "Berta, don't you see God's hand in this? Your home has *changed.* Your life can change too, with these new people to help, these missionaries. Don't you see? You can go home to Ana now. It's been months. Nothing will harm you. That man that kidnapped you won't come around. This place is God's place. It will be protected by Him and His kind, good people. I know in my old bones you are safe to go back. I *believe* it, Berta."

Berta sat in silence as she let the words sink in. Maybe the widow was right.

"And if I recall, there's probably a young man still pining away for you. Just as you have been for him. Go find them now. It's what you need to do."

Berta hugged the woman and grabbed the newspaper up. Without giving it another thought, she packed her suitcase and stuffed the paper in. "Are you sure you will be okay? I hate to leave you so suddenly."

"I'm fine, girl. Knew you were here for a reason and that has now come to an end. Don't you worry about me. Just write me a letter from time to time, okay?" The old lady's voice cracked with her final words. "I love you, Berta. Now go, before I change my mind. Take my umbrella with you."

A tearful sob escaped Berta's throat. "Oh, Mrs. Tucker! How can I ever thank you—" Berta gave her one last hug before reaching for the umbrella and leaving.

Stepping onto the creaking porch, the first raindrop plopped to the ground. Opening her umbrella, Berta took the quickest route to the train station and purchased the next train to Seal Harbor.

Within eight hours, she stepped foot off the train's platform and took in the scene around her. A wave of fear enveloped Berta as painful, scary memories washed over her. *No, I won't give into fear. God is my shield.*

Having to restrain her feet from running through town to the fence that separated the two distinct sections of Seal Harbor, Berta made haste to *Rita's Place* and Ana. No, it was now *Rita's Hope.* And that is what surged through her the closer she got to her old home.

Raising the umbrella at the onslaught of rain, Berta nearly walked by the white house with the gray trim. Realizing she was in the right area, she looked up and gasped at the changes that had taken place. Cars gathered in the parking lot to the left of the building. Shrubs and flowerpots were spilling color and greenery everywhere. Rockers and chairs lined the long porch as people exited the door to *Rita's Plate.* The new name brought a smile to Berta's lips. This was a different looking crowd too. Families, not rough looking men came out the door. Berta could hardly take it all in.

The sign that spelled out *Rita's Hope,* just like the newspaper said, beckoned to her. Entering that door, Berta took in the busy kitchen, unchanged in appearance, but in a flurry of activity.

And there she was. "Ana!"

Nearly dropping the basket of rolls she was carrying, Ana squealed when she spotted her sister. A sweet mixture of tears and hugs enveloped Berta as Ana finally let go for the others to grab her next. Then she saw the older couple in the center of the room, taking it all in.

The woman greeted her warmly. "You must be Berta! Oh I have heard so much about you, and now you are back home! We are so glad you are here! God has answered our prayers for your return."

"You prayed for me?" Berta was stunned.

"Yes, when you first went missing, our friends called us and had us begin to pray immediately and when we came here the girls told us the story and we have all prayed for you."

"You all prayed?"

Faces glowed all around her with something unmistakable in each set of eyes peering back at Berta. She knew that look, that longing for life and more. Berta could see peace and hope in their faces, peace that had never been there before. Gratitude overwhelmed her. God was at work even here while she had been away.

Ana wouldn't leave Berta's side as the other girls had to go about serving in the restaurant and cooking, the countenances of them all forever changed. Pulling her sister aside, Ana questioned her about the ordeal of her kidnapping, her one night stay with Markus, the letter she had Markus deliver, and about Berta's time at Barkersville. The story quickly poured out of Berta with the promise of more details later.

Finally, Ana asked, "Will you go see Andrew? I know for a fact that he wants to see you. He has been so upset since your disappearance. You have to go! Last I heard, he was staying in Seal Harbor and working a short term job in town. Berta, you need to go to Sergeant Walker at the AST office and ask him where Ed Hamilton lives. Ed was with Andrew constantly before marrying, and he can tell you where to find Andrew. Go now! But as long as you promise to come back."

A sad smile crossed Berta's face. "I hope you are right. What if he has moved on to another location or another girl?"

"Trust me; he hasn't."

"Okay. I will see you later, Ana." Hugging her sister once again, the two had mingled tears on their cheeks. "I am so glad to be back and excited to hear more about all the changes here."

"Go. Then we will talk soon."

Stepping out onto the porch, Berta still needed her umbrella though the rain was nothing more than a drizzle. Raising the black umbrella over her head, this time she allowed her feet to do as they wish.

So she ran. As quickly as she could to the man who would get her one step closer to Andrew.

Wrapping up his day's work, Will was put out that someone was entering the office right as he was about to leave. An umbrella-covered figure stepped inside. Lowering her covering, a girl looked him straight in the eye and said two words that nearly caused him to go weak in the knees.

Glancing at his name tag, she spoke, "I'm Berta."

Mouth hanging agape, Will was speechless.

"Sergeant Walker, do you know who I am?"

"Yes—yes, I'm sorry. I honestly never expected to see you, much less you find your way to me. Excuse my lack of words, but I am truly shocked."

A slow smile crept over the girl's face. She extended her hand to the chair behind her.

"Yes, of course. Have a seat. You have a lot to tell me I gather."

The next half hour Berta answered all of Sergeant Walker's questions. Finally she had one of her own. "Sergeant, how can I get in contact with Andrew?"

"You are in luck. He's staying at the local hotel and working for a man from town for another week. Want me to walk you over?"

"No, I know where it is. But thank you."

"Young lady, I must tell you. You are an answer to prayers."

Smiling broadly, Berta beamed at his comment. "You aren't the first person to tell me that today."

With that, Berta left the door bell ringing as she headed to the hotel down the street.

Still raining lightly, Berta walked into the hotel's entry and folded the umbrella. Her back turned to the front counter, she heard a familiar voice behind her. Turning, her eyes confirmed what her heart hoped for.

Andrew.

Head down and walking in her direction, he nearly ran over her in his attempt to exit the hotel. Looking up at the last second, he sputtered, "Oh, excuse me, Miss."

A sharp intake of breathe.

A look of startled realization.

His knees grew instantly wobbly as he grabbed her arm. "Ber—Berta? Is it you?"

"Andrew!" It was all she could get past the growing lump in her throat.

"Dear God in Heaven.....I don't believe it! You are really here?" Andrew grabbed his chest as he tried to still his racing heart.

Laughter bubbled past the tears in Berta's throat. "It's me. It really is."

Consumed by his own fit of laughter, Andrew scooped Berta up in his arms and twirled her around the hotel's lobby, unashamed of his joy. He whispered one word in her ear. "Redemption. *This* is what it means." Finally setting her down, Andrew pulled Berta to a more private corner with a table and two chairs.

"What do you mean by that, Andrew? Redemption?" Berta's face frowned in concentration.

"Something I have learned about and am just now experiencing. When God gives you something good in exchange for what you don't deserve. I don't deserve you coming back to me, Berta.

But God has heard my prayers and is giving me a second chance to do what I promised I would. Remember what I promised you? That I would rescue you from the life you had at Rita's and take you away so we could start over?"

"How could I forget that? I just had a hard time believing. Not because I doubted you, but because I couldn't see myself in any other way. But now I do. I will have to tell you about my friend, Widow Tucker and what she taught me." Berta shyly brushed her hair away from her eyes.

"Berta, I have to change my promise to you. I didn't get to rescue you from Rita's. God used a bad situation, a kidnapping, and you are free. But I really don't want to run away and start over somewhere else. I like it here now and I don't want to separate you and Ana again. What if we start over here in Seal Harbor? Close to your sister and close to my family? Only we get to start over redeemed. New. What do you think, Berta?"

Standing to her feet, Berta pulled Andrew up in front of her. She gingerly kissed him on the lips and said, "Nothing would make me happier, Andrew. Nothing at all."

# A WORD TO MY READERS

If I could throw a party right now I would! And I would invite YOU, my readers! We would celebrate several things. First, the fact that this newbie author finished her first book series, and secondly, that you stuck it out in these pages with me! It's a scary thing to do the unknown, to be vulnerable, and to decide to be uncomfortable. Who wants to do that?

Those of us who want to risk and dream and fly.

Me and you.

Trust me, it's worth it. Even if everyone doesn't like you or approve or applaud. It's ok. My deepest desire with every word I write is to do just what the first words of these books say: *MAY MY PASSION BRING YOU FAME!*

If I have brought awareness to my Lord and Savior, Jesus Christ, if I have praised my Creator and my God, and if anyone sees the power of the Holy Spirit among these pages, then I have brought HIM fame! And my goal is met.

I hope you have enjoyed this series as much as I enjoyed writing it. Please do me the favor and spread the word about these books by rating them on Amazon, by telling your fellow-readers, or by giving my books as a gift to someone you know who might need what you found within the pages.

As you could see when you first met Rose, she needed a *rescuer*. Needed to be *rescued.* The onslaught of questions, both answered and unanswered, drove her to find answers and embrace who she was. We can drown in the sea of the unknown and fear, flailing and struggling our whole lives or we can cry out and find that hand of rescue extended to us. I was like Rose; I needed rescuing from my own self, from fears and darkness and brought into the truth and light. Reach out for your Rescuer. He's right there.

If you read the second book in this Alaska's Aleutian Island Series, you met Andrew in desperate need of returning to God and to his family. Mistakes often destroy us, but they don't have to. If our mistakes don't destroy us, then they will define us, which can be nearly just as detrimental. Thank God for people like Ed, huh? If you haven't met Edward Hamilton in Book 2, you need to! Hopefully you have an Ed in your life or are being an Ed to someone in need of help. We all need that shining light to help us find our way back home.

And finally, in the third book, you meet several characters in need of redemption. Don't we all need that? A complete exchange in our lives, handing over our messes and receiving a "do-over" and a second chance? Rita's girls got just that. I hope you found a little bit of yourself in the characters of all three books. We are all there, lost, alone, imprisoned, desperate, rejected.

But I have hope for you! For me! We have a Rescuer, One who wants us to return to Him, and One who will redeem all our mistakes!

*It's in Christ that we find out* **who we are** *and* **what we are living for***. Long before we first heard of Christ and got our hopes up,* **he had his eye on us***, had designs on us for glorious living, part of the overall purpose he is working out in everything and everyone. (Ephesians 1:11-12, The Message, emphasis mine)*

Don't we all need to know that Someone has their eye on us? Don't we long to know who we are and what we are living for? I do! If you want to personally email me with any questions about that Someone, about God and His Son, Jesus, you can contact me at truloveswords@gmail.com

One last word, a dear friend once told me, "The only thing that will get in your way is *you.*"

Dare to dream. Find the courage to act on that dream. Then go do it!! It's worth it; trust me!

# ABOUT THE AUTHOR

Trudy Samsill is a resident of Paradise, Texas. She is wife to her best friend and soul-mate of 29 years and mother to 3 wonderful sons and 1 sweet princess. Trudy has been a home-school mom for 23 years, having graduated 2 sons and continuing to homeschool the last two, a junior and 7th grader. She recently graduated from Louisiana Baptist University with her Associates of Arts in Elementary Education in the Spring of 2013. Her first passion is writing, desiring her written words to touch her readers, to bring hope and inspiration towards greatness. She has a great love for nature, especially birds and wildflowers that flourish on their 11 acre homestead. Trudy is passionate about her relationship with God, above all else, giving Him all glory for this gift of words entrusted to her.

Trudy can also be found on her author website and blog at mytruwords.com.

This year she began a website encouraging older women to mentor younger women through coffee, tea, and heart-chats. See her latest blog posts and ideas here: talkingteacups.com

Please check out her first e-book venture, a short story, Glass Marbles. Here is the link to this book sold on Amazon: http://www.amazon.com/Glass-Marbles-ebook/dp/B00ASFMKO6/ref=sr_1_1?s=books&ie=UTF8&qid=1377523047&sr=1-1&keywords=glass+marbles

Don't miss <u>RESCUED</u>, *Alaska's Aleutian Islands Series (Book 1)* and <u>RETURNED</u>, *(Book 2)*. Both can be purchased from Amazon in e-book format or paperback:

<u>http://www.amazon.com/Rescued-Alaskas-Aleutian-Island-ebook/dp/B00ET9WFQA/ref=sr_1_1?ie=UTF8&qid=1382545934&sr=8-1&keywords=rescued+trudy</u>

<u>http://www.amazon.com/Returned-Alaskas-Aleutian-Islands-2/dp/1500270180/ref=sr_1_2?ie=UTF8&qid=1440109013&sr=8-2&keywords=trudy+samsill</u>

Made in the USA
Middletown, DE
22 December 2023

46640368R00190